THE STORM

If no one can get in, can any of them get out?

Gemma Denham

Cahill Davis Publishing

Copyright © 2025 Gemma Denham

The moral right of Gemma to be identified as the Author of the Work has been asserted by her in accordance with the Copyright, Designs and Patents Act 1988.

First published in Great Britain in 2025 by Cahill Davis Publishing Limited.

First published in paperback in Great Britain in 2025 by Cahill Davis Publishing Limited.

Apart from any use permitted under UK copyright law, this publication may only be reproduced, stored, or transmitted, in any form, or by any means, with prior permission in writing of the publishers or, in case of reprographic production, in accordance with the terms of licences issued by the Copyright Licencing Agency.

All characters in this publication are fictitious and any resemblance to real persons, living or dead, is purely coincidental.

ISBN 978-1-915307-26-2 (eBook)

ISBN 978-1-915307-25-5 (Paperback)

Cahill Davis Publishing Limited

www.cahilldavispublishing.co.uk

For my wonderful husband, Gary. Whose support and encouragement gave me the confidence to write this.

The footsteps were slow and steady. They became softer as they reached the carpet of the lounge, but the room remained shrouded in darkness. No flickering or sweeping torchlight.

She could hear them shuffling about, searching blindly. She desperately wanted to look. Just a quick peek to see if she could see who it was and what they were doing. But she couldn't even see her hand in front of her face. She knew it was darker back here, crouched in her hiding spot, but she also knew there wouldn't be much more light out there. No. It wasn't worth it. She needed to stay put. Stay still. Not risk any movement that could make a sound.

The air grew heavy as they drew nearer. They were definitely close to her now. She instinctively pushed herself backwards, shrinking further from the threat, trying to meld with the wooden shelf behind her. It dug into her spine.

Soft shuffles on the carpet. The slow but deliberate moving of furniture as if searching. For what? For her?

She felt rather than heard them approach where she sat crouched. Even though it was dark, she screwed her eyes shut as if the act of not seeing would make her invisible to her attacker. They were right behind her. She felt it. Almost felt their breath tickle across her skin. Down her neck. She shivered. She imagined it to be a man, but her mind wouldn't picture who.

Trying to shrink into herself, she curled her body inwards and crouched into a tighter ball, making herself as small as possible, and prayed that they couldn't see her. What was taking so long? Why weren't they moving? Why weren't they doing anything? Could they see her? She tensed her body ready to spring up in either a counterattack or to make a run for it. Poised, the wait was intolerable.

CHAPTER 1

Two weeks ago

Lizzy awoke under the weight of Luke's arm. She shifted uncomfortably, opening her eyes to be met with his eager, smiling face.

'Morning, beautiful,' he purred.

She gave a small jolt and gasped. 'Jeez, I do wish you wouldn't do that,' she said, laughing. He nuzzled into her warmth as she absentmindedly stroked his arm, her thoughts racing. She needed to get on; there was no time for lying around. Carefully, she removed his arm and slipped from the covers.

'Oh come on, Lizzy,' he protested. 'Just a quick snuggle before the day begins?' He looked up at her with pleading eyes and stroked the space she had just vacated.

'As tempting as that is, I have a busy day. Far too much to get through for me to be indulging in such fanciful behaviour.' She winked and threw a pillow at him. Then a serious note replaced her playful tone. 'Sylvie has been on at me again for the final draft of this bloody manuscript.'

'And?'

'And I'm still way off. It's just not flowing.'

'What you need, Miss Adams, is a more creative and bigger workspace. If we—'

'Luke, please,' Lizzy warned, walking from the room and shutting down the conversation before it could begin. They'd had this same conversation over and over recently. 'We should move out of the flat, Lizzy; buy a house, Lizzy; somewhere nice to raise a family, Lizzy.' It was all too much, too fast, too much pressure. She liked her little flat. She stopped moving, just a momentary pause, her brow furrowing and heart sinking a little. Her flat, she realised. In her head, it was still hers, not theirs. That wasn't a good sign.

When Lizzy emerged from the shower, the covers on the bed had been straightened and a coffee was waiting for her on the kitchen counter. Luke had already left for work. She instantly felt guilty and regretted snapping at him. She should be ecstatic that this lovely, gorgeous man wanted to commit and lay down roots together. What was wrong with her? She loved Luke, she really did. So why did the very thought of commitment feel so damn suffocating?

She dressed quickly in grey sweats and a black long-sleeved tee, scooped her long dark waves into a messy bun, then sat down at the little flip-down corner unit she called her office desk and opened her laptop. Her first book had been quite a success and her publisher was eager to get book two out while there was still interest. Book two, however, was proving to be difficult. It sometimes felt as if she'd used up everything she had in the first one and had nothing left to pour into this one. She was too distracted – that was the problem.

She read through the last few paragraphs of where she'd previously left off, trying to get back into the story, fingers poised over the keyboard, adding and deleting a few words here and there to make it flow better. As much as she tried though, she couldn't help but think back to her conversation with Luke. It played in her head like a broken record and, too often, she caught herself staring into space or flicking onto Instagram.

The Storm

She pulled herself back once again, typed out a couple of lines, then deleted them. Her focus was shot. Oh, bugger it, she thought, hitting save on the file and changing into her running gear.

Locking the flat behind herself, Lizzy emerged into the brilliance of the day. It may have still been August, but the mugginess of summer had already lifted and the sun on her face felt invigorating instead of repressive, unlike the last few days. It was a welcome relief.

Lizzy started off at a jog, easing her muscles into an easy rhythm, slowly building her pace until her feet pounded the streets. She was going too hard, too fast, whizzing past the chaos of the city; shops, offices, and people rushed past her in a blur. Traffic stop-starting, getting in her way, everything crowding her. Busy and loud. Grey and oppressive. Her legs burned with the effort, but she pushed on harder still, only slowing as the city opened up, died down, ran out.

Green spaces slowly replaced the grey as buildings gave way to trees and fields. Only when she reached the park did she finally start to feel at ease. She dropped back down to a jog, then slowed to a walk before stopping to stretch out on a bench and catch her breath.

What the hell was she running from? It wasn't like her to be so wound up, so stressed. She wasn't sure it had been intentional to come here, but now, she was glad. She had always loved Fletcher Moss Botanical Gardens. The green space, rambling paths, beautiful blooms, and the peace.

Who was she kidding – she knew what she was running from. For so long now, she had been avoiding Luke and her feelings. She didn't know how to process it all, how to decide, how to know anything with him forever breathing down her neck. Demanding so much of her. She took time over her stretches, letting her heart rate settle, then took off at a slower pace. This was better. This allowed thoughts.

Lizzy took a path along the river, enjoying the serenity and drinking in the peace and tranquillity. The leaves were already turning, the park beginning to burst into the oranges and reds of the fast-approaching autumn. She watched a few flutter to the ground as she ran, enjoying their dance on the breeze. There were always a few people along here at this time of day – an elderly couple resting on a bench, a mother and child feeding the ducks – but most others were at work or school. As she ran, she hoped the quiet would allow her to think, but she still found her thoughts spiralling.

A run was never going to be enough. She needed time. Time away from Luke, she realised. Him pestering her was only adding to her defiance and stress. She decided that when she returned home, she'd look into her options for a solo vacation, a little writing retreat. Although there was still the mammoth task of persuading him to allow her the space she so desperately needed.

'Hello, gorgeous.' Luke's face instantly lit as he walked in and saw Lizzy. A cheeky, dimpled smile amidst his stubble. So full of love and admiration. He hung his blazer on a hook by the door and popped his laptop bag down beneath it. 'Good day?'

'Yeah, not bad.' Although now she wasn't sure if she regretted what she'd actually done today – not only looked into a solo writing retreat but actually booked it. She'd spent the past half hour nervously nibbling and picking at her fingers, watching the clock, and doomscrolling as she awaited his arrival. And the nerves had only intensified.

He came over and planted a kiss on the top of her head from behind, hands light on her shoulders, dropping into a hug as he leaned over the back of the sofa, his cheek brushing hers. 'How was your run?'

She'd showered and changed an hour ago. She hadn't told him she was going out today, hadn't known herself for sure until she was doing it. She pulled away and looked at him, a prickly heat flooding her cheeks.

'Fletcher Moss, wasn't it?'

The Storm

And there it was. How he knew. He'd tracked her phone again.

'It was fine,' she replied, her voice small. She cleared her throat, giving more confidence to her voice, and turned in her seat to face him, tracking him with her body as he came round to sit with her.

'I've been looking at writing retreats. I've been struggling with this book a while now, and if I keep going as I am, I'm never going to finish in time. I thought it would be good for me to have some time away to really knuckle down, you know? Just by myself.'

'By yourself?'

'Yeah... just to give me a chance to finish this book. No distractions; ultimate focus.'

His eyes drooped as his face fell.

'It's only one week.' She laughed. 'I'll be back before you know it. It'll give you chance to see the lads and do something fun. Give Jake a call – you've not seen him in ages. Go out for a few beers, enjoy yourself.'

He rubbed a hand over his chin and loosened a couple of his shirt buttons. He didn't look convinced.

'And on the plus, I shall return a lot less grumpy. I know I've been a bit snappy of late, and I'm sorry.' She gave him the baby-doll eyes. 'Sooo?'

He finally looked at her again. Stopped his fiddling. 'Sure,' he conceded. 'Of course. Whatever you need.'

He gave her a smile that didn't quite reach his eyes, but it was all she needed. The relief was so immense she wrapped him in an embrace and kissed him. For the first time in a long time, she felt good, free, as though she was taking back control.

Luke relaxed into the kiss, and it intensified. She let him lead her to the bedroom. A weight had been lifted from her shoulders, and she fully gave herself to him, briefly feeling the excitement that had consumed their dating days.

CHAPTER 2

"Notebook, pens, underwear, purse…" Lizzy ticked off her list in said notebook and then checked she'd remembered everything for what felt like the hundredth time. Finally, she closed her notebook and carefully packed it all into a bag. She didn't need all that much – it wasn't exactly a holiday.

Happy that she did indeed have everything, she zipped it closed and took it, along with her laptop bag, out into the living room, where Luke sat pouting. He'd taken the morning to come and wave her off and sprang up when he saw her.

'A week is going to feel so long,' he whined as he picked her bags up and carried them outside, carefully loading them into the boot of her Mini. 'I can't believe I can't even call or message you.'

'It's no distractions for a reason.'

She had purposely booked the most remote hotel she could find. One with no phone or internet signal. Not only would it mean there was nothing to do but write, it would also stop Luke from bombarding her with messages. She needed space and time, to finish the book, yes, that hadn't been a lie, but also to come to a decision about the whole house thing. It wasn't fair to keep shutting him down and cutting him off every time he brought it up. He deserved more from her. Whether she could give it or not, well, that was the question.

'It will fly by. I promise,' she said.

His look was pure sorrow, and he hugged her as if he were a child leaving for his first day at school. It felt almost cruel to break it off, but she really had to get going. It wouldn't take all that long to get there really, she just couldn't bear the sorrowful puppy-dog eyes any longer.

She peeled him off and slipped into the Mini. Luke gathered himself together and plastered a smile on his face.

'I love you, Lizzy Adams, have a lovely time. Go write me a bestseller.'

'I love you too,' she called, strapping herself in and blowing him kisses through the open window. And she did. But that drive down the road, the drive away from the flat they shared, felt very much like her drive to freedom.

Motorways and civilisation gave way to rolling hills that increased in size and beauty as Lizzy neared the Lake District. She had always loved this part of the country. It reminded her of the camping holidays of her youth, of being dragged up mountains under protest by her over-enthusiastic dad, the views being much more the reward than the soggy picnic could ever be. It felt as if she were coming home. The air felt cleaner, lighter, fuller of life even from inside the car. Every exhale seemed to take more of her tension away with it.

With the mountains now surrounding the car, the roads grew smaller and windier, and even with the satnav, she managed to miss her turn. It took another twenty minutes of driving before she found anywhere big and safe enough to turn in, but, eventually, she was back where she was supposed to be and, by crawling slowly enough, she managed to spot a sign for the hotel before she passed the turning a second time.

The turn took her onto a single tree-lined track that the satnav didn't even identify as a road and led her the last few miles down to Briar's Crag – a four-star country hotel overlooking one of the many glorious lakes the area was famous for. As she approached the hotel, the purple slate of the structure seemed to loom straight out of the brilliance of the water, the sun that glittered over the lake reflecting from the windows in magnificent fashion. Lizzy couldn't help but break into a beaming smile. She pulled her car round on the gravel driveway and parked in a small bay set to the side along with two others.

Retrieving her meagre case and laptop bag from the boot, she stood back and took a moment to appreciate the stunning scenery. The hotel was set into a valley with mountains surrounding and hugging each side of it. With the brilliant blue sky they had been blessed with today, it more than lived up to the photos posted on the website.

Lizzy shivered and hugged her jacket round herself as she made her way to the entrance. A big, old wooden door stood open, welcoming her inside, where it was equally impressive. Oak beams and floral regency wallpaper adorned the walls, and the roaring fire that greeted her in reception was most welcome. Her boots tapped on the parquet floor and echoed round the room as she stepped further in, the chill leaving her body.

The hardwood desk standing to the side of the room was beautifully panelled and functioned as reception desk and check-in. A vase of fresh flowers sat on top alongside a shiny brass push bell that Lizzy so desperately wanted to ping despite the manager standing next to it, talking on the phone. She decided it was probably not the best idea as she made her way over and stood waiting patiently. His name badge identified him as Gideon. He was dressed smartly but relaxed, in a shirt and thin knit jumper. It was a look that was professional without shouting about it. His six-foot frame towered over Lizzy's five-foot-five, and his strawberry blond hair was styled into a natural-looking side sweep that unnaturally didn't move or waver. Behind him was a large board with room keys hanging from it.

He ended his call and turned his attention to Lizzy. 'Good morning and welcome to Briar's Crag.'

'Morning. Checking in, please. Lizzy Adams.'

The Storm

Gideon tapped a few keys on the computer in front of him. 'Ahh, yes, here we are.' He peered closely at the screen and then straightened. 'I'm afraid your room won't be ready until 2 p.m.; you're a little early. But the rest of the hotel is open to you – the lounge, bar, and dining room.'

'No problem at all, thank you.'

'I'll just get you a registration form to fill in.' He turned to the drawers behind him and took out a single form, which he placed on the desk with a pen. 'You may also want to check out the grounds while we're blessed with the sun. The lake is just a short walk out the back and we've many footpaths to explore. There's a storm moving in, so make the most of it while you can. The forecast warns it could be with us a few days.'

As Lizzy opened her mouth to reply, a middle-aged man barrelled down the stairs and into reception. He wore a rumpled suit that was snug on the belly of his slightly overweight frame but a little baggy in the arms. His salt-and-pepper hair was short and either gelled or greasy, and his chin was adorned with day-old stubble. His eyes bulged and his face was flushed.

'What kind of a hotel doesn't have bloody Wi-Fi?' he spat as he stomped across the room. 'Do you realise how many important business calls and emails I'm going to miss? And this sorry excuse for a hotel not only doesn't have Wi-Fi, I can't get a bloody signal either.'

The red of his face increased in intensity as he spoke, and as he got to the desk, he all but shoved Lizzy out of the way and slammed his hands down on the smooth surface. She stumbled to the side in her haste to avoid colliding with him. Not wanting to redirect his anger and get on the receiving end, she held her tongue at the sheer rudeness.

'As I explained to you earlier, Mr Franks, this hotel is run as a complete break and retreat from the outside world. It is advertised as such, and it clearly states on the website that we have no phone or internet signal. Now—'

'And as I told you, my bloody secretary booked it, not me.'

'Then I suggest you take it up with her.'

Mr Franks threw his hands up in the air and stormed back up the stairs, muttering under his breath. The manager sighed and rubbed at the bridge of his nose. A door slammed overhead, making Lizzy jump slightly. She quietly slid the long-forgotten form from the desk, and, offering a tight-lipped smile of compassion, took herself off in search of the lounge.

The lounge fed off the reception to the right, and in complement to reception, it was snug and inviting. Sofas, armchairs, and side tables were artfully arranged in the space, and the plush Jacobean carpet and mulberry walls gave the room a luxurious feel. A fire crackled in this room too, and paintings portraying the area's natural beauty hung on the walls. Only a couple, who appeared to be in their mid-twenties, were using the space. The girl was slim, with long caramel hair, and wore beige skinny trousers and a soft cream cashmere jumper. She had on white pump-style trainers and seemed to be entwined with her partner – a clean-shaven man with dark wavy hair and a cheeky grin. He wore ripped jeans and a college sweater. They screamed lovesick, and Lizzy wondered if they were here on honeymoon or having an affair. They didn't notice or acknowledge her arrival.

Lizzy set herself up in one of the armchairs and manoeuvred one of the tables in front of her. She quickly scribbled her details onto the form, then opened her laptop bag and got out her laptop ready to set about working on her manuscript. She'd drop the form back later when she formally checked in.

CHAPTER 3

At precisely 1:30 p.m., Lizzy was interrupted from her flow by the arrival of another guest in the lounge. An elderly lady who walked with a cane but brandished it as if it were a fashion accessory. She oozed flamboyant style and entered the room as though she had just been announced onto a stage. Her high-cheek-boned face was heavily made up, and she tottered on kitten heels as if they were a second skin.

'Where is that boy Evan?' she demanded, swooshing her shawl over her shoulder in a grand flourish.

Lizzy looked around, suddenly realising that the couple had left her at some point. By process of elimination, the lady must be addressing her.

'I'm sorry, I don't know an Evan. I've only just arrived.'

'The boy, you know.' She tutted. 'Half past one, a glass of brandy before luncheon,' she continued, somewhat irate at Lizzy's inability to produce said boy.

Just as Lizzy was about to reply that, once again, she didn't know anyone called Evan, a young man of about twenty sauntered in. He wore a partially untucked dark grey shirt with black trousers and scuffed his feet as he walked. His curly mop of hair was cut short on the back and sides, and his close-knit brows and snarled lips gave him a permanent scowl. He slowly slipped behind the bar area that sat at the far end of the lounge as though he couldn't care less who was waiting. This appeared to anger the lady further, who was clearly used to getting exactly what she wanted.

'It's 1:35 p.m. now, Evan,' she shrieked. 'Brandy is at 1:30 p.m., one-thirty precisely. Oh, I feel so faint.' She raised the back of her hand to her head dramatically and engineered a very careful fall backwards into one of the waiting armchairs.

Evan rolled his eyes. He poured the drink and placed it on the bar, managing to slosh some of the amber liquid over the side as he did so. The lady looked horrified and leapt out of the chair with surprising speed. She stood to her full five-foot height to command him.

'Well, what good is that? Pour me another at once,' she demanded. 'I can't drink that one.'

'Deidre, it's fine—'

'It's Miss Malone to you,' she shot back, batting at the glass, sending it flying over the bar, where it smashed on the floor. 'I hope that comes out of your wages, young man. Maybe then you'll be more inclined to do it properly.'

Through gritted teeth, Evan poured a fresh one, muttering expletives as soon as she moved out of earshot.

Not wanting to be left alone with this vile woman, Lizzy packed her laptop away and, slinging her bag over her shoulder, headed to the dining room for lunch.

The dining room was bright and airy, with sunlight pouring in through two ornate bay windows that overlooked the grounds to the rear. The highly patterned carpet continued into this room, but the walls were papered in a subtle cream floral design. A long, heavy wooden table sat along the far wall, covered with a wonderfully prepared hot and cold buffet. A large, bald chef kept dipping in and out, topping up the platters and rearranging them. The couple from earlier, Lizzy saw, had moved to here, and the girl was busy feeding morsels from her plate to the man. Lizzy couldn't remember ever being that wrapped up in someone. She wondered if the man actually enjoyed it or was just putting up with it. She supposed that Luke would probably like that kind of behaviour.

Lizzy picked up a plate and helped herself to some food before finding a seat at an empty table. Instinctively, she reached for her phone, taking it from her pocket for a little banal scrolling before remembering that it was no good to her here. She saw she had five messages and had missed two calls from before the signal dropped, all from Luke. She opened the first one and sighed. It had been sent mere minutes after she'd left.

```
10:05 a.m.  Miss you already. Love you
lots xxx
10:35 a.m.  You're going to do great, I
just know it! xxx
10:45 a.m.  Let me know you have arrived
safely. Or give me a call before you
lose signal xxx
11 a.m. I love you so much, this week is
going to be so long! xxx
11:30 a.m. Are you there yet? Everything
ok? xxx
```

Lizzy powered off her phone and chucked it into her bag. Thank God there was no signal here. It was sweet that he cared so much, but jeez, give a girl a little breathing room.

She picked at her lunch as the stress from the past few weeks slowly ebbed its way back into her body. After five minutes of moving food around her plate, she conceded that she'd lost her appetite and left, stepping out the front door for a bit of fresh air.

'Whoa, steady there.' A man quickly stepped sideways, a suitcase in hand, and waited for her to pass, pushing his thick-framed black glasses up to sit properly on the bridge of his nose.

'Sorry,' she muttered, moving past him to stand out of the way of the door.

Within seconds, he was back outside, hefting a second, larger, suitcase out of the boot. He had short grey hair and a stubbly beard. Lizzy put him at early fifties. In contrast to his reasonably trim frame, the next person to step out of the car, who Lizzy assumed to be his wife, was quite overweight. Her auburn-dyed hair was cut into a straight bob that framed her face, and she wore a cotton dress and chunky cardigan that accentuated her ample bosom and tipped her over to frumpy.

Yet to leave the car was a teenage girl. She sat slouched in the back seat, door hanging open, her feet resting on the headrest in front of her. She held an iPhone that was plugged into her ears. Lizzy hoped that her parents had prewarned her about the lack of signal here, or they were surely in for one hell of a tantrum later.

CHAPTER 4

Eighteen-year-old Ellie Barker dragged herself from the car and was immediately handed a travel case by her beaming dad. Smile all you like, she thought, doesn't change the fact that I hate you right now. She narrowed her eyes and gave a snide smile in return. Of all the places her parents could have picked to go on holiday, they chose the bloody Lake District. Were they trying to ruin her life?

She slung her bag over her shoulder and took the handle of her travel case. It bumped and juddered over the gravel. Ellie gave it a sharp tug, causing it to tip sideways awkwardly. She stumbled, turned, and growled at it, then pulled it harder still.

Once inside, her parents approached the reception desk, leaving Ellie standing there like a spare part.

'Paul and Fiona Barker,' her dad announced. No 'hello' or anything. Ellie rolled her eyes. What a knob.

She left them to the paperwork and surveyed the room. It gave off old country vibes. Still, at least it looked decent enough. If you liked that kind of thing.

Her dad turned and dangled a key in front of her face, mock bowing. Ellie snatched it and turned away. Why did parents have to be so bloody embarrassing?

She turned, looking for the lift, but found none. Another strike. With a huff, she took the stairs, banging the case on every one of them as she dragged it behind her. At least she was getting her own room. That was one small saving grace. If she'd had to share with her parents, she would have seriously considered suicide. It was bad enough that the place didn't have Wi-Fi. That was a nice little bombshell they'd dropped on her halfway up the motorway. Some shit about reconnecting as a family and getting away from technology. Spending some 'quality time' together. That had to be down to Mum. She highly doubted Dad would have come up with anything like that. God, her Insta feed was going to take a serious hit. If she lost followers because of this, she would be seriously pissed. Not that there was anything to post a photo of up here anyway. No beaches, no bikini-clad selfies, no sunset cocktails.

She sighed. This was going to be the week from hell.

CHAPTER 5

Lizzy had followed one of the many rambling, tree-lined footpaths that ran from the hotel and was sat by the water's edge, skimming stones into the lake and enjoying the sun on her face. The setting was idyllic. The vast expanse of water in front of her mirrored back the peaks and trees that surrounded it. Birds swooped and sang in the blue sky overhead. There was certainly no hint of the threatened storm so far. It was picture-postcard beautiful. Perfect. Every time the tranquil setting started to ease her stresses though, Luke popped back into her thoughts and she was right back to the ball of tension she'd started as.

Did she love him? Yes.

Did she enjoy spending time with him? Yes.

Did she want to buy a house with him? No.

But was that no to moving out of the flat or no to it being with Luke? This was where she always stalled. No real leaning either way. Should that tell her all she needed to know? If it wasn't a resounding yes, then surely it was a no. No?

She picked up a rock and lobbed it into the water, trying to send as much of her frustration as she could with it. With her lips set into a thin line, she stood and started the walk back to the hotel. At least she should be able to get into her room now and do some writing in peace.

Lizzy had been handed a good old-fashioned key on a fob, which she placed on the bedside table of her room. It was more modern up here than on the ground floor, the décor simple but still luxurious, if a little tired, and she could easily imagine that this had once been a grand house.

Her room was pleasant – a decent-looking double bed shrouded in white linen, ample built-in wardrobe, and the standard hospitality tray you would expect to find. The moderate en-suite was modern enough to have been decorated in the last decade, and she was lucky enough to have been blessed with one of the hotel's corner rooms that boasted a beautiful bay window. A wooden desk was nestled into the nook it provided, overlooking the surrounding peaks out of the front of the hotel. The view was stunning. Lizzy stood back in admiration and breathed it in. She could never have enough of this.

After unpacking the essentials, she set up her laptop and notebook on the desk and got back into her work. It was slow and steady, but she found that here, the work was at least constant. She revelled in the peace and quiet. No beeps from her phone, no notifications pinging up on her screen, no Luke constantly bothering her. A house with a separate workspace would make it easier to shut him out, she mused. Wait, that wasn't exactly the right way to think about it though, was it? She shook her head and mentally berated herself for allowing her mind to wander back to Luke again.

Lizzy arched her back, flexed her fingers, and began again. Hours quickly passed, and before she knew it, her stomach was signalling that it must be nearing dinner time.

The dining room was already a hive of activity when Lizzy arrived. She was shown to a seat by a young waitress whose name badge read Poppy. She wore the same grey shirt and black trousers as Evan, only neater. Her long black hair was

The Storm

tied back into a ponytail, but tendrils hung loose to frame, or rather hide, her pale face. Her heavily black-lined eyes nervously skirted around the room, never meeting Lizzy's. Poppy held out a menu, which Lizzy took with a smile, then she mumbled something that Lizzy couldn't quite catch.

'I'm sorry?'

'Would you like to order a drink?' Poppy asked again, slightly louder this time.

'Oh, yes, yes, I'll have a white wine, please. Chardonnay, thank you.'

Poppy gave a small nod and hurried away. Lizzy felt for her. Clearly, front of house was way out of her comfort zone.

The rude man she had briefly seen in reception earlier, Mr Franks, was sitting in a corner, still in his rumpled suit and wearing an expression of pure contempt. Lizzy wondered if he was still fuming or if this was how he always looked. He was eating steak whilst furiously flicking through paperwork, his face flushed with either stress or drink. Evan sauntered over and deposited what looked like a tall glass of Coke in front of him, then made his way over to the two lovebirds, who at this moment in time looked anything but in love. Their voices remained low, but the urgency of their exchange suggested that maybe all was not rosy. As they registered Evan's arrival, they drew back and plastered smiles on their faces.

The family Lizzy had bumped into at lunch sat on the other side of the room. The girl, who was clearly in a sulk, picked at her plate while her parents ate in mechanical silence.

Happy families all round, thought Lizzy, casting her eyes over her menu.

Though there were two wait staff service was incredibly slow. Evan loitered around the room without actually doing anything or speaking to anyone, looking busy doing nothing, and Poppy stood to the side, fidgeting from foot to foot whilst picking at her fingers and avoiding eye contact should anyone even think of trying to interact with her.

It wasn't until Gideon noticed and gave her a nudge that she moved and disappeared into the kitchen.

As Poppy arrived back at Lizzy's table with the chardonnay, Deidre arrived.

'Good evening, everyone,' she purred loudly. Everyone looked up and, pleased she had everyone's attention, she sashayed into the room.

Evan, whether finally gathering a little focus or just happening to find himself at her side, showed her to the table next to Mr Franks.

'No, not this one,' she hissed. 'I want my usual one. I'm not sitting next to him.'

'Well, piss off, then,' Mr Franks spat back.

Deidre's eyes widened and her jaw dropped at being spoken to in such a way. With a trademark swish of her scarf, she bumped into his table, toppling his drink. The sticky liquid saturated his papers and overflowed the tabletop into his lap.

He jumped up, face puce and spit flying. 'You bloody cow. Look what you've done.'

'Oh dear, accidents happen I suppose.' Deidre could barely contain her grin.

'Do you have any idea how important these are? You've probably cost me the deal now.'

Gideon was over in a shot, ushering Evan and Deidre away and mopping down Mr Franks with a very unsubstantial paper napkin.

'Mr Franks, I'm so sorry. Poppy will get you another drink, on the house. Let me help you with your papers.'

'Oh, sod off, will you?' He batted Gideon away as if he were an annoying fly and shook his dripping papers, which were clearly ruined. A vein pulsed in his temple as he threw them to the floor before pointing a stubby finger at Deidre. 'You'll pay for this,' he snarled before hastily gathering his things and leaving the room.

'Did you hear that?' Deidre asked of the room. 'Oh, I shall need a brandy to recover.' She fanned herself theatrically,

The Storm

but the smugness that shone through her eyes far outweighed her show of indignation.

CHAPTER 6

Fiona sat in silence and watched as her husband slowly drank himself into oblivion. What could she say? She was the reason behind this uncharacteristic change of behaviour after all. She felt bad for Ellie. What must she be thinking? Had she noticed? How could she not. Fiona longed to talk to her daughter. If she could just chat banal gossip over dinner like normal, just sweep everything under the carpet and pretend they were a normal loving family again. But no. It was too risky. To utter a single word would risk opening an invitation of rebuke. Even if those words were said to her daughter and not to him. If she didn't speak, he would have no reason to respond. To question. To argue. While he remained quiet, so would she. You don't poke a sleeping bear.

CHAPTER 7

Lizzy's table was bare all but for her half-empty wine glass. She idly brushed at a few crumbs on the table linen as she mentally debated a dessert. The evening felt a little less tense without Mr Franks' presence. The lovebirds seemed to have made up during their meal, and after getting a bit touchy feely, they had gone off up to bed. The teenager had apparently caught Evan's eye, who when he wasn't hovering around her like a fly, was sneaking glances. It appeared the girl's parents had yet to say a word to one another. The father, who had been filling the silence with drink, sat with a steely glare, while his wife, eyes cast downwards, looked quite stoic. No wonder the girl is so surly. Poor kid having to endure that atmosphere.

As soon as Evan had collected the plates from their table, the girl quietly rose and left. Her mother followed soon after without uttering a single word, leaving the father alone. He didn't appear bothered by this, only offering the briefest glances at their retreat. Deidre, unusually quiet since the earlier drama, sat sipping sherry. She reached into a clutch bag and drew a cigarette from a slim silver case. Gideon was over before it reached her lips.

'Now, Deidre, you know you can't smoke that in here.'
'Oh pish posh.' She tutted, waving him away.
'Let me escort you to one of our lovely outdoor seating areas.'

With a satisfied grin, she accepted. She rose on wobbly legs and took Gideon's arm. 'The shock, my dear,' she said in way of explanation. 'That Mr Franks really is quite rude.'

With her head held high, they left through French doors that led out onto the patio. Lizzy wondered how much of that 'shock' had come from the many glasses of brandy Deidre had consumed.

CHAPTER 8

Ellie shut the door behind her and leaned back against it. She had left dinner as soon as she was able and not a moment too soon. She didn't know what she had done, but she had clearly upset her parents somehow - neither had uttered a single word to her all night. Well, fine with her. She was still cross at them for forcing her on this holiday. Bloody Lake District.

She plopped down onto the edge of the bed and let herself fall backwards. At least the bed was soft. She ran her hand over the linen, which was unimaginatively white, then grabbed it into fists. She squeezed it tight with a scowl before releasing it and shuffling herself higher up the bed. She plumped the pillows with a good punch and then arranged them behind her so that she was comfortably propped up.

She had been in a mood about coming here, she couldn't deny that, but she hadn't been that terrible about it. Had she? She'd said her piece and then remained quiet. She'd definitely said and behaved worse before. Maybe they'd had a row. That was probably more likely. Something had clearly changed between arriving and dinner and she'd barely been with them.

There was a click of a door out in the hall but no voices as Ellie heard one or both of her parents return to their room. She'd been very tempted to ask for a room change when she found out her parents were in the room next door, but in the end, she couldn't be bothered to trek all the way back downstairs. She hoped they would make up before morning but hoped to God that it wouldn't involve make-up sex. She quickly turned on the TV just in case and turned the volume up high. For good measure, she hopped into the shower.

Shit, this was going to be a long week.

CHAPTER 9

Neither Evan nor Poppy came to enquire about dessert, so Lizzy made her way back to her room. There was a beautiful roll-top bath she had big plans for, and after all the travelling and drama, she was quite looking forward to an early night.

She ran the bath as hot as she could stand and lay luxuriating in the soothing bubbles until the water started to cool. The flat only had a shower, so it really felt like a pampering treat. She decided that tomorrow she should plan ahead and bring her book and a drink in with her. Make the most of it while she could.

After bathing, she quickly dried her hair before slipping beneath the cool, crisp sheets. They were clearly good quality and felt lovely against her skin. Out of habit, she found she was on the right side of the bed, but realising she was alone and it was all hers, she spread herself out and snuggled into the middle.

She ignored the TV remote and picked up her book, reading until her eyes started to droop. Just as she was about to turn off the lamp, a series of bangs and the thuds of heavy, uneven footfall emanated from out in the corridor. She crept from the bed and made her way over to the door. Peering through the spyhole, she surveyed the landing area. From where her room was, she could just see the top of the stairs to her left, the landing to the majority of the other rooms rounding the corner away from them. Stumbling up the stairs was the father of the family. He swayed a little at the top, walked towards Lizzy's room, then with a confused but determined look on his face, he turned and headed round the corner in the opposite direction.

CHAPTER 10

Lizzy arrived at breakfast the following morning to see the buffet table was back. She had slept well and woken ravenous, full of optimism and energy for the day ahead, so she was delighted to see it laden with everything anyone could ever desire for breakfast. Half of the table was made up of hot trays filled with all manner of full English delights – sausages, bacon, hashbrowns, mushrooms, tomatoes, and eggs in every variety. The other half held baskets of pastries, bread for toasting, fruit, and a selection of cereals and juices. Forever health-conscious, Lizzy opted for muesli and an orange juice. Then drawn in by the many delights on offer and reconsidering her options, she decided to treat herself and added a croissant and jam.

She took the same table she'd had the night before as Poppy appeared brandishing coffee. The waitress hovered uneasily and held up the pot as way of offering rather than speaking.

Lizzy smiled. 'Please.'

Poppy nodded and poured the coffee before shuffling off to the next table. There was already a small jug of milk and pot of white sugar cubes in the middle of each table. She poured some milk and stirred her coffee gently, ignoring the sugar.

Evan, she noted, was wafting around like a fart again, trying to look busy without actually doing anything in what was fast becoming apparent to be his usual manner. Lizzy was starting to wonder if either of them had actually received any training for their roles or had just been thrown into them.

Mr Franks was down already, plate piled to the rafters and reading a newspaper. His complexion was a much more human colour this morning, but he still wore a persistent frown.

The mother and daughter of the family group were also present and had both opted for cereal and toast. Neither spoke, but it seemed to be a comfortable silence of two people who had run out of things to say. They sat relaxed in each other's company and looked to be in no hurry to leave when they finished eating. Tea and coffee were topped up as the girl played on her phone and the mother appeared lost in a daydream.

It was a good half an hour later that the father made an appearance. His face looked ashen and he moved gingerly as he walked. The mother seemed to stiffen as he approached the table and watched from the corner of her eye as he slowly lowered himself into a chair. The girl glanced at him, but that was all the welcome he got. No one spoke and the mother's posture remained stiff, as if she were expecting an argument. He accepted a coffee when Evan came over, though once he had it, he only took baby sips, leaving it alone for the most part. The plate in front of him remained empty.

No Deidre yet. She's probably waiting until everyone is down to make her entrance, Lizzy mused.

Lizzy was just finishing up when the two lovebirds arrived hand in hand and beaming at each other. The way they constantly gazed at each other and always had to be touching was far too cutesy for Lizzy's liking, and she found that their affection for one another disgusted her. She wondered what kind of person that made her. Envious? Resentful? A bitch most likely. Was she just a horrible person?

Not wanting to dwell on those thoughts, Lizzy left the dining room and made her way back upstairs. In her room, she sat at the desk and opened her laptop, gazing out of the

The Storm

window behind it at the landscape that beckoned beyond. She should have gone for a run before breakfast, she realised. Air and exercise before working often helped with her concentration. She was far too full to even contemplate one now.

She was just considering heading out for a walk instead when an ear-piercing scream came from down the corridor. Lizzy stood, almost toppling her chair in her haste to get to the door. Flinging it open, she paused on the landing, but everything was quiet.

The scream hadn't sounded close enough to be the room closest. She closed her door and started to walk slowly down the corridor, towards and then past the stairs, looking around and trying to fathom the direction she'd heard the sound. Nobody was there and all the doors she passed were shut, no noises coming from within. Then she heard faint crying coming from her left. Following the sound, she rounded the corner, taking her to the other side of the hotel. There was a housekeeping cart in the corridor and the door to room two stood open partway.

'Hello?' Lizzy knocked gently on the door.

There was no response.

'Are you ok in there?'

No sound other than more crying.

Lizzy slowly pushed the door open further and cautiously stepped inside. Poppy stood shaking by the window. Tears streamed down her face and her breath was coming in ragged gulps. White towels and hot drink sachets were scattered on the floor around her.

Lizzy rushed to her side, eyebrows knitted in concern. 'Poppy? Whatever's the matter? What's happened?'

Poppy didn't look up. She didn't even seem to know Lizzy was there. Instead, she remained staring straight ahead with unblinking eyes.

Lizzy followed her gaze to the bed, previously hidden from view by the door. More accurately, she gazed at the form that lay upon it. Deidre was still dressed in last night's clothes. They looked slightly rumpled, as though slept in, even though she lay on top of the covers. Her milky eyes stared straight ahead and her mouth gaped slightly. Lizzy didn't need to feel for a pulse to know she was looking at a dead body.

'Oh.' She gasped, recoiling. Her hand flew to her mouth. She had never seen a dead body before, and she found herself taking short, sharp breaths. As if to breathe deeply would be to inhale death itself. Deidre's skin had a waxy sheen to it that made it look almost clammy, and it hung loose on her face, like the muscles had already given in to gravity. Lizzy tried to look away, but her eyes wouldn't obey. It was as though she were watching a horror film, where you know something horrific is about to happen and yet your eyes are glued to the screen despite the incoming scare. Except this was real life. And something horrific had happened.

The sound of Poppy crying broke Lizzy out of her trance. She looked up, but Poppy was still fixed on Deidre. Lizzy looked around for something to cover Deidre's face, and not wanting to pull the linen from underneath the body, she collected one of the fresh towels that lay at Poppy's feet and gently laid it over the deceased. But no matter how much she stared at the towel, wanting to see just that, the image of Deidre's face was fresh in her mind, a memory she was sure would never dull. And she knew Poppy still saw it too.

'Come on,' she said gently. 'Let's go downstairs and get you some tea.'

Poppy moved like she wasn't in control of her legs, and Lizzy was convinced the poor girl was still yet to blink. She put a supporting arm under Poppy's and all but carried her out of the room. Her wailing had died down to a whimper now.

They stepped out of the room as Gideon arrived on the landing. He had a face of pure thunder that quickly fell pale on seeing the two girls.

'What's happened? Poppy? Are you ok?' He put a reassuring hand on her shoulder, leaning into her slightly as if encouraging her to open up. 'What's going on? What was all the noise?'

Poppy gave a small shake of her head – the only response she could seemingly manage.

'Oh, Gideon,' Lizzy started, taking over. 'I'm afraid it's Deidre. She... well...' She pinched the bridge of her nose as she focused on holding back tears. 'She passed away in the night. Poppy just found her. She's had quite the shock... we both have.'

Poppy continued to whimper quietly.

'Oh, good lord.' Gideon made a move towards the room.

'Wait.' Lizzy put a hand out, stopping him. 'I don't think you should go in there. Don't we need to preserve the scene or something? I don't know. We need to call someone. An ambulance or the police. I'm not really sure who needs to come in a situation like this.' Lizzy's words tumbled out too fast as the thoughts popped into her head. Getting louder as she spoke. More urgent. She tried to slow down, take deeper breaths, remain calm. Panicking wouldn't help.

'Yes, yes, of course. I'll make the call.'

'I locked the room and then called nine-nine-nine. They're sending an ambulance.' Gideon poured tea into three cups and added a generous amount of sugar to each.

Lizzy never normally took sugar in her drinks, but the shake of her hand as she brought the cup to her lips told her it was probably necessary. She took a small sip and returned it to the table in front of her, then tried and failed to relax back into the lounge sofa. She was too tense, and her muscles wouldn't obey.

'I called your mum as well, Poppy.' Gideon moved so that he was on Poppy's level and made an effort to make eye contact as he spoke. 'She's going to come and collect you, ok?

I think you probably need a bit of a break after this. Take the rest of the week off if you need it. Ok?'

Lizzy wasn't sure Poppy was hearing a word he said. She sat staring ahead, her gaze fixed on something neither of them could see. She no longer made any noises, but her tears continued to fall steadily and her lower lip trembled.

It took a little persuasion, with Lizzy physically placing the cup in Poppy's hand and tipping it gently to her lips, but eventually, they got her to take some tea, and she drank slowly and rhythmically. Lizzy sat back and picked up her own cup, noticed it was already empty, and refilled it from the pot.

The three of them sat in silence until the crunch of tyres on gravel announced Poppy's mum's arrival.

Gideon slowly got to his feet. He only made it as far as the doorway when Poppy's mum hurried into the room and enveloped Poppy in a huge hug. Poppy rose on unsteady feet, guided by her mum, and together, they walked out in zombie-like fashion, her mum supporting and leading her. Gideon followed them out, leaving Lizzy alone in the lounge. She watched through the window as they helped Poppy into the car and then stood in mumbled conversation.

Lizzy looked away, then a few minutes later, heard the engine start and the gravel kick up a little as they drove off. She didn't quite know what to do with herself. What was she supposed to do? Wait for the ambulance to arrive, she supposed. She imagined they'd want to talk to her. She had been in the room after all. If they didn't, the police would. The police would be coming too, wouldn't they?

Gideon came back into the lounge. He stood and ran his hands over his face and through his hair, exhaling loudly. He looked as unsure as she felt.

'Gosh, it's just so awful. Can I get you anything? More tea, Miss…?' He paused and rubbed his temple, then brought his hand down to rest a finger over his lips. 'I'm so sorry, in all the drama, I've quite forgotten your name.'

'It's Lizzy.'

The Storm

'Lizzy. Thank you. For your help with Poppy, I mean.'

'No worries. Poor girl.' She looked at the teapot, but she wasn't sure she could stomach another drink – a mix of the sickly sugar and image of Deidre stuck in her head. 'And no… to the tea. Thank you though. I think I might go for a little walk. Just in the grounds. If anyone comes and, you know, needs to talk to me. I won't be far away, but, it's just… I think I need a bit of air.'

Lizzy pushed out a long breath as she stood, then slowly left the room, walked through the reception area, and wandered to the front entrance and out into the day. She felt in a daze herself and shook her head in an attempt to dislodge the image of Deidre on the bed. She had no real aim or destination, she just knew she needed to be outside; the hotel had suddenly become hot and claustrophobic.

The fresh breeze that hit her face as she walked down the steps was refreshing. She stood and inhaled deeply before moving on, walking on autopilot, not really aware of her surroundings until she found herself in the same spot by the lake as the previous day.

There was a small beach-like area of shingle here where the water gently lapped at the land. Towards one side was a crop of rocks, and choosing a large flat one, she climbed up and sat staring off over the lake and into the distance. The cold from the rock seeped through her leggings, and she drew her knees up instinctively and hugged them, feeling a sudden urge to phone Luke or her mum. To seek comfort from someone close to her.

A breeze suddenly picked up, causing Lizzy to draw her knees closer. There was no blue sky or cheery birdsong today. Clouds loomed overhead, mirroring her mood.

After a while of deep breathing, the initial shock wore off and her swirling mind calmed. She released the grip on her legs a little as her body relaxed. The thoughts of Luke and her mum were still there but less urgent, fading away into the background. Feeling stronger, she got to her feet and started wandering back to the hotel, following the winding path of freshly fallen leaves still soft underfoot.

It didn't feel as though she had been gone all that long, but as she neared the hotel, Lizzy could see the unmistakable fluorescent livery of the ambulance winking through the trees. It seemed unnaturally bright given the gloom that was setting in. It stood closed up and silent. No blues needed for this callout.

Inside, the hotel was equally quiet and still, though an undercurrent of activity hummed through the air. Lizzy padded her way up to her room and quietly closed the door. To make noise seemed disrespectful, though she wasn't really sure why. Given Deidre's nature, there should surely have been a fanfare playing to announce her departure or the hallways should have been lined with grieving women shrouded in black.

After removing her shoes, Lizzy left them by the door and went over to the small desk. She sat and opened her laptop, but her mind was as blank as the screen that greeted her. Despite feeling calm only a few moments ago, the sight of the ambulance had unsettled her.

She left the page she was on and went back to a previous section that needed editing. It should have been an easy task. Would have been on any other day. It didn't need much – a little more description, a better choice of words – but the words swam across the page in a blur. She shut her eyes, opened them to try again, but all she saw was the ambulance in her mind's eye. She shut the laptop, then looked up at the sound of a car approaching.

CHAPTER 11

A trio of red-faced boys stood in front of PC Anna Blackwell, staring at their feet. She glanced at her partner, PC Colin Myers, and let out a quiet sigh. They'd only taken some chocolate bars and a couple of cans from the fridge, but apparently, it was becoming a habit. The Village Shop in Braithewaite was where Anna often shopped. It was a small, white-rendered, converted cottage packed to the rafters with every essential the small village could need and every treat, drink, and ice cream the passing tourist could want. And as with a lot of other shoplifters she'd dealt with, the trio were just bored kids in a small village with nothing to do.

Her radio buzzed against her chest. She gave PC Myers a small nod before stepping outside, leaving him to finish up. He was currently giving the little buggers hell and scaring the life out of them. He was soft as shite to all who knew him, but his stocky six-foot figure could be a looming presence when needed. His late fifties, cantankerous attitude could be a big help too. Especially when dealing with ten-year-olds.

'This is Bravo two seven four receiving,' she spoke into the radio as the door clicked shut behind her.

Control gave Anna their next call as she got back into the car to wait for Myers. She was just fastening her seatbelt as he emerged and walked round to the driver's side.

'Little shits,' he mumbled, lumbering back into the car.

'Call through. Sudden death over at Briar's Crag hotel.'
'Oh, bloody great. Just what I needed today.'

The hotel cut an impressive structure in the surroundings once they had weaved their way down to it from the main road. It still amazed Anna that there were properties like these hidden down the small paths that snaked off the beaten track. Lovely in summer, but she betted it was a right bitch through winter.

As they pulled up and parked, one of the ambulance crew emerged to meet them. A tall, smartly dressed man hovered in the doorway behind. The manager or an overeager guest, she supposed, hoping for the former. They were both keen to get this call over with and move on with their day. These things had a habit of dragging on at the best of times without a do-gooder trying to be helpful or coming up with conspiracies.

'PC Myers and Blackwell,' Myers said by way of greeting. 'What do we have?'

'Elderly female found dead this morning at around 8:30 a.m. by the chambermaid. She's now left the premises – the chambermaid that is – taken home by her mother. Looks like natural causes; there're no obvious signs of injury or a struggle.'

'Left?' Myers' eyes looked impossibly wide and the word came out exorbitantly loud.

The paramedic held his hands up in surrender. 'Before we got here.'

'Shit, paperwork?' Myers asked, shaking his head.

'Just finishing up.' He nodded towards the hotel as his colleague emerged. She had a brief exchange with the man in the doorway before wandering over to them.

'Looks pretty open and shut,' she said, handing Myers the paperwork.

He idly flicked through and signed the handover as the paramedics packed up.

The Storm

'We good?' she called, slamming the rear doors.

'Yeah, yeah. Thanks. Right, then, Blackwell, let's get it over with.' He strode purposefully to the hotel with Blackwell following. They were met by the hovering man.

'Thank you for coming out. I'm Gideon, the manager of Briar's Crag.' He held his hand out to Myers and then Blackwell to shake. 'What do you need from me? Can I get you a drink? A tea or a coffee, maybe?'

'Aye, a tea would be lovely, ta. Milk and two, please,' Myers said. 'Shall we go through to your office?'

'Yes, of course, come through.'

'I'm PC Myers, and this is my colleague, PC Blackwell. She'll have a tea n'all, just milk.'

Gideon led them to his office, which was behind the reception desk. It was noticeably cooler in there away from the open fire in reception. The walls were plain magnolia and an oak desk sat on the worn hardwood floor. A monitor and keyboard lay centre stage, surrounded by piles of paperwork. Framed prints adorned the walls, each portraying the beautiful lake's scenery.

As the officers took a seat, Gideon left momentarily, and after some brief mumblings outside the door, to which they supposed he was getting some lower-grade staff member to play tea maid, he returned and sat awkwardly at his desk. First, with his hands perched on crossed legs, and then into a thinking man's pose. Finally, he rested his elbows on the desk, leaning into them.

Myers raised an eyebrow at Blackwell as she took out her notebook.

'So,' Myers began, 'let's start with the basics. The deceased's name?'

'Deidre Malone.'

'And when did Miss Malone check-in?'

'Last Thursday, the twentieth. She's a regular of ours; always comes up late summer and stays for a few weeks. Leaves before the cold sets in.'

'Travelling alone?'

'Oh yes, she's been widowed over thirty years now, I believe. No one else has dared take her on since.' He chuckled, then stopped suddenly, bringing his hand to his mouth. 'I am so sorry. I... I didn't mean—'

'Quite alright. Can you explain what you mean by that? Bit of a character, was she?'

'Well, erm... yes, but I... she...' He fingered his collar as if it were suddenly too tight around his neck. 'Oh dear. Miss Malone, well, I guess you would call her eccentric.'

'In what way?'

'She enjoyed being the centre of attention and she was very particular – where she sat, how her food was cooked, that sort of thing. Everything at a set time and in a set way. I mean, she was no bother really, not when you got to know her, knew how to handle her.'

'Anyone she did bother?'

Gideon relaxed a little, sitting back in his chair, eyebrows knitted slightly as he considered the question. 'Not really, not properly... She could rub people up a bit, but nothing serious. She liked to put on a show, but that was all it was. Most of the time, she kept to herself.'

'And how was she yesterday? Still on top form? Well?'

There was a bump at the door followed by a bang as it was manhandled open. Evan walked in with a tray on which sat three cups of tea and a pot of sugar cubes. A good deal of tea had slopped over. He looked for a place to safely set it down, gave up, then plonked it precariously on top of a pile of paper. He left again as the officers took their cups. Myers plopped a couple of sugar cubes in his and took a good slug, keeping hold of it. Blackwell watched tea slowly drip from the bottom of her cup onto her uniform. She set hers back down.

'She was fine as far as I know. Came down to breakfast at 7:30 a.m., she sat and read in the lounge for a bit, then went to her room. She takes... took brandy in the bar at 1:30 p.m., then lunch at 2 p.m. We don't usually see much of her after that until dinner. She sometimes walks…' He sighed. 'Walked in the grounds but not far, as she has…' He frowned, refusing to correct himself a third time. 'A stick. Dinner at 7:30 p.m. Last night, she sat outside for a bit to smoke. I think she went up to bed around nine-thirty or maybe 10 p.m., but I can't be sure.'

'Do you know what she ate yesterday?'

'No, but Evan will. He served her.'

Myers nodded, making a mental note to speak with him. 'Was she close to anyone at the hotel? Anyone she would chat to?'

'Not really, no. To be honest, I think all her bluster and show was just to get some interaction. I think she was actually quite lonely.'

The door to Deidre's room was closed but unlocked following the paramedics' visit. Blackwell covered her mouth with her hand as Myers opened the door, suppressing a gag as she smelt, and then saw once she was inside, that Deidre's bowels and bladder had clearly evacuated themselves. She hung back as Myers approached the deceased, lingering behind him and watching over his shoulder. As a fairly new recruit, she had yet to build up the cast-iron stomach Myers had developed over his years.

'Poor lady,' Myers said, shaking his head as he leaned over her, checking for any obvious signs of injury.

Even though the paramedics had examined her, it was procedure and needed to be adhered to. There were no injuries that they could see – no cuts or bruising, no defensive wounds, not even a broken nail. The bedclothes were largely undisturbed and the space as a whole was in a neat and orderly fashion. A place for everything and everything in its place, as Anna's grandmother used to say to her when she'd made a mess as a child. They checked the door and window for any evidence of tampering, but the window was locked and secure and the door and its locks were unmarked. There were a couple of prescription bottles in the bedside drawer. Sleeping tablets and blood thinners. Anna bagged them as protocol, but the paramedics were right – it looked pretty open and shut. Just a poor old lady who'd slipped away in her sleep.

CHAPTER 12

Lizzy had tried to lose herself in work several times, but to no avail. Eventually, she had shut the laptop and picked up her book, but after reading and rereading the same sentence over and over, she gave up on that too.

She assumed the police would want to talk to her at some point and couldn't settle for the waiting for it. Time was moving like sludge, and she paced the room like a caged animal. It was like waiting to be called to the headmaster's office. She'd seen the paramedics leave from her window. It surprised her that they hadn't taken the body. Isn't that what normally happened? The body. How awful to think of her like that. She was still Deidre. Only, she wasn't.

Lizzy lay starfished on the bed, making faces out of the ceiling rose when the bedside phone rang. She grabbed the receiver hastily.

'Hello?'

'Lizzy, it's Gideon. I'm with the police. Would you mind coming downstairs to answer a few questions?'

'Be right there.'

Replacing the receiver, she smoothed down her clothes, gathered herself together, and headed downstairs, where they had taken over a corner of the lounge. Two officers sat at one of the wooden tables at the far end, facing the doorway. Presumably, it was the most neutral and friendly setting, somewhere to put the guests at ease as they were questioned. They were in quiet conversation but stopped and looked up as she approached.

The lady officer immediately stood up to shake her hand. 'Hello, I'm PC Blackwell, and this is PC Myers.' She was trim and petite and wore her blonde hair in the neatest bun Lizzy had ever seen. She had a warm and friendly face.

The man, Myers, seemed huge in comparison. He reminded Lizzy a little of her dad. She guessed they would be about a similar age, and he held the same strength and protective aura as him. Myers' smile was friendly, but it didn't quite reach his eyes. Beaten down or respectful of the situation? she wondered.

'Thank you for coming down. Would you please take a seat?' Myers gestured to a chair.

Lizzy sat facing them.

'Could you just walk us through this morning, Lizzy?' Myers asked. 'I understand you were at the scene with Poppy, in Deidre's room?'

Blackwell flipped open a notebook as he spoke and sat with her pen poised, a sympathetic look on her face. Lizzy suddenly felt nervous, though she had no reason to be. She shifted in her seat.

'Yes. Of course. I went back to my room after breakfast. I was just getting ready to go for a walk when I heard a scream, so I went out into the corridor to see if everything was alright. I found Poppy in Deidre's room – the door was open. She was in a right state, bless her.' Lizzy's hand went to her collarbone, and she rubbed at it absentmindedly. 'Deidre was on the bed. It was obvious she was dead. Poppy was hysterical. I tried to calm her and coax her from the room. Then Gideon, the manager, came up, and we took Poppy down and called you guys.'

'So, the door was already open when you got to the room?'

'Yes.'

'And Poppy was inside?'

The Storm

'Yes. She'd gone to clean the room.' Lizzy stopped her rubbing and dropped her hands into her lap. 'Well, I assume – there was a cleaning cart outside.'

'Did you touch Deidre? Or see Poppy touch her at all?'

'No.' She looked up suddenly. 'Oh, wait, I didn't touch her exactly, but I did lay a towel over her face.'

Blackwell glanced at Myers, who remained looking at Lizzy. His face had changed. What was it? Confusion? Suspicion? It had been the wrong thing to do, she realised. She should have left her alone.

'Poppy was in such a state. I covered Deidre's face so she couldn't see her anymore. To get Poppy to move, to come away. Sorry. It was a stupid thing to do; I should have thought.'

'That's ok. As you can appreciate, it's just vitally important that we know who did what and who touched what. Did you touch anything else in the room or the body, sorry, Deidre herself?'

'No. Well, I imagine I touched the door or the handle when I first got there, but after I covered Deidre's face, I just concentrated on getting Poppy out of the room.'

'Ok, thank you. Now, how did Deidre seem to you last night?'

'Fine, as far as I know. I only arrived yesterday, so I didn't know her, I only saw her a couple of times really.'

'But on those occasions, she seemed well? Nothing looked amiss? Nothing worried or concerned you about her?'

'No. Not at all. She looked a little tipsy at the end of the evening, but that was all. A little unsteady on her feet, but she wasn't drunk. She walked with a stick though, so I don't know how much was actually drink and how much was normal for her. As I said, I'd only just arrived and met her.'

'Ok, thank you, Lizzy, that's very helpful. That will be all for now. We'll be in touch if we need any more.'

Lizzy rose to leave.

'Are you staying here long? Holiday, is it?' Myers called before she turned away.

'For the week. Just a little break.'

Myers nodded in response, and Lizzy took that as permission to leave. It made her uncomfortable that she was essentially being asked about her movements. She had half-expected to be told not to leave the area. Was she a suspect? Were there suspects? Did there need to be? The questions she'd been asked didn't lead that way. The police were probably just being thorough. Still, it unnerved her.

CHAPTER 13

Myers and Blackwell had so far spoken to the manager Gideon, Lizzy from room seven, and the couple Jenny and Alex from room eight. In a rather long and torturous interview, Evan had eventually been able to provide them with a list of everything he had served Deidre food- and drink-wise. None of them had raised any concerns for the victim so far or thrown up anything suspicious.

The family from rooms five and six were currently out, which left John Franks from room three – the adjoining room to Deidre – and chambermaid-cum-waitress Poppy, who they would need to visit on their way back to the station.

'I'm pretty sure he's still in the hotel; I haven't seen him leave.' Gideon smiled nervously before calling Mr Franks' room again, but once more, there was just an endless ring tone.

'He's still not answering,' he said, replacing the receiver.

'Then I guess we'll take the party to him,' Myers said, getting to his feet.

Myers and Blackwell headed upstairs to Mr Franks' room. Blackwell knocked firmly on his door, but when that still failed to summon him, Myers pounded on it with enough force to shake it in its frame. Eventually, there was movement.

'Fuck's sake,' someone muttered from within.

A few moments later, they heard the lock disengaging with a clink. Mr Franks threw the door open with such force that there was almost a suction of air pulling Anna into the room with it.

'What can't you understand about do not dist...' His flushed face calmed slightly and the puff went out of his chest. 'Oh, what do you want?'

'Sorry to disturb you, Mr Franks. I'm PC Myers and this is my colleague PC Blackwell. I'm afraid I must inform you that there's been a death in the hotel during the night, so we just need to ask everyone a few questions. Ok if we come in?'

Myers strode straight in, forcing the man to step aside.

Mr Franks was unshaven and had the air of dishevelment about him. His room likewise. In contrast to Deidre's, it seemed nothing had a place in here. Clothes were strewn about the floor, papers littered the desk, used tissues lay on the bedside tables, and a nearly empty bottle of what looked like whiskey lay poking out from under the bed. The whole room smelt warm and heavy. Anna had to resist the urge to open a window.

'Well, if you must,' Mr Franks said, following them further into the room. 'But I am very busy. Who is it, then? Who died?' He seemed largely unconcerned by the news he'd just been given. No sign of shock or even curiosity. He stood with a bored expression and made a show of folding his arms over his chest.

'A Miss Deidre Malone, from room four. The room next to yours,' Myers answered.

He looked mildly amused. 'Ha. That old bat.'

Both officers looked at him, but he made no move to apologise. He either didn't realise he was being disrespectful or didn't care. Anna took a seat on the desk chair – the only space available – and opened her notebook to take notes, leaning the pad on her lap for want of anywhere else she could place it.

'You two didn't get on?' Myers asked.

'Couldn't stand the woman. Good riddance, I say, stupid bitch. I've only been up here two days and she was a pain in my arse for both of them.' He shook his finger, emphasising his displeasure.

'Can you tell us your movements last night, Mr Franks?' Myers continued.

'From when? When she ruined my papers and nearly cost me the deal, or when I came to my room?'

'Well, let's start with the papers, shall we?'

'Stuck up bitch wouldn't sit at the table next to mine. Knocked my drink over all my paperwork in protest.' He shook his head and looked away. 'I came to bed, had a couple of drinks, went to sleep. Not much to tell.'

'And did you see Deidre again after you left the dining room?'

He shot them both a fierce look. 'No. They were bloody important papers and it pissed me off, but they weren't worth killing over, if that's where you're headed.'

'Just trying to get all the facts, Mr Franks.' Myers cast his eyes around the space. 'Did you leave your room at all in the night?'

'No.'

'Did you hear anything outside your room after you retired for the night?'

'No. Now, is that all? Only, I am very busy.'

Myers looked Mr Franks square in the eye with a steely glare. With barely concealed annoyance, he said, 'I'm sorry that this is inconveniencing you, Mr Franks, but a woman has died.'

Though Myers' voice had remained calm, it held a weight that commanded he be listened to. Mr Franks snorted like a bull about to charge and stared him out. Myers returned the stare and continued.

'Your room shares a wall with the deceased. You heard nothing at all last night? Not even the door opening or closing?'

'As I already said, no. I heard nothing. Now…' Mr Franks stood and gestured to the door, ushering the officers out of the room and all but slamming the door behind them.

'Well, he's a charmer,' whispered Blackwell, staring at the closed door. 'Can't see why anyone wouldn't want to sit next to him.'

'No, quite. So, what's your impression?'

'Mmm, well, he was definitely keen to get rid of us. But he looked more like a man on the verge of a breakdown, if you ask me.'

CHAPTER 14

A day of fell walking had not improved Ellie's mood. Her parents still weren't talking to each other and she had traipsed and trailed after them all day in awkward silence. Not that she had wanted to talk to them. But the fact there was clearly something going on bothered her. She hated it here. This was not a holiday. A holiday involved beaches and swimming pools and sun. This was cold and bleak. She looked up at the gathering clouds, grey and ominous above them, and snarled as if to emphasise her distaste. She knew her friends all had better plans than her. While they lay sunning themselves in far-off places, she had trudged through muddy bogs, almost losing a boot, and panted her way up hills she had no desire to climb.

She looked down at her new Zara jeans, now splattered with mud, and scowled. It was her parents' fault they were now ruined, as they'd dragged her up here, so they could buy her some new ones when they got home.

She kicked and stomped at the muddy path, sending bits of stone flying as they descended the latest hill. At least leaving the hotel had briefly restored her signal and data. Once out of the valley, she had managed to get back into her feeds, and every so often, she idly scrolled and updated herself on all the latest social media posts. She purposely hung back behind her parents as she did this, knowing they would only moan if they saw her on her phone. It wasn't worth it. Her bikini-clad cocktail-sipping friends smiling back at her only served to sour her mood further. It wasn't fair. How could she compete with that here?

The wind started picking up, bringing a cold drizzle with it. She hadn't brought any gloves with her, and before long, her fingers ached with cold and started turning white and numb at the ends. Gritting her teeth, she angrily stuffed the phone back into her pocket, keeping her hands in them, hoping they would offer some protection.

Today had shown her that she would be getting signal at least some of the time though. If she could just get some decent photos she could upload every time they left the valley. She had thought long and hard, but all she had managed to come up with so far was an adventurer-explorer angle. Maybe a few photos of her on a mountain or by a lake. She had to admit the scenery was stunning. When it wasn't obscured by mist or rain. A few artsy shots of a map, maybe her walking boots. It wasn't in the same league, but at least it was original. Who knew, it may even win her some followers from different circles.

They saw the police car sitting on the driveway as they walked up to the hotel, the livery shining in stark brightness against the grey day surrounding it. Her mum's eyebrows raised at the sight and her dad frowned, but they still didn't speak. It was starting to feel like a competition of who could be stubborn the longest. The police car piqued Ellie's interest, but not for long – it was bound to be something dull. With her luck, they would be checking in to stay there. Maybe they'd have some good stories though.

They passed it and carried on into reception, trailing bits of the fell behind them on the polished wood floor. The owners of the vehicle, two uniformed officers, stood as they entered, causing Ellie's heart to skip a little. They approached and introduced themselves, though Ellie didn't take in their names, then ushered them into the lounge, getting them to sit at one of the tables. Ellie was suddenly nervous and sat giving

The Storm

them her full attention, waiting for the bombshell. They were clearly not here to bring them good news.

'I'm afraid we must inform you that there's been a death in the hotel during the night. Nothing to worry about, we just need to ask everyone a few questions if that's alright?' It was the man speaking. Mayor or Myer or something. Ellie's eyes grew impossibly wide.

'Oh, how awful,' her mum gasped, bringing a hand to her neck. She looked genuinely distraught, as if she'd actually known the woman.

Ellie's mood softened a little out of empathy for her mum, but not enough to show it. She was stubborn like that. Stubborn and hot-tempered and... sorry for her mum. She crossed her arms tightly. No, it was her dad's job to comfort her mum. She looked at him, but he made no effort to. No arm around her shoulders, no hand to hold, he just sat there like a mannequin.

She was vaguely aware of him asking how it had happened, but their voices became blurred and distant, as if she were watching the scene from afar. Last night. Deidre had died last night while they'd all slept just a few doors away. She felt sick at the thought and looked away from them to the walls, the floor, the hanging pictures, anywhere but at the people talking. If she focused her eyes elsewhere, maybe she could pretend it hadn't happened and her mind would stop picturing it.

'Ellie,' her dad's voice broke through the bubble she had placed herself in.

'What?' she answered sharply, annoyed at being brought back to face it. She quickly tried to soften her voice as she realised how disrespectful she must appear. 'Sorry.'

The police officer, the male one, cleared his throat. 'I was just asking if you heard anything last night? Anything at all that may have seemed a bit odd. Even if it didn't at the time but does now in light of things?'

'Oh... no.'

'Or if you noticed anything unusual. How Deidre was behaving, or anyone else for that matter.'

'No.'

She answered each question posed to her as short and direct as she could, hoping to get it over with as quickly as possible. Finally, the questions came to an end and they left. She stood, ready to leave, desperate to get back to her room, to some solitude, but her dad was on his feet too, eyes blazing and jaw clenched. He stared at her, hands on hips, an expectant expression on his face.

'What?' she spat.

'What? What. How bloody uncooperative could you be?'

She clenched her fists. 'I answered their questions; what more do you want from me?'

'How about a bit of bloody respect? They're police officers, for Christ's sake. A woman has died.' He exhaled loudly and shook his head. 'You need to grow up, Ellie.'

She set her mouth, silently fuming and trying not to react. God, he was a hypocrite. Her grow up? He'd been giving Mum the silent treatment all day – that was hardly mature now, was it? She waited a beat to make sure he had said all he needed to say, then she turned and stomped up the stairs to her room. She needed a shower to rid herself of this awful day and this horrible news. She was also desperate to get out of her muddy clothes.

CHAPTER 15

Lizzy sat at the large wooden desk and opened her laptop. The morning's events still clouded her mind, but having now spoken to the police, she was feeling much more settled. She took a brief few moments to read through and remind herself of where she had got to and then finally managed to start typing. It was good too, not fractured as before, but prose that flowed and enhanced her work. She found it flowed so well in fact that she grew completely immersed as her fingers flew over the keys.

'Chapter fifteen,' she said, then smiled at just how far she'd got. This was more like it. She was more focused, less distracted, and she was finally making a dent.

Her stomach growled angrily at her, snapping her from her workflow. She checked the time in the bottom right corner of her laptop screen. 4 p.m. Damn, she'd missed lunch and dinner was still a couple of hours away.

She hit save and shut her laptop, then sat back, looking out the window. She frowned as she noticed a black van on the driveway. It didn't look like the average vehicle of a guest to her. Lizzy's mind flicked between maintenance or delivery, then her eyes widened. A private ambulance. Deidre was leaving.

She turned away from the window, quickly wondering if there was some show of respect she should be adhering to. Like in the olden days, where she imagined people would remove their hats or bow their heads. She had no hat to remove, so she bowed her head briefly. Then she arched her back and massaged her neck, cracking it to each side for good measure. Not for Deidre, rather for too much sitting in one position and too much screen time.

Lizzy changed into her running gear and headed outside. The clouds were so low it looked as if they had fallen from the sky and were grazing the surrounding mountains. It was a bizarre sight. Beautiful and dramatic.

She ran towards the lake and followed the path that skirted it. It was an easy run, the terrain fairly flat and the scenery simply stunning. Each footstep took a little bit of stress away with it. Lizzy ran until the path started to climb and get scrambly, then stopped for breath and a stretch by a waterfall. God, she loved it here. It was so freeing being outside, being in nature, being… alone.

She haltered on that last thought. Did she mean that? Was she enjoying a break, or was she deciding her future? Two days… that wasn't long enough to decide. She was just enjoying a break; no need to be rash. Still, the thought unsettled her. She loved Luke. On paper, he was the perfect man. Reality didn't always live up to expectations though. She mentally scolded herself and turned back as the first fat drops of rain fell. By the time she reached the hotel, she was sodden.

CHAPTER 16

'I think this might be it,' Myers said, pulling the car to the side and coming to a slow stop as he squinted out of the side window.

Blackwell looked at the slate brick semi and the number four on the door and nodded.

It looked a little tired, but it was neat enough and the cottage garden in front seemed to have been tended to with love.

'Ready to go again?' Myers asked.

Blackwell sighed. It had taken an age for the undertaker to arrive and the body, which they'd had to sign over, to leave their charge, allowing them to leave. They had been warned by the hotel manager that Poppy was in quite a state, so they had decided between themselves that Blackwell should take the lead on this one. Though she was the less experienced of the two, she would be the least threatening presence.

'I suppose,' she said, getting out of the car.

Myers joined her, and they made their way up the path to the door. Flowers of every colour overflowed the borders to decorate the original-looking stones. They brightened the somewhat dull day and still managed to look cheery in the gloom.

Blackwell rang the bell while Myers stood a step behind her. After a few moments, the door was answered by a woman in her late forties. Concern was etched into her features and she hugged a long cardigan round her curvy frame.

'Mrs Flintwood?' Blackwell began. 'I'm PC Blackwell and this is my colleague PC Myers. Could we step in and talk with Poppy, please?'

The woman looked a little flustered, patting her chest lightly with one hand and almost flapping the other, but she swung the door open and showed them through into a cramped living room. It was cosy rather than cluttered and felt warm and homely.

'I'll just fetch her; she's upstairs in her room.'

Blackwell sat on one of the floral-print sofas, while Myers, always the detective, had a good snoop around the room. He'd gotten as far as eyeing up the photographs on the mantel when advancing footsteps sounded through the door. A girl they took to be Poppy entered the room. She wore black leggings with an oversized grey hoodie. Her long dark hair hung loose around her face, which she used as a shield to hide behind. She appeared shy and nervy and eyed them suspiciously as she sat in an armchair, bringing her legs up onto the seat as if she were trying to curl into a ball.

Her mum followed her in. 'Tea or coffee?' she asked.

'I'm good, but thank you,' Blackwell replied.

'Aye, that would be lovely, thank you. Milk and two sugars, please,' Myers said, never one to turn down a cuppa.

She nodded politely, then turned and left, presumedly for the kitchen, leaving the three of them alone.

'Hello, Poppy, how are you doing?' Blackwell began.

Poppy looked up at Blackwell with black-smudged eyes and shrugged.

'I'm PC Blackwell, and that man over there is PC Myers. I know you've been through a lot today already, but we need to ask you a few questions about it, ok?'

Poppy nodded and started chewing on the cuff of her sleeve.

The Storm

'Now, if you can think back for me, was Deidre's room locked when you got to it this morning?'

Poppy nodded.

'So, you had to use a key to get in?'

Another nod.

'And what happened when you let yourself in?'

Poppy took a few seconds to think and compose herself. To find her voice. Even so, it still came out barely above a whisper. 'I took her some clean towels. I always knock first, in case. No one answered, so I let myself in.'

'Do you have a key to all the rooms, or is it a master key?'

'A master.' She'd moved on from chewing her sleeve to picking at it. Evidently, she had made a hole and pulled at the ragged ends of it.

'And do you keep that, or is it kept somewhere at the hotel?'

'The hotel. There are two in reception and I think Gideon has one in his office.'

'So, you knocked, then went in? Then what?'

Poppy looked away as tears started streaming down her face. 'The room was dark, so I opened the curtains. When I turned around, I...' The tears turned into gulping sobs.

'It's ok, Poppy, you're doing really well.'

Poppy's mum arrived with Myers' tea. She placed it on a side table and went to her daughter. Perching on the arm of the chair, she hugged her close.

'Do we have to do this now?'

'I'm sorry, Mrs Flintwood, but it's important we ask these questions as soon as possible,' Myers interjected.

She grimaced but nodded her consent for them to continue.

'So, Poppy, you opened the curtains...'

'She was on the bed just... just lying there, and... I thought she was asleep, but... but she looked wrong...' Her words came in hiccuppy bursts as she struggled with the memory. 'Her eyes.'

Blackwell knew what she was talking about. The eyes of the dead were unmistakable. Milky, unseeing, and totally devoid of life. It was an eerie thing to see and it must have been such a shock – first to find somebody in a room you thought was unoccupied and then to find them dead.

'Did you touch anything in the room? Did you go to Deidre at all?'

Poppy shook her head and tried to get her crying under control. Every time she seemed to have calmed, her face crumpled and she started over.

'Wait, yes.' She sniffed. 'Well, just the door and the curtains. I think. I don't remember touching anything else. I don't think I did. I definitely didn't go to her… I… I couldn't.'

'You've done really well. That's great. Thank you, Poppy.'

Blackwell turned her attention to her mother. 'I think we can leave it there. Thank you. We'll show ourselves out.'

PC Anna Blackwell secured her locker and clocked off for the day. A few of them were going to the Ship for a pint, but she really didn't fancy it. It had been a dull and draining day, plus it was now lashing it down out there. All she wanted was to get home and snuggle up with a takeaway.

Deidre and the guests at Briars Crag still played on her mind. The poor woman hadn't been likeable, it seemed, but apart from a minor altercation with Mr Franks, there seemed no reason for anyone to wish her ill. Besides, after a quick call with his boss, it would appear there was actually no deal to ruin – Mr Franks had in fact been recently suspended pending an internal investigation by HR. All shirt and no trousers, Anna thought. The bloke couldn't let go of his own egotistical jumped-up image of himself.

The Storm

She and Myers had determined there was no suspicious activity and filed the relevant paperwork. All that remained now was the obligatory post-mortem, which was scheduled for tomorrow morning. God, she wished for a bit more excitement tomorrow. Give her a joyrider or a mugger any day.

CHAPTER 17

Dinner at the hotel was a much more sombre affair that night. Conversations were hushed or non-existent. The only real noise came from the pounding of the rain and the howling of the wind. In Poppy's absence, Gideon was waiting tables along with Evan. He brought a much speedier and efficient service than had gone on before. Lizzy sat shivering slightly. Even after taking a long bath, she still felt chilled. She ordered the slow-cooked lamb stew in the hope it would warm her from the inside and a red wine to go with it.

Mr Franks was at his usual table, beer in hand and a burger and chips in front of him. He had no papers with him tonight; instead, he just sat staring at his food, which he ate with a ferocity that made it appear he was angry with his meal. The man looked like a heart attack waiting to happen.

The lovebirds were thankfully less lovey-dovey tonight. Their faces held compassion and the girl tenderly stroked the back of the man's hand as they quietly ate. Lizzy thought it was a very soothing gesture and found herself suddenly jealous of the action. Of them. Her head was all over the place right now.

Get it together, Lizzy, she thought.

Gideon arrived with her food and placed it in front of her.

'Thank you.'

He nodded and left.

The Storm

She tucked in, thankful for the distraction. It was good, just what she needed, and she enjoyed every mouthful of it.

She was just finishing up when the family of three arrived. They looked a little uncertain as they entered the dining room, hovering by the door as if unsure whether to come in or not. Evan, in a boost of efficiency, went straight to them and seated them at their usual table. He went to fetch menus, lingering over handing Ellie hers, then left them to consider their options. The parents once again sat in stony silence, stoic and grave, but there was a different energy about the girl tonight. A sparkle almost. She seemed to have noticed the attention she was getting from Evan and threw him smiles and glances whenever she could. Evan, clearly smitten, reciprocated whenever possible, grinning at her like a Cheshire cat and making sure he was never far away from their table – certainly always looking at it at least, or rather at Ellie. In contrast to Gideon's speed and efficiency, this resulted in a more clumsy and painfully slow service than usual from Evan, as he largely ignored the other tables and mixed up orders when he did actually attend them. Lizzy could see Gideon watching him as he bustled about picking up the slack, his face setting harder and jaw clenching as he became more irate with Evan's behaviour as the night went on. Finally, he took Evan aside, both of them returning moments later with faces of thunder. Evan's service improved slightly afterwards, though his temperament did not. He stomped from table to table with a look of sheer indifference.

As with the previous night, the girl left as soon as she had eaten, leaving her parents sitting alone at the table. Lizzy wondered if they sat in the comfortable silence that came with years of marriage or in awkwardness. Looking at their faces, she suspected the latter.

CHAPTER 18

Fiona sat nursing a white wine. Their meal was over and their plates cleared away, though she made no move to leave. Her husband remained seated at the table also. He may have been by her side, but he was there in body only. He may as well have not been; in fact, she would have probably preferred that. His presence was simply a reminder. They didn't speak. Not to each other. Hadn't for the past few days now. Another day of silent stewing passed. Another day of regret and betrayal. Tomorrow would no doubt be the same. At least Ellie seemed to be in a better mood today.

She played with the stem of her glass. How could she have done this to her family? How could she have been so stupid to think that Paul would never find out?

This holiday was supposed to be special. Their last as a family before Ellie headed off to university. Before she was fully grown and no longer needed them. Not that she needed them now. Not really. It had taken enough persuading and guilt-tripping to get her to even come this week.

Fiona wondered why they'd bothered. Ellie seemed to be in an almost permanent scowl with them – nothing they did was right or good enough anymore, everyone else's parents were way cooler, let them do more, let them stay out later, let boys come over. It was never-ending.

A last holiday to be a family. A last chance to bond with her daughter. And what had she done? Ruined it all before they'd even arrived. She cursed herself for letting this happen.

The Storm

All her fault. All her stupid, stupid fault. She needed to fix it. But how? Speak to Paul and clear the air? Speak to Ellie and get her version in first?

Fiona relished neither choice.

CHAPTER 19

Ellie sat heavily on the bed, drawing her knees up to rest her head on them. Being around her parents was becoming unbearable. Whatever they had going on, she really hoped they'd get over it soon. She sighed. Maybe they'd let her do her own thing tomorrow. She could go off exploring. Get some shots done ready to upload. She started mentally going through possible settings, picturing the grounds of the hotel and the lake, places she could get to by herself. Then she heard movement out in the corridor. Approaching footsteps, the click and then soft thud of a door. Her parents returning.

It was still early. Now that they were up here, maybe she could go back down, have a bit of fun. Evan had been giving her the eye all night, and she wondered if there was something there. He was kind of cute. Not in a boyfriend way, but maybe in a fun-on-holiday way. She checked herself in the mirror, freshened her lip gloss, then silently opened and closed her door and slipped downstairs, hoping he was still around.

She found Evan still in the dining room, clearing the tables and resetting them for the morning. She could have gone directly to the bar without coming in here, but by walking this way round, she'd made sure he'd notice her. She sat by the counter, waiting. He was behind the bar before she even got comfortable on the stool.

'Vodka and Coke, please,' she said, letting a smile play on her lips. This was going to be fun.

CHAPTER 20

'I can't believe you could be so fucking stupid. So callous. Has our whole marriage been a sham? Was I just a bloody joke to you?' Paul's whole body shook with his words, spit flying from his mouth like a barking dog. His hands flew from his head into tight fists and back again as a vein pulsed in his temple.

Fiona sat sobbing on the edge of the bed. Big, ugly, gulping sobs. He'd seemed so much calmer tonight at dinner. Subdued in his drinking rather than the angry drunk of the previous night. She'd thought it was her best chance of talking him round, of explaining. How wrong she'd been.

'I... I'm so s-sorry,' she wailed.

'Sorry? You're sorry? Bit late for that, isn't it?' he spat. 'About nineteen bloody years too late, if you ask me.'

'It... it doesn't have t-to... change anything. We can still be a f-fa-family.'

'God, you're unbelievable.' He threw his hands up into the air and paced the room. He stopped inches from Fiona's face, suddenly speaking quietly. 'I wish it had been you that died last night, you poisonous cheating bitch.' He pointed a finger into her face, jabbing as he spoke. 'If you ever, ever use this to take Ellie away from me, you will sorely regret it. I have raised that child from birth. I am her father, and I will always be her father. And so help anyone who gets in my way.'

The venom with which he spoke sent chills down Fiona's spine, and she shrank into herself with every word. She couldn't be small enough. Couldn't get away. She was utterly trapped in this horrible situation, and the worst thing was that it was all her own making.

Paul backed away. Leaning against the wall, he took a couple of steadying breaths, then crumpled before her, sliding onto the floor as his tears came.

She couldn't bear to see him like this. To see what she had done to him. To see what she had done to them. She loved him so much that she felt as if her body were shattering underneath the weight of it. She wrapped her arms around her torso, holding tight, as if she could hold herself together and stop it from happening. She desperately wanted to go to him, to hold him and soothe him and make everything alright. For everything to go back to normal. But there was no getting over this, was there? She had destroyed her family before it was even made. One stupid drunken night nineteen years ago. A one-night stand. Their beautiful daughter. Only, she wasn't Paul's beautiful daughter.

Fiona got to her feet and fled the room. She could no longer stand the sound of her husband's breaking heart. It was tearing her own in two.

CHAPTER 21

Behind the bar, Evan tried to look busy polishing glasses and moving things around while he clearly struggled for something to say. Ellie kept watching him and smiling, enjoying his discomfort and the power she seemed to be holding over him. The lights had slowly been extinguished around them and even Gideon seemed to have disappeared and left them to it. At last, he spoke.

'So... how long are you staying for?'

Ellie laughed. 'Seriously? Ten minutes of polishing that glass and that's all you can come up with?'

Evan looked taken aback and then his brows knitted into a scowl. She felt bad for teasing him and relented.

'I'm here for a week, and in case you were wondering, yes, I'm single,' she purred. She looked away smiling and took a sip of her dwindling drink. She didn't believe in dancing around the issue.

Evan's cheeks coloured slightly and he grinned. He looked at the glass in his hand as if just realising it was there and finally set it down. 'Can I get you another?' he asked, motioning to her glass.

Ellie nodded.

He began refilling as noises from upstairs filtered through the ceiling. They paused, looking up. All they could pick up was muffled shouts. No words, no sense of direction or ownership. A definite row though.

'Jeez, someone's going for it tonight,' Evan said.

They looked at each other and giggled. The awkward tension dissipated in that moment, and they relaxed into themselves.

'So, and genuine question I swear, this is not a line. What are you doing in a place like this? I mean, there's fuck all to do here. Like, seriously. It's dull as shit. It doesn't really seem your kinda place.'

'It's not. Like, at all. No offence.'

'None taken. You think I'd be here if I didn't have to be?'

'It was my parents' idea. I start uni in a couple of weeks and Mum had this great plan of one last family holiday, all bonding bullshit 'cause their "little girl is growing up".' She rolled her eyes. 'All my friends, and I mean all of them, have flown off to somewhere amazing, and I'm stuck bloody fell-walking.'

Evan gave a compassionate wince. 'Yeah, that sucks.'

'And what is with the signal here? There is literally nothing to do. How do you survive?'

'Shit, isn't it? The whole valley's in a black spot. Gideon uses it as a marketing ploy to sell the "ultimate retreat and escape from technology". It's a total ball-ache. We have signal up in the village though.'

Behind them, feet clattered down the stairs and then the front door clicked open and shut. It wasn't long until they heard it click again.

'Bloody wind,' Evan scowled, rolling his eyes. With a huff, he threw the towel down and bustled from the bar to go and secure it.

CHAPTER 22

Fiona hadn't really thought about where she was going, only that she needed to be out of that room. The rain was falling hard, and not having planned to come outside, she hadn't thought to grab a coat when she'd fled. Fiona ran round to seek shelter in the smoking area. It was little more than a wooden roof on legs, and the wind carried the rain through the open sides. She pulled her clothes tightly around herself, trying to stave off the cold. It was a futile attempt, and she was soaked through and shivering within seconds.

What was she going to do? She wasn't sure how she would ever be able to face her husband again. She had known he would be furious, but she really hadn't foreseen just how venomous he would be.

She took a deep breath. God, she was shaking. Not just from the cold but the build-up of emotions. She couldn't go back into that room until he was in a much calmer state. She couldn't exactly stay out here in this either though. She could slip back inside, sit in the lounge for a while and dry off. Get a brandy to steady her nerves ready to face him again. Or wait until he was asleep.

No. They needed to sort this tonight. It wasn't fair on Ellie to keep going how they had been. Fiona wasn't sure she could keep going like this either. It was destroying her, it was destroying her husband, and it would for sure destroy Ellie.

A shadow fell across the corner of her vision, and she turned as a presence edged round the hotel. Someone was approaching slowly and steadily, as if unsure of her reaction or scared of startling her. He'd already calmed, she thought, breathing a sigh of relief. He was ready to talk.

'Oh, Paul,' she gushed, rushing forwards to meet him.

CHAPTER 23

Lizzy sat at breakfast foggy-headed. She'd had a very disturbed sleep, which had left her feeling somewhat disjointed from her body. Like the physical and the mental weren't quite aligned. She had a bowl of fruit and yogurt in front her and a coffee strong enough to stand a spoon up in. She brought it up to her face and savoured the aroma as she surveyed the room, her eyes immediately being drawn to the table occupied by the family. The father looked like a withered version of his former self. He wore the haggard expression of someone who had been up all night and held his coffee cup like he was trying to warm his hands and summon life from it. His daughter was plugged into her phone, immersed in whatever she was listening to and spooning heaps of cereal into her mouth. She seemed happy enough at least. Either she hadn't heard them going at it last night, or it was a common occurrence that she had grown desensitised to. The mother wasn't down yet. Lizzy wondered if this was due to embarrassment or necessity – they hadn't exactly been subtle or quiet. Lizzy could fully sympathise with not wanting to make an appearance this morning after the show they'd put on. It was also possible that they hadn't made up yet. Maybe she couldn't stand sitting at the same table as him. Lizzy wondered, intrigued, as to what could have set them off so spectacularly. Which one of them was in the wrong? What was it all about? Then she had a horrible thought. What if he'd hit her? What if she was upstairs hiding a black eye?

Lizzy looked away embarrassed, realising she'd been staring. The lovebirds were back to feeding each other. Or rather, she was trying to feed him. She was smiling sweetly, trying to be cute while he looked to be quickly tiring of the game. The whole scene gave Lizzy the appearance of a mother trying to feed her child. Lizzy smiled at the thought, taking a sip of coffee to stop herself from giggling. Definitely a new relationship, she decided. They hadn't worked each other out yet.

Movement at a side table caught Lizzy's eye, and she turned, surprised to see Poppy laying it with silverware. She wondered if she had heard Gideon offer her the week off or chosen to ignore it and keep busy. Maybe her mother had insisted. She appeared to be functioning again though, moving in her normal skittish way. It was only her face that had changed, her still puffy eyes rimmed red instead of with black kohl eyeliner. Lizzy felt sorry for her and made a mental note to check on her when she got the chance.

Breakfast helped to clear her head, or rather the caffeine hit did, and Lizzy left the dining room feeling much more human. As she passed through reception, heading for the stairs, Mr Franks barrelled down in the opposite direction and bumped roughly into her shoulder, spinning her to the side. Even though she had seen him coming, her reaction could not match the speed with which he travelled.

'Ow,' she exclaimed, rubbing the spot he'd hit.

He gave a brief backwards glance, but that was all. Not even a muttered apology.

'Excuse you,' she called back after him with a scowl, her face blushing with heat.

The Storm

He really was quite infuriating. At least he had finally changed out of that horrible crumpled suit. He was wearing an equally awful one, but at least this one was clean. He'd washed his hair too. Without all the grease, it looked a whole shade lighter. That's where the improvements stopped though. His hair, although clean, hadn't been combed, and his stubble was getting longer by the day. Lizzy wondered what kind of business would choose to have him representing it. He must be a phone and email kind of guy, not a face-to-face meeting sort, she surmised.

CHAPTER 24

PC Anna Blackwell had just come on shift. She sat at her desk, surrounded by a sea of others all clacking away at their keyboards, typing up her own reports to the background hum of office chatter punctuated by ringing phones. She hit save on the file as her own phone rang.

'PC Blackwell,' she answered.

Myers, sitting silently across from her, watched as her face fell and she closed her eyes.

She hung up and exhaled loudly. 'We fucked up.'

'We? What do you mean? How? What have we done?'

'The death at Briar's Crag is no longer looking like natural causes. We missed something.'

'Missed what?'

'I don't know, but facial bruising had developed by the time the pathologist received the body and they found cotton fibres in her mouth.' The fibres could have been explained by Lizzy covering the face with a towel, but the bruising suggested suffocation.

She banged her hand down on the desk. 'Shit. Final nail in the coffin - her hyoid bone was fractured and there were petechial haemorrhages on the lungs. The official cause of death was recorded as asphyxiation.'

She leaned back in her chair, covering her face with her hands, then running them over her head until she met with her bun. She held onto it momentarily, then sat forwards, elbows

The Storm

on the desk, her head rested on praying hands. The report in front of her was forgotten now; her thoughts consisted solely of Deidre and how this would affect her career.

Myers exhaled and scratched his head. 'It happens. Don't get beat up about it.'

'We ballsed it up though, didn't we?'

'Look, we did everything by the book and went with the information and evidence we had at the time.'

'Yeah, but—'

'No. End of. The scene was kept secure, and unless the hotel manager has fucked up, it should still be locked and untouched. We did our jobs, now we hand it over to CID.' His tone was light, relaxed.

Anna still didn't like it, but she didn't feel as if she had a choice. She felt as though she'd failed an exam. She'd not been in this position before, but she guessed that she'd be called in to explain herself. They both would. Would it be together as partners or individually to see if their stories matched up? If this really was murder, and it looked bloody likely, then they'd missed something and heads would roll.

'Well, don't just stand around; make yourself useful.' Myers waved his mug at her.

She rolled her eyes but stood and took it anyway.

CHAPTER 25

The rain continued to lash outside as the storm reached full force. Even though it was now midmorning, the sky still held no light, albeit for the odd random flash of lightning. Another rumble sounded overhead, and Gideon's monitor flickered along with the lights. He silently willed the power to hold. The remoteness of the hotel made it a real draw in the summer months, but during weather like this, it became a curse. All that gave it charm turned bleak. The wonderful surrounding scenery was walled off by fog, mist, and rain. People's endless freedom shrank into a claustrophobic prison. Nobody would be venturing out today, which made it more imperative that the power hold. His guests would need some sort of entertainment, and it looked as though TV or radio would be their obvious choice. The hotel lounge was stocked with a full selection of books, cards, and board games should any of them feel the need to venture from their own four walls. Gideon had asked Evan and Poppy to place candles on every common room table just in case the worst should happen. They remained unlit but ready. Power outages were common here in bad weather, but thankfully, they were usually short. He expected the bar would be getting hit hard later.

The trill of the phone broke Gideon from his mental checklist of preparations. The reception was patchy and the voice on the other end faded in and out in a stuttering fashion.

'Good morn…thi…Detective…Cumbr…Police…can…

yo...request...room...to remain... sealed...we wi...further questions...ask...no one leave.'

He heard enough to get the gist of the call before the line died. He hung up, then tried the phone again. There was a click, but he was met with silence. No dial tone.

'Bloody perfect,' he said as he slammed the receiver down.

CHAPTER 26

Lizzy faced the rain-streaked window, laptop open and busily typing away on her edits. She was pleased she was here to work and not here on holiday; it was truly awful out there. The storm had moved in so much so that she could barely see out now; however, it was doing wonders for her focus, and in just a few short hours, she had achieved more than she had done in the entire previous week. She found she was at one with her writing here, with herself. She wondered if she would be sorry to return home or if she would return refreshed and invigorated. She feared for the former and wished for the latter. Still, the Luke question buzzed round her mind like a wasp. As much as she told herself that it was too early to decide, that she hadn't had enough of a break yet, she realised that she had yet to miss him. To want him. They had been together for two years. She should be feeling something different than relief. Though that is what she did feel. Relief. At not always being held and touched. At not explaining every movement of her day. At not being bombarded with calls and texts whenever they were apart. He was lovely, and she knew it all came from a good place, but he was exhausting and she was relieved to be free of him.

Lizzy wiped at her face, suddenly aware she was crying. Then she moved to the bed and lay down. Curling herself into the foetal position, she hugged the duvet close to her chest and let the tears fall. She allowed herself a few minutes of self-indulgent crying, then got up and went to the

The Storm

bathroom to give her face a good wash in cold water. Feeling better, she sat on the bed, her thoughts spinning. She went through a mental checklist of the good and bad points of their relationship. There were many good memories – mainly of their early dating days, even of him moving into her flat. He'd been so romantic and attentive, and she had been so blissfully happy. But things had slowly changed. She couldn't pinpoint when or even what had happened. She didn't even know if it had been him who had changed or her. But their relationship had morphed. The attentiveness felt claustrophobic. The romance felt forced.

She used to love every minute they spent together. But now, he wanted to be with her all of the time, which had been sweet – was sweet, flattering even. But she still needed time to herself. And lately, he was becoming resentful of any time he wasn't with her, whether she was alone in the flat or, God forbid, had gone out somewhere without him. She would have to provide him with a full itinerary of where she was going, who she was going with, what time she would be back… The list was endless.

And it didn't even stop there. He would text to make sure she had got there safe, call to say hi to everyone, text to make sure she was having a good time, text to check when she would be back even though she'd already told him. And she realised she did miss Luke. But she missed the old Luke. The carefree one. If the question had been about him, then it wouldn't even be a question. She just didn't know how to get that version of him back or if she even could. And that's where her dilemma lay. She wasn't ready to give up and say goodbye to the sweet Luke who she knew was still in there.

CHAPTER 27

Lizzy was the first one down to lunch and went straight to the buffet-style food, helping herself to all the warm offerings before taking a seat. With little else to do today, the other guests soon piled in after her. The storm had dissipated to a steady shower that extended the small view outside the windows somewhat. Rivers of water had sprung from multiple points around the grounds and were running down towards the lake. It pooled on the driveway in places and puddled on the grass. It was miserable, but at least it seemed to be breaking.

At the table in front of her, there was still no sign of the mother. Lizzy started to wonder if maybe she had left last night, as she would have needed to eat and the hotel didn't offer room service. The father had more life in him at least. His cheeks had regained some colour and he chatted a little to the girl in the awkward way that some fathers do with their teenage daughters. Still, he was trying at least. It was definitely progress. The girl was less forthcoming in her efforts and offered little in response. Shrugs and grunts mainly. Unless Evan was around, of course, then came the smiles and the coy looks. The man from the cutesy couple had noticed her too, it seemed, as his gaze kept wandering from his ever-talking girlfriend. Lizzy guessed it probably had something to do with the low-cut top the girl was wearing today that her breasts practically spilled out of. Lizzy even caught herself looking on a couple of occasions. The father seemed to notice the leering eyes upon her as he looked up and around the room, then started angrily whispering to the girl. Her lip curled and she rolled her eyes, then shrugged a hoodie on and sat pouting, arms crossed.

Mr Franks sat quietly in the corner, absorbed in a newspaper. The plate in front of him was incredibly modest compared to normal, and even that looked untouched.

Lizzy finished her meal, a squash and barley quinoa with lemon cod, then picked up her coffee and took it through to the lounge. She had the room to herself and settled into one of the plush armchairs, watching the last of the rain ebb away. It was quite relaxing. Meditative almost. Especially as a small fire had already been lit. Poppy scurried through but was gone before Lizzy could call to her. She had to give her her dues, she was coping a lot better than Lizzy had thought she would, given her state yesterday. She decided she'd still check on her if the right situation arose but no longer felt the need to seek her out.

A cup of coffee later and with her jacket on, Lizzy wandered outside, where the rain had almost stopped. The weak light danced on every leaf and blade of grass, reflecting each drop of rain and making everything sparkle. With the mist still lying low, the whole place looked quite magical and ethereal. Looking up at the still dramatic skies, Lizzy decided that it was best not to go too far. It did feel good to be back outside though. The air was so clean and fresh. Lizzy inhaled deeply, savouring it.

The grounds of the hotel weren't huge – a covered smoking area set to the side, a flagstone patio with cast-iron tables and chairs, a grassy area dotted with shrubs and bushes. They didn't need to be big. Not when they were nestled amongst such beauty. The mountains hugged the grounds and the lake was practically a stone's throw away. Wandering footpaths led in all directions, begging to be explored. There were a couple of outbuildings to the back of the hotel and a second car park. Presumably, those were just for staff.

Lizzy took the nearest path and wandered down towards the lake, careful to avoid the many rivulets of water cascading in the same direction. Everything was saturated, but the ground held solid. Still, Lizzy trod carefully – she hadn't exactly brought walking boots with her, so she was conscious of slipping or getting a foot caught in sludge.

After a hundred yards, the footpath disappeared into a small copse of trees, and when she emerged on the other side, the lake suddenly appeared in front of her. Even with the looming sky, the water glittered with what little light there was in spectacular fashion. Every time Lizzy saw it, and from whatever angle, the beauty of it always amazed her.

The footpath spidered out further here as it petered down towards the water's edge. The heather that clung to the higher edges of the path was in partial bloom, and the sight made her smile as she walked past.

The Storm

As Lizzy neared the lake, she suddenly became aware of something bobbing in the water a few yards from the shoreline. It was partially submerged, but even from here, Lizzy could see it was quite large. She frowned and tutted, thinking someone had fly-tipped or that the storm had blown in a bag of rubbish or a patio umbrella. But as she drew closer, the shape became apparent and she detected limbs.

'Shit.' She gasped as she dashed into the water.

The cold hit hard, taking her breath away, and the muddy bed sucked at her trainers, threatening to claim them. Pulling harder with her legs, Lizzy ploughed on, wading deeper and deeper into the lake, each step chilling her further and making her pant harder. Adrenaline coursed through her veins keeping her going, keeping her moving. She had to get to them, had to save them. They hadn't looked all that far out, but the water reached her waist by the time she got to it.

Lizzy reached out to them and turned the body, desperate to give them air. She gasped, immediately letting go. The face that looked back at her showed all too clearly that she was too late. Her breaths started coming hard and fast and tears sprang to her eyes. Lizzy stood stock-still, her heart hammering, unsure of what to do as she stared down at the bloated face and auburn bob that haloed out from around it.

CHAPTER 28

Lizzy took a few deep breaths to try to compose herself. She was shaking violently now, the cold penetrating her core and the effects of shock beginning to set in. She needed to get out of the water. And she needed to… She looked away and bit her lip, fear taking over. It would be easy to run back to the hotel, get help, leave her in the water in the meantime. So easy, right?

She took one step away from the body, closer to the shore, then screwed her eyes tight for a second before turning back around with a deep sigh. She was a woman, probably a daughter, maybe a sister, aunt, a cousin… but definitely a wife and a mother. How would she feel if someone left her mother's body dead in the water, where it could potentially float away?

I need to get her out of the water.

With shaking hands, Lizzy tentatively touched the body again, just fingertips on clothes. The poor woman's face was bloated and marbled, her skin wrinkled and already looking loose, especially on her hands. Lizzy's lips trembled and she suppressed a gag. She held on to the lady's cardigan, fearing the skin would slough off in her hands if she touched it.

The Storm

Trying not to look at it any more than she had to, Lizzy slowly and carefully started pulling the body back through the water, towards the shore. The water held the weight, but the mud underfoot made progress incredibly slow. Each pull of a foot took incredible effort and strength as the suction worked against her. Twice, Lizzy slipped, plunging herself into the icy water and earning herself a mouthful of lake, the presence of the body in it making her gag and choke on more than the water itself. As the water grew shallower, the body grew heavier, which wasn't helped by the lady's weight.

Lizzy paused at the shoreline to catch her breath before pulling at her, trying to get the body up the bank far enough so that it wouldn't be in danger of slipping back in. The muddy ground gave the body some lubrication, but it took every ounce of effort and strength that Lizzy had to finally get it high enough. She collapsed onto her knees, panting, then immediately threw up.

Lizzy wiped her mouth with the back of her hand and struggled to her feet. She took a few shaky steps back up towards the path and then broke into a feeble yet determined run.

Lizzy burst into reception trailing mud and water in her wake. Gideon stared at her from behind the desk, his mouth agape.

'What in God's name…?'

She stood in the middle of the room, trembling and panting hard, trying to get enough air into her lungs to enable her to speak. She was completely sodden, and mud encased her hands, splashed her face, and matted her hair.

Gideon started to move towards her but then stopped, looking her up and down. 'Did you slip into the lake?' His voice held concern.

'There's... oh, God... there's a body, in the lake... I...' She brought shaking hands to her face. 'The lady, from the family. I found her in the lake. I...'

Gideon's hand flew to his mouth. 'Oh, Jesus.'

'Can you phone for the police? I've dragged her out, but... shit.' Lizzy shivered uncontrollably and her teeth chattered so much that her jaw hurt. She looked at Gideon with pleading, desperate eyes, as if she needed him to take the burden from her. To take control of the situation.

'The lines are dead. The storm has brought them down.' He began pacing, breathing heavier, glancing at the phone as if wishing for it to suddenly work. 'Dear God, what do we do?' He suddenly stopped and stared at her, his mouth slightly opening as he retook her in. 'Oh, let me get you a towel. We need to get you warm. Here, come and stand by the fire. Evan. Evan. Quick, we need a towel.'

Evan wandered in from the dining room with an almost audible eye roll, saw Lizzy, tutted, then trudged upstairs to fetch a towel. Gideon helped her remove her outer garments. They sucked at her skin as he peeled them off her and discarded them on the floor. The T-shirt and jeans she was left standing in felt heavy and restrictive, but she was loathed to remove them in front of Gideon, and thankfully, he didn't try.

'What are we going to do?' Lizzy said, her voice small. 'We need to get help. We need... oh, God, we need to tell her family.' A tear rolled down her cheek as her heart broke at this realisation.

The Storm

Evan sauntered back down the stairs with a towel in his hand as though he had all the time in the world.

'For Christ's sake,' Gideon scolded, snatching it away from him and wrapping it around Lizzy's shoulders. She hugged at it desperately, smearing muddy handprints all over it.

'I pulled her out of the water, but she needs to be moved. We can't leave her there. Not like that.'

Evan's face paled.

'No, no, of course. Let me worry about that though. You need to go upstairs, have a hot bath, get warm.'

'Water? Who was in the water?' Evan flicked his gaze back and forth between them. 'Are they ok?'

Lizzy closed her eyes and silently wept with trembling lips.

Gideon looked down with a solemn face. 'There's been an accident. Fiona Barker, room six. She's been found in the lake.'

'Found?' Evan repeated. 'She's...?'

Gideon nodded. He put his head in his hands and started pacing one way to form an idea, then back again, dismissing it with a shake of his head. 'Evan and Carl can help me,' he finally said.

Evan's face fell with numb horror.

'Three of us together. I'm sure there's a trolley or something we can use. Where is she, Lizzy?'

'I took the first path from the patio. Between the flower boxes.'

'Right. Well. Ok. Evan, can you fetch Carl, please? He may still be in the kitchen. Both of you will need coats and boots. Get dressed and back here as quick as you can.'

Evan floundered, turning this way and that before getting a hold on himself. He suddenly moved with purpose in the direction of the kitchen.

'What about her family? Her husband and daughter?' Lizzy asked.

'I think it's more important we move her first. Get her somewhere safe. We don't want them running out there to find her.'

Lizzy paled as the image of the bloated face came back to her. The water had turned that loving mother into something not even her worst nightmares could have conjured. No, she thought. No, we definitely don't want them to find her.

CHAPTER 29

With limbs of lead, Lizzy made her way upstairs. Her muscles screamed at her with every step and her body shivered so much it hurt. She arrived at her room and locked the door behind her before starting the shower running. Her numb fingers fumbled with the fastening of her jeans, and she cried in frustration, trying to tear them from her body. There was no doubt in her mind that she would never wear any of these clothes ever again.

Once off, she kicked them into the corner of the bathroom and sunk to the floor sobbing – for the mother, for her family, herself, for the men going out there to deal with it and bring her back.

She hugged her legs close to her chest and longed to call Luke. She needed so strongly to be wrapped in his love, for him to smother her with hugs.

Finally drained of emotion, she rose and stepped into the steaming shower. The spray needled her numbness, turning her cold painful. She scrubbed at her skin, she shampooed her hair. Then she ran a bath and repeated the process. She wasn't sure she would ever feel clean again.

Lizzy dressed in leggings and layered up a T-shirt with a chunky knit cardigan and scarf. She was no longer numb, but she still couldn't get warm, not even by the radiator. What she really wanted was to get her PJs on and climb into bed, sleep, forget today had ever happened. But she had a feeling Gideon or the family would want to talk to her, and night attire would really not be appropriate.

She sank onto the edge of the bed and stared vacantly ahead, wondering where the poor lady was now, if the men had managed to find her, if they had got her back safely. She should have gone with them, she suddenly thought, shown them exactly where to find her and helped them. Taken Evan's place. He may have only been a few years younger than her, but he still seemed so young, still holding on to his teenage angst. He didn't need to see that. To do that. Lizzy had already seen and touched. Was already covered in mud and... She ran to the bathroom as images of the body came flooding back to her, leaned over the toilet bowl, and retched until she had nothing left but bile.

CHAPTER 30

The rain had started up again. It had never truly stopped. Just dwindled to something insubstantial. Now though, it fell in a heavy shower from a sky blackened with the promise of more. Unable to settle, Lizzy went back downstairs to find Gideon. To find anyone. Her need for human companionship overrode her need to be alone.

She scanned the empty reception area, then turned at a sound, but it was only the hiss and spit of the fire. Her heart sank. She wondered if they had returned yet. It was a fairly short walk away, but if they had no equipment to transport the body, it would take them a long time even with the three of them.

The fire crackled again invitingly, and Lizzy moved closer to the warmth. The parquet floor had a sheen to it, all the mud and water she had trailed in earlier mopped away. Scrubbed clean as if nothing had happened. She wished she could wipe her memory of the day just as easily.

She stood holding her hands out to the fire, turned to warm her back, then sank down in one of the armchairs to the side of the fire to wait. Barely a minute had passed when she heard feet approaching quickly and nimbly on the stairs. Gideon arrived freshly laundered, his face flushed and his hair still damp.

Lizzy rose. 'Is she—'

'Yes.' He paused. 'We've put her in one of the outbuildings.'

Lizzy's face fell.

'I know it doesn't seem all that respectful, but she'll be safe and dry in there. Until the police can come. It's better than leaving her by the lake in the storm.'

Lizzy had to concede he was right. The danger of the storm washing her back into the lake or of an animal sniffing around her was too great. It didn't seem right, not by a long shot, but it was the best choice they had available to them at this moment in time.

'The phones are still out, so Carl's going to drive over to the station once he's cleaned up. Report it and get someone out.'

'Right. Good.' Lizzy sank back into the chair with a sigh of relief.

'Are you ok? You're looking much better.'

She may not have felt it, but she did look it. Her face had regained colour, and after the mud-covered swamp monster she'd been, she could hardly have looked worse.

'Much better, thank you. Are you ok? Evan?' Her eyebrows furrowed. 'I'm so sorry, I should have gone back with you, shown you, helped... I—'

He raised a hand to stop her. 'It's fine. We're fine. We'll... be fine. You were exactly where you needed to be, getting yourself dry and warm.'

Lizzy gave a small nod, then looked away into the fire. 'Have you spoken to her family yet? Have you told them?'

'No, not yet. I needed to get cleaned up first. And, well, I was hoping the police would do it. When they arrive.'

'Yes, of course. I suppose that would be best.'

A bald man Lizzy recognised as the chef strode in through the main doors, his dripping raincoat peppering the floor with droplets. He rubbed his hands over a serious and grim expression, shaking his head like a dog ridding itself of water. Lizzy stood in anticipation of his news.

The Storm

'Ahh, Carl, just setting off?' Gideon asked.

'Just back. It's unpassable; storm's brought a landslide down, blocking the road. No one'll be coming in or going out for a while.'

'Shit.' Gideon rubbed the bridge of his nose as Carl disappeared into one of the offices behind the reception desk. He returned moments later minus his coat and headed towards the kitchens.

'There must be somewhere we can get a signal here. If we walked far enough or started up one of the peaks, got higher?' Lizzy said.

'The black spot stretches farther than you'd be able to safely get in this weather.'

Lizzy sat back on the armchair, sinking into the umber tweed. Gideon joined her by sinking into the opposing chair.

'We have to tell them,' Lizzy said. 'They have a right to know.'

CHAPTER 31

'He'll be down in a moment,' Gideon said, taking a seat near Lizzy in the lounge. She'd chosen seats near enough to the fire to feel the heat without risking them feeling uncomfortable.

They had decided they would tell the father first, reasoning that he may be better placed to break the news to his daughter himself and possibly even prefer to. If not, he may at least be able to offer her some comfort after being allowed to recover from the initial shock himself first. It was still early, an hour before dinner, so they were unlikely to be disturbed. Plus, Gideon thought it likely he would be in need of a stiff drink once they'd finished.

After a good five minutes, Paul arrived looking worn and tired, the stubble he had arrived with now looking like a lazy oversight rather than a fashion choice. He landed heavily on the sofa opposite them.

'What's this about, then?' he asked.

Gideon took the lead. 'I'm afraid I have some rather bad news, Mr Barker... Paul. It's about your wife.'

'Fiona? What's that bitch done now?'

Gideon exchanged a worried glance with Lizzy. Lizzy nervously took over, wondering how the hell you broke news of this nature to somebody.

'Paul, this afternoon, I found your wife at the lake. Or rather, in the lake.'

The Storm

Paul's eyes flicked between the two of them with furrowed brows. 'And?'

'And...' Lizzy took a deep breath. She had hoped he would have understood her hint so she wouldn't have to say it out loud. 'I'm so sorry, Paul. She's dead.' She stared at Paul with searching eyes as he stared dully back at her.

His eyes narrowed and his forehead set in a frown. 'Dead?' He leaned forwards as if he hadn't heard her correctly, then looked at Gideon with a puzzled expression.

Gideon nodded.

His eyes started darting round the room as he tried to take it all in. To understand. 'When? How?'

'Well, we believe she drowned,' Lizzy said.

Gideon rose and made his way to the bar. He poured a healthy measure of whiskey, then set it down in front of Paul. Paul stared at it but didn't drink. Didn't move. Didn't blink.

'We've moved her out of the water. She's somewhere safe and dry, but I'm afraid the phone lines are down so we can't call anybody out just yet. We will keep trying though,' Gideon assured him.

Paul still hadn't moved.

Lizzy leaned forwards, trying to meet his gaze. Nervously, she said, 'Would you like us to tell your daughter for you? Or to be there with you when you do?'

Paul's head snapped up, and he looked at her with pure fury. 'Nobody tells Ellie,' he spat. 'Nobody. Do you hear me?'

The outburst was so unexpected Lizzy jumped back in her seat. 'But, Paul—'

'No. She is my daughter, and this is our holiday together. Our last holiday. And nothing and nobody is going to ruin that. Ok?' With a shaky hand, Paul picked up the whiskey and downed it in one. He slammed the glass down so hard that Lizzy was surprised it didn't smash. He stood, staring at them both with a look of hatred.

'You are not to breathe a word of this to her. Either of you. Do you understand?' His tone was quiet but firm, and he pointed a trembling finger at each of them as he spoke, his eyes boring into them as he flicked between the pair. Then he strode quickly from the room.

CHAPTER 32

'That wasn't the reaction I expected,' Lizzy finally said after at least ten minutes of complete stunned silence.

'Me neither. I guess shock affects everyone differently though.' Gideon walked over to the bar and poured another whiskey. This time, for himself. 'Want one?'

Lizzy shook her head.

'I know I shouldn't, not while working, but...' He shrugged and drank half down in one gulp.

She couldn't blame him. She would have one too if she thought her stomach could handle it. Her dad was a whiskey drinker, and she always had a tot when she was feeling a bit down or under the weather. The taste and aroma would immediately transport her back to her childhood home. To evenings snuggled up with her dad on the sofa, watching old James Bond films or a good old family game show. It was like having a hug from him when he wasn't there.

'I will take a tea though. If there's one going?'

Gideon nodded and wandered off towards the kitchen, eventually returning with a tray. Ever the professional, it was laden with a teapot, cup, milk jug, and sugar bowl. A mug would have sufficed, she thought, it was enough that he had made it for her. He may well have been acting on autopilot, but she smiled at his kindness, nevertheless.

'Thanks.' She poured a cup, hesitated at the sugar, then added one anyway. It didn't bring the comfort of her dad, but it did bring her some comfort and was very welcome. She held it cupped in her hands, feeling the heat radiate through her body.

'I told Carl while I was in there. Explained what Paul had asked of us.'

'It's so unbelievable. I mean... how can he not tell her? She has a right to know,' Lizzy said, her eyes almost pleading, though it wasn't Gideon she needed to convince.

'I know, but however strange we find his decision, it is his decision to make. She is his daughter, and we need to respect his wishes.'

'But it's so messed up. How exactly is he planning on having a lovely family holiday with that hanging over them? She'll surely ask after her, wonder where she is. And what about when the police do come?'

'It's the shock, I imagine. I think he may well be in denial. I'm sure he'll come round after it's sunk in a bit.'

Lizzy supposed what Gideon was saying made sense. She hoped so.

They sat in companionable silence while they finished their drinks.

'I should go and find Evan,' Gideon said, rising. He placed his empty glass on the low table. 'Make sure he doesn't mention it either.'

Lizzy gave a half-smile and nodded as she poured herself a second cup. She had no desire to return to her room alone. Her body still felt leaden and it was warmer down here. Her thoughts swirled and drifted, and she fought the urge to close her eyes.

CHAPTER 33

Voices and footsteps floated in from reception and roused Lizzy from sleep. She looked around the room, disoriented, taking in her surroundings. She was still in the lounge, though the tea tray that had been in front of her had disappeared. She really hoped she hadn't been snoring or asleep with her mouth agape. She rubbed her hands over her face to brush away the last remnants of sleep and found drool on her chin. Great.

A quick look at her watch told her the noises were probably the other guests coming down for dinner. She stood and stretched out the knots that napping upright had given her, then headed through to the dining room. She wasn't convinced she was hungry, feeling physically and mentally wretched and drained from the day's events.

It had been Mr Franks and the lovebirds she'd heard come down. Paul and Ellie's table lay empty, all three seats still around it, one waiting for a mother who would never return. Lizzy turned away with tears in her eyes.

Mr Franks sat surveying the menu. He already had a pint in front of him and some kind of spirit. Lizzy wondered what kind of businessman would stay so long in a hotel where he couldn't connect to the outside world. How was he working? Maybe he wasn't. There were papers and folders laid out on his table again though, so he presumably was doing something. He would occasionally rustle them, flick through, and scrawl notes in the margins. Most of the time, he just stared at them as if deep in thought, a lost expression clouding his face or his features thunderous. Mr Franks didn't seem to have a neutral face, and Lizzy still hadn't seen him smile yet.

The lovebirds were unusually quiet tonight. She looked solemn and he looked bored. Neither spoke. Their actions and mannerisms were open and friendly though, so it didn't appear that they had fallen out. Maybe too long kept cooped up. Or maybe too long for the length of the relationship. Lizzy was pretty convinced now that her first assumption of honeymooners was way off and decided that their relationship was definitely fairly new. No one who had been together any length of time would act the way they had been. Or was she being cynical? Wasn't it more likely that she would never act the way that they had been?

Lizzy dropped her head into her hands and sighed. She suddenly felt that coming here had just been running away from her problems and that now she needed a retreat from her retreat. But it had helped, hadn't it? Was helping? She was definitely making huge headway with her writing. Her mind was free and flowing in that regard. And on Luke? Well, that was still a seesaw of emotions. Just when she'd come to accept one way of thinking, something would turn her thoughts upside down and she'd be right back to where she started. It was a battle between her heart and her head. Unfortunately, both were strong-willed and persuasive. She shook her head free of her thoughts and glanced at her menu, still unsure if she even wanted anything.

Poppy came by the table a few minutes later. She stood holding her order pad and pen but didn't actually speak.

'Hi, Poppy, just the soup and a roll, please,' Lizzy said, deciding that was probably a fairly safe option. 'Oh, and a sparkling water. Thank you.'

She tried to catch her eye, but the contact Poppy gave was so fleeting before she scurried away that she wasn't able. Lizzy thought she looked terribly pale and drawn, but then she had before all of this happened. She would have liked to talk

The Storm

to her a little if she'd allow, to ask how she was and offer her support. She doubted Evan would be a caring shoulder to cry on, and Gideon, as sweet as he seemed to be, was her boss. Poppy looked to be late teens, early twenties tops. Not the sort of age to be friends with an older male boss.

Lizzy kept a lookout ready for an intercept and clocked Poppy on her way back with her water. As she neared her table though, Lizzy's attention was suddenly diverted to Paul and Ellie entering the dining room. The water was deposited and Poppy retreated all without Lizzy noticing. Paul looked tired, his face and eyes puffy, his expression neutral. Ellie, by contrast, was as fresh and dewy-faced as ever, wearing her usual look of indifference. There were no red eyes or blotchy face. Her makeup looked full and perfectly applied.

'He hasn't told her,' Lizzy whispered to herself. Part of her had hoped he would have come to his senses after the initial shock wore off.

She was aware she was staring, but she couldn't look away. Paul glanced around the room, and they locked eyes. His expression turned thunderous, and she looked away, wishing she'd brought her book down with her. The time it was taking her food to arrive stretched and she felt the need to fill it with something.

The soup didn't take all that long to arrive, but by the time it did, Lizzy had lost all confidence in herself.

'Thank you,' she said quietly to Poppy and let her leave without probing.

After taking a few tiny mouthfuls, Lizzy found she was actually ravenous, and when Poppy came to take her bowl away, she ordered a side of chips. She risked a glance towards Paul and Ellie's table and then quickly looked down at the white linen tablecloth. She decided she was being ridiculous. She hadn't done anything wrong, so why was she so afraid of looking? She looked back up.

It appeared that Paul was attempting some small talk. Ellie sat with one earphone in, picking at her food, clearly uninterested in whatever her father was saying. She kept casting flirty smiles over at Evan every time he passed, but they were not reciprocated tonight. He was trying hard to look anywhere but her table. Who could blame him? He'd just moved her dead mother's body from a lake and wasn't allowed to talk about it. Easier to not let anything slip if things were kept professional. Lizzy had a feeling Ellie wasn't the sort of girl to let him get away with snubbing her though. She hoped Evan was prepared.

Paul suddenly thumped a fist down onto the table.

Everyone jumped and stopped what they were doing, turning to stare at the interruption to their evening. A stunned silence filled the room, allowing even more volume for Paul's words.

'Could you at least have the decency to show me even the tiniest bit of attention when I'm talking to you?' he bellowed.

Ellie sat back, eyebrows raised and hands up in mock surrender. 'Sor-ry.'

The silence stretched as everyone sat waiting for the next outburst or reaction. None came. Slowly, murmurs of conversation started up again.

Paul ran a hand up his face and through his hair. He looked over at Evan, who stood rooted to the spot, unable to tear his eyes away. He glanced between Evan and Ellie, clearly unhappy with either of them showing interest in the other. 'A bit of respect, that's all,' he said firmly but quietly. Then he stood and, looking daggers at Evan, left the table and walked out.

Evan dashed back into the kitchen and Ellie, red-faced, sat staring down at the table, clenching her jaw. She looked a little unsure of what to do. Lizzy considered going over and sitting with her, but she wasn't sure she'd be able to keep her mouth shut. As she debated back and forth, Ellie made the decision for her and left. It felt as though the whole room breathed a sigh of relief.

The Storm

'Well, that was the best entertainment I've seen all day,' Mr Franks bellowed followed by a hearty laugh and swig of his beer.

Tactful as ever, Lizzy thought, rolling her eyes. She finished her chips and decided that maybe now was the right time for that whiskey.

CHAPTER 34

Ellie slammed the door behind her and threw herself face down on the bed. She screamed into the pillow, then flipped over onto her back. Bloody men, she thought, frowning at the ceiling.

She wanted to talk to her mum, but that would involve knocking on their door and no doubt it would be Dad who answered it. She had no desire to see him again tonight after his little outburst at dinner. What an embarrassment. The whole dining room had looked at them. Everyone. They'd all stopped eating and talking and just stared.

And what the hell was with Evan? They had spent a good part of last night in the bar chatting and getting to know each other. After getting a little tipsy, they'd even had a kiss and a bit of a fumble. Was that what this was about? Was he regretting getting involved or pissed off at her for not going further? God, men played some stupid mind games. No, not men, boys. That's all he was. A silly little boy playing silly little games. Well, she'd show him. No one treated her like that and got away with it.

CHAPTER 35

Warmed from the whiskey, Lizzy snuggled under the duvet, wriggling down and pulling it up under her chin. She felt a lot better for eating, but she was keen to put the whole horrific day behind her. After turning off the bedside light, she closed her eyes and tried to get comfortable. She lay on her back, then her side, trying one way and then the other. It didn't matter where or how she positioned herself though, lying in the dark, the memories returned to haunt her and refused to let her rest. Every time she closed her eyes, Fiona's bloated, marbled face swam in front of her vision like it was rising up through water towards her. It didn't help that she had fallen asleep earlier either. It may have only been twenty minutes or so, but it had messed with her body clock. She was both wide awake and dog-tired.

Lizzy sat up, put the light back on, flicked the TV on, and scrolled for something banal to watch. The news popped up, showing images of the landslide down the road. She sat up a little straighter, taking in the scene from the drone footage. Jesus, what a mess. Mud and rocks of varying sizes had been sloughed off the hillside and now covered the road. She hadn't quite realised the extent of the accident when Carl had told them about it earlier. Most likely, he hadn't been able to tell himself from the driveway. Apparently, it had been in danger of going for a few years and local residents were up in arms about it. It covered one hell of an area and had in parts taken some of the road away with it. It would take a few days to clear enough access for emergency vehicles to pass but would be closed to passing traffic for a few months while they made the area safe. Lizzy could only imagine the horrendous detour this would bring to the locals. It wasn't the most direct route anywhere as it was. She then worried about getting home; would they be able to clear enough road in time for her departure, or would they all be stuck here for weeks? No, of course they wouldn't. There would be emergency procedures for such things. They wouldn't be trapped.

She flicked again, looking for something to take her mind away from it, and landed on a nature documentary. Perfect. She watched for a few minutes to calm her racing mind, then snuggled back down into the bed, shutting her eyes to the furry rodents that scurried on the screen as she drifted off to David Attenborough's dulcet tones.

Lizzy woke with a start. The room was in darkness albeit for the glow of the TV still playing though the documentary had ended and rolling news lit the screen. Her heart thudded in her chest and sweat prickled her brow. How could they have missed it? Why hadn't it occurred to them before? In all the drama and panic, she realised they had all missed one glaring fact. Two deaths in two days. What was the likelihood of that happening? Pretty slim, she reasoned. Especially Fiona's death. She was late forties, early fifties maybe. Still young. And strong. She wasn't a feeble woman. The chance of her accidentally drowning in a lake seemed very small.

The more Lizzy thought about it, the clearer it became. From the moment she was last heard of until the moment Lizzy found her, there had been a raging storm. No one would have willingly ventured out in that to walk beside a lake, so unless Fiona had gone out there with the intention of ending her life, someone had taken it from her. And with the road out impassable, it meant that someone was staying in the hotel.

The Storm

Lizzy gathered the bedclothes up to her neck and switched the lamp on. She sat shaking, breathing hard, unsure what to do with this information. Everyone would be asleep by now; it was the middle of the night. Unfair of her to wake everyone up with her ravings and scare them. But even worse if she didn't and someone else died. And awful for her if the first person she woke up to tell ended up being the murderer.

She switched off the TV and listened to the night. Outside, the storm continued to rage, lashing the windows with a steady drumbeat. She slipped from the bed and over to the door to look through the spyhole. The corridor lay in darkness. Lizzy pressed her ear to the wood. Nothing to be heard. She thought about going out there to... to do what? Hand on the doorknob, she paused in deliberation. Then she turned in retreat.

With frantic eyes, she scanned the room for something big and heavy. With the wardrobe being built-in, the desk would have to do. It would certainly be easier to move than the bed. She hurriedly removed the hostess tray and kettle from the top, placed it on the floor so that it wouldn't fall, and started pushing it towards the door. With a potential killer in the building, there was no way she was trusting the flimsy hotel locks to keep her safe. The desk was a solid unit though and heavier than it looked. She got into position and leaned all her weight against it. After the effort of moving Fiona's body earlier, every muscle in her body screamed in protest. Pushing from a standing position resulted in little progress, so she got down lower with her shoulder up against the end. It still hurt and it took a little while for her feet to find traction against the carpet, but when she did and it started to move, it slid fairly steadily. The desk hit the door with a dull thump, and Lizzy sat back panting. She was absolutely exhausted, but she felt a whole lot better having created a barricade. Still, she worried about the potential of what could be happening beyond her door.

She climbed up and knelt on the desk, ear to the door once more. Nothing. A last look through the spyhole. Darkness. She sat like that for a few minutes, letting her eyes grow accustomed to the darkness and the fisheye view, looking for any sign of movement. There was nothing to be seen, and the only sounds were the beating of her heart and the heaviness of her breathing.

She got down and padded back to bed. She left the TV off this time so that there was nothing to mask any sounds. She did, however, leave the light on.

CHAPTER 36

After a fitful night, Lizzy awoke with the dawn chorus. She hadn't had much sleep, but at least she had managed some. Though the sleep she had gotten had been filled with nightmares. Reliving finding Fiona in the lake. Being chased through the hotel by a knife-wielding intruder. In one particularly bad one, she had taken hold of Fiona and started to pull her out only for Fiona to grab hold of her and drag her into the lake with her. Lizzy had woken gasping for air, tangled in the bedsheets.

She rolled over but knew no more sleep would come. Her eyes felt like sandpaper and she had the dull beginnings of a lack-of-sleep hangover. The rain was still falling, but at least it had quietened to a steady shower now.

Dragging herself from the bed, she hurriedly dressed in last night's clothes that littered the floor and set about moving the desk back. Pulling it was a lot harder than pushing it had been, and it seemed to take ages just to move it a few inches. Several times, Lizzy had to stop for breath and to rest her arms. The ache in them had intensified in the night, and they burned with the effort. She worked on getting it far out enough to squeeze in behind and push from the other side, and then she only moved it enough to enable her to open the door. She did so with reserve, inching it open and peering out before venturing into the corridor. Coast clear, she hurried down to reception in search of Gideon.

The hour was early and Gideon was not at the reception desk yet. Should she try to find him or wait in reception? Waiting would be best. She had a good view of all the rooms linked to this one from here, multiple escape points, and full visibility of the stairs.

She sat on one of the fireside chairs and looked from door to door, the stairs constantly in the corner of her eye, although she knew she would easily hear someone walking down them. The fire was unlit, the hotel still sleeping.

She lasted all of a minute before feeling too much of a sitting duck. Was wandering around a good idea? She wasn't sure, but she couldn't help feeling impatient and useless just sitting there doing nothing.

She scouted the rooms downstairs – the lounge, the bar, the dining room. She even peeked into the kitchen. None of the staff were up yet, not that that surprised her at only 5:30 a.m. They had no reason to be.

She shuddered, suddenly realising how cold it was. Wrapping her arms around herself, she crept back upstairs, opened her bedroom door, and squeezed into her room. There was no way she'd be able to focus on work while she waited for everyone else to awaken, so she tiptoed into her bathroom and turned the shower on to heat up, hoping the hot water would take the chill out of her body.

She didn't like the idea of showering without her barricade, but she also couldn't bear to move it again – her arms were leaden from her last efforts, her strength completely sapped. She realised now how much easier it would have been to try to wedge the chair underneath the handle. Did that work with swivel chairs? She wasn't sure it would or that she could trust it. To try would also involve moving the desk further away from the door. She decided it wasn't worth the effort.

Instead, she removed a drawer from the desk and placed it on the floor between the desk and the door. It left a six-inch gap. Not enough space to allow the door to open far enough for anyone to pass through. Not stealthily at least. She was certain it would break under pressure, but it would take a massive slam or someone trying to kick it in. It would certainly prevent anyone from sneaking in undetected.

The reception desk was still empty when Lizzy ventured downstairs again at 6 a.m., now dressed in fresh clothes, but this time, she could hear shuffling papers interspersed with the click of a keyboard in one of the offices behind it. She leaned on the desk, hands on the wooden top to push herself closer, and called out. It wasn't enough. She was too quiet to be heard. She didn't want to shout or ring the bell in case she disturbed any of the other guests, so she slipped behind the desk and rapped gently on the door. It was only pushed to so she nudged it open, revealing a wide-eyed Gideon.

'Lizzy.'

'Sorry, I did call, but…'

'Not a problem, sorry, you just made me jump, that's all. You're up early. What can I do for you? Everything alright?' Gideon was hovering behind his desk, bent over a mess of papers with another mess of them in his hand. His shock made him look like a caught-out schoolboy.

'Yes.' Her body sagged. 'Actually, no. can we talk?'

Gideon motioned to the chair in front of Lizzy and lowered himself into the one behind the desk.

'I've been thinking about Fiona,' she began.

'Oh, gosh, me too. Just awful. I barely slept a wink last night. I imagine you didn't either.' He yawned, as if to prove his point.

'No, it's not that. Well, it's not just that. It's the nature of it all. I mean, two deaths in two days. Doesn't that seem a bit suspicious to you?'

'I haven't really thought about it, to be honest. But, well, Deidre was quite an old lady.'

'She was. But Fiona wasn't. And why would she be out by the lake in a storm? It doesn't make any sense. It can't have been accidental, surely? She either went there deliberately or else that decision was taken from her.'

He sat back suddenly, taller, straightening his back and frowning at her. 'Wait, you're not saying someone potentially killed her?'

'I think they were both killed, Gideon.' She leaned forwards and looked deep into his eyes. 'It came to me last night, and I can't believe we never saw it before. I've been up half the night thinking about it, and the more I think about it, the more it makes sense.'

Gideon sat back, placing steepled fingers to his mouth as he seemed to process what Lizzy was saying. 'I suppose it would make some sense of the police call I received.'

'What call? Are the phones working again?' Lizzy asked, suddenly animated.

'No, no, this was yesterday morning. No, the lines are still as dead as a dodo. They called first thing, but the line wasn't great. I could only catch the odd word, but I gathered they had more questions for everyone and asked that no one leave the hotel.'

'Shit. And that didn't raise any alarm bells? Jesus, Gideon.' Lizzy was up out of her chair and pacing the room.

'Well, it seemed inconsequential at the time. I just supposed it was box-ticking, finishing off the forms and whatnot. We don't know that there was anything suspect. Don't you think you may be jumping to conclusions just a little? Look, you've had a horrible shock, gone through a traumatic experience and barely slept. Could it not be possible that your imagination is running away with you a little?'

Lizzy stopped pacing and rested her hands on the back of her chair. She took a few deep, steadying breaths and closed her eyes. She ran through it all again in her head. No, she was still convinced that something wasn't right.

The Storm

'I don't know about Deidre, but Fiona's death was not an accident. Either she went out there and took her own life or someone staying here took it from her. We need to get the police out here as soon as possible.'

'Yes, we do. As I said though, the lines are still out at the moment. They tend to drop in and out when we have a bad storm, but I'll keep trying throughout the day. If that's all it is, they should be back on before long. The thing is that with the landslide out there though—'

'Shit, the landslide. I forgot about that. Is there any other access to the hotel?'

'No, we're nestled in a valley. One road in and out. The only other way is over the mountains, but that could take days. And you'd probably be looking at a death wish in this weather.'

'What about the lake? Surely, you have a boat there? Can we get across the lake?'

'We did have a boat. Well, we do have a boat. It's just not seaworthy, as they say. It's currently down at Sourpool Wyke being repaired.'

'So, we're stuck until they can clear a path?'

'I'm afraid so.'

Lizzy's face fell as she sank back down into the chair and mentally went through their options. It was a short list that only consisted of sitting tight and waiting out the storm – in the figurative and literal senses.

CHAPTER 37

Lizzy sat cradling the remnants of a tea that had long gone cold. Gideon had brought it in a while ago in an effort to calm them both while they decided what to do. His reserve must be slipping, she thought as she stared into the cup – no tray service and teapot this time.

They had argued back and forth about telling everyone their suspicions. What it came down to in the end though was what evidence did they have? None. Quite simply, at this point, it was the ravings of an overtired, traumatised woman. Gideon was polite enough not to say it in such words, but the message was clear. He reasoned the deaths every which way he could to explain the multiple reasons why they could be very unfortunate accidents. He had nearly convinced her a few times. She was so tired that it was easy to accept that she could be overreacting. Still, something didn't sit right. In the end, she had agreed to keep quiet. At least for the time being. It was Ellie who had swung it. The poor girl had lost her mother. What further trauma would it cause her to hear Lizzy shouting about suicide or possibly murder? After exhausting every angle, they sat in silence, deep in their own thoughts.

'You'll have to excuse me,' Gideon said at last, rising from his seat. 'The hotel still has to be run and the hour is getting on.' He motioned towards the door.

'Oh. Oh, yes, of course. Sorry, Gideon.' Lizzy gently placed her cup on Gideon's desk and walked out into

The Storm

reception, feeling quite dazed. The hour really was getting on she noticed as Poppy skittered past towards the dining room where the sound of cutlery clinking and the smell of breakfast emanated. She went in and sat at her usual table, eyeing everyone around her.

Mr Franks was shovelling food into his mouth from a plate piled high with what Lizzy thought was far too much for one person. No work papers on his table today; instead, a newspaper lay in front of him that he read with intense concentration. Lizzy wrinkled her head in confusion. The road in and out was closed – no deliveries. Surely, this was the same paper he'd been reading yesterday?

His face seemed a little less red today but still held a permanent scowl. He occasionally flicked his gaze up to his fellow diners, but for the most part, he looked fully engaged in his activities.

Paul and Ellie were down. He was chatting to his daughter in a hushed tone that Lizzy couldn't pick up. He looked just as dishevelled as he had yesterday, though his face was a healthier colour. For most of yesterday, he had looked near meltdown, his face passing through every hue known to man. Ellie sat half-listening while she tore at a jam-covered croissant. The tears were slow and precise, as though each one took a lot of concentration. Every few seconds, she popped a piece into her mouth and chewed lazily. She contributed to the conversation with grunts and eye rolls. Lizzy looked closely at her face. Fresh as a daisy. He still hadn't told her, then. Lizzy felt the rage bubbling inside her. She started to rise in her seat when a hand clamped her shoulder and pushed her down.

'Coffee?' Gideon asked, instantly pouring her a cup regardless. He bent to her ear and whispered, 'Now, in front of a dining room full of guests, is not the time.'

Lizzy sat like a chastised child, silently fuming but not saying a word.

'We are all trapped in here until the storm passes or they open the road. Please don't make it a terrifying experience. Unless we have proof of anything, we say nothing.' He stood, his eyes holding hers as he tried to stare her down. She had never felt hatred for anyone like she was suddenly feeling towards Gideon in this moment.

'Fine,' she said through gritted teeth.

Gideon wandered off, handing Poppy the jug as he left the room.

After regaining some composure, Lizzy headed up to the buffet table. She reached for the muesli, then withdrew her hand. Healthy eating be damned today, she thought. She took a warm plate from the stack and proceeded to load it with sausages, eggs, bacon, and beans.

The end of the line took her close to Mr Franks' table, where he was consuming his breakfast with all the finesse of a bulldozer. The noise he made drew her attention, and she looked over in revulsion. He'd be better placed with a trough, she thought. Her eye caught the paper, and he looked up, sensing her behind him. He slammed it shut, but not before she had seen the job section in front of him.

CHAPTER 38

Ellie had listened to her dad drivel on and on for what seemed like an eternity. It appeared that he had turned into super dad overnight and now he had a million things they needed to do together – museums, slate mines, a wildlife park, rambling, an art gallery, a boat trip. She had remained quiet, letting him babble on, not wanting to upset him. That could wait for another day, one when they weren't trapped together on holiday. She was practically an adult and about to head off to uni. Could he not see that she no longer needed to be entertained? That she could be left to her own devices? Would even quite possibly prefer it to being cooped up with her parents? At least he was talking to her again though. She had to admit that was preferable to the past couple of days. Just.

'Where's Mum?' she asked, glancing at the empty seat next to her. Sure, they had packed some food, but it was just snacks – some crisps, bread, ham, cheese, and chocolate. Surely, it wasn't enough for her mum to avoid every meal every day. And she knew her mum had a decent appetite.

'Oh, uh, she has a migraine,' her dad mumbled.

'Again?'

He nodded before jumping straight back into talking about their special father-daughter bond.

To add to her low mood, Evan hadn't looked at her once since they'd come down this morning. She had specially selected her outfit in an attempt to draw his eye again. Grey joggers that hugged her buttocks and a cropped T-shirt that showed off her trim navel with a neckline that more than hinted at the amble bosom beneath. He glanced with a bowed head but didn't linger. This wasn't how things worked. Boys chased her and she was the one to let them down. What had happened to suddenly scare him off? What had she done?

Her dad stood, and she followed him towards the stairs, though the corner of her eye was still on Evan.

'Oh, I've left my earphones,' she said, stopping suddenly just before the door and making a show of patting herself down. She let him carry on towards his room with promises to meet back in reception in half an hour for God knows what bonding activity.

Evan was clearing their table, his back towards her as he loaded a tray with plates, so she didn't have to fake a show of where she was going just in case her dad was watching.

'Hey, stranger, you've been awfully quiet.'

Evan spun round on his heel so fast he momentarily lost grip on the plate he was holding. He regained control at the last minute and stood gripping it tightly. His face drained of colour and beads of sweat dotted his forehead.

'Jeez, what's wrong with you?' Ellis asked with sudden concern.

'I... er... erm...'

'Okay, how about hi, Ellie?'

'Yeah, hi. Sorry, I have to go.' Evan turned, placed the plate down, and picked up the tray he had loaded with items from the table.

He started to walk away, but Ellie moved in front of him, arms crossed, keeping him between herself and the table. 'Yeahhh, I don't think so. What's going on, Evan?'

Evan went to speak, then his eyes flicked over her shoulder. She turned to see what he was looking at. Her dad hadn't left. He stood there, hands on hips, staring in from the doorway.

'Evan?' she began, turning back. But he had already slipped past her and was practically running to the kitchen.

The Storm

She looked back towards her father to see his retreating legs on the stairs. Ahh, so her dad didn't like the thought of them together, was that it? Had he had words with Evan? Tried to scare him off? Well, screw him. He didn't get to decide who she saw. And he couldn't keep tabs on her twenty-four hours a day.

CHAPTER 39

Lizzy had watched the exchange between Evan and Ellie. If it weren't for Evan's secret, it would have been amusing to watch. Young love and the turmoil that went with it. Everything was such a drama at that age, she thought. Then she remembered her own troubled love life and decided not to pass judgement. She sighed and speared the last piece of sausage. She had savoured every mouthful, but now the meal was over, she felt greasy and bloated. She signalled to Poppy, who came over with a tray and started taking her plate.

'Could I get a mint tea, please, Poppy?' she said, wanting something to cleanse her palette and ease her digestion. Poppy's almost imperceivable nod was the only indication she gave of having heard the order. She took the tray and quickly left Lizzy alone again.

Lizzy looked at her fellow diners now that Ellie and Paul had left. At some point during them leaving the dining room and then Ellie's exchange with Evan, the male of the lovebirds had come down. He was sitting alone at the table, quietly sipping at his tea, his face calm and pensive. In front of him, a full plate of breakfast sat untouched. Lizzy looked towards the breakfast buffet, then around the room, but the other lovebird wasn't in the dining room at all.

Lizzy's whole body flushed hot and her pulse quickened.

No, please, no. Not another one.

The Storm

She stood with such speed that she sent her chair toppling backwards to crash on the floor. The room fell silent as the rest of the diners looked towards the commotion.

Mr Lovebird stood and walked over. 'Here, let me get that for you,' he said, righting the chair. 'Are you ok?'

'I'm—' Lizzy choked on her words as the toilet door opened and out walked his girlfriend. 'Yes, sorry… spider.' She laughed. 'Saw a spider, that's all. Hate the things. It's run off now.'

Mr Lovebird eyed her suspiciously but smiled and nodded as his girlfriend joined him. Lizzy went to leave, her face burning with embarrassment, as Poppy appeared with her tea.

'Oh, thank you, Poppy. I think I'll take it in the lounge if that's ok?'

Poppy nodded, carried the tray through, and placed it on one of the tables while Lizzy followed. She needed to get a grip.

She sank into one of the plush armchairs and thought, not for the first time this break, how she wished she could phone Luke. His overbearing nature was exactly what she needed right now. With a potential killer in the hotel, she imagined that his possessive love would feel reassuring. It wasn't about the love though, was it? Not if she was being honest. What she was craving was protection. She internally chastised her selfishness.

Sipping her tea, with tears in her eyes, what she wished for most was a phone call with her mum.

CHAPTER 40

Ellie met her dad as promised in reception at the allotted time. He was dressed in full outdoor gear of wellies and waterproof coat. He looked tired, but his face lit briefly when he saw her descend the stairs. It soon became a scowl when he saw her coatless and in trainers.

'Well, that's no good, is it?' he said, throwing his arms out with a shake of his head and gesturing to her attire.

'What?'

'You'll not get far in this weather dressed like that.'

Ellie looked to the window and the rain still falling steadily outside. 'We're not going out in that. What's the point?'

'Fresh air and exercise. We didn't come here to sit in the hotel all day.'

'We didn't come here to get soaked and miserable either.' She placed a hand on a jutted hip to emphasise her point.

'Look, I'm sure it'll be fine when we get going. A bit of rain never hurt anybody. It'll probably blow over soon anyway.'

'Blow over? It's a full-on storm, Dad. It has been for the past two days. I doubt it's just going to blow over.'

'Ellie—'

'No, you do what you like, but I'm not going.' With that, she turned and started back up the stairs. She didn't see her dad's shoulders sag as he breathed out a resigned sigh.

The Storm

Back in her room, she closed the door, then moved past the piles of discarded clothes on the floor to stand by her window, waiting to see if her dad went without her. Her view wasn't great, most of it taken by a wall, but she reckoned she would just be able to catch a fleeting glimpse if he left. She saw nothing but the falling rain, then five minutes later, she heard his footsteps out in the corridor and the open and shut of her parents' door. He hadn't, then. Damn it – that would have made things a lot easier.

Undeterred, she removed her trainers and tiptoed to the door. After easing it open, she slipped out and carefully pushed it closed behind her as quietly as she could. It made the softest click that was barely audible. She padded down the corridor towards the back of the hotel. With the road out and the staff unable to leave, Evan and Poppy were forced to stay in a couple of the empty rooms. Evan had told her as much the other night at the bar. If she remembered right, his was the one by the back stairs. He had complained about the noise of people using them when he was trying to sleep.

She rapped on the door. There was movement inside before it opened slowly. As soon as it reached a few inches, Ellie pushed on it and stepped inside, shutting it quickly behind her.

Evan stumbled back into the room wearing nothing but black joggers. His brows shot up in surprise at the intrusion and he crossed his arms over his body, wrapping them around his waist, she assumed in some effort to hide his body from her. Ellie ran an appraising eye over it and smiled.

'I know what's going on, and you don't have to be scared,' she purred.

Evan blanched and backed away. Eventually, he reached the bed and fell back, landing upright on it.

She began walking forwards. 'My dad doesn't rule me. It's my life and I'll spend my time with whoever I want.' She now stood inches away from him. Suddenly, and to Evan's horror and delight, she sat astride him.

'I won't tell if you don't,' she whispered.

Ellie cupped his face and gave him a long lingering kiss before he could utter a protest. He resisted at first but soon relented, kissing her back with increasing passion. His hands, which had been resting on the bed, stroked up her legs and round to her buttocks. As he caressed her, she felt him harden beneath her. She wiggled back and forth on his lap as they kissed, making him whimper. As his hands started upwards towards her breasts, she removed her top and pushed him backwards before climbing off him. She made a show of removing the rest of her clothes, slowly easing off each piece and letting it fall to the floor.

Evan sat wide-eyed in stunned silence. Then he jumped up and, in a hurried, clumsy fashion, removed his own. He stood in front of her as if he was waiting for permission – not knowing what to do next and not daring to make the next move. Ellie smiled and took his hand, guiding him back to the bed. It was all the coaxing he needed. He suddenly regained his confidence and took control. All previous thoughts from the past twenty-four hours were forgotten; his focus was very much in the present as he slipped under the covers with her.

CHAPTER 41

A prickly sensation tingled over Lizzy's scalp and ran down her spine the moment she got back to her room. She froze for a moment, listening and looking for anything out of the ordinary. Anything that immediately looked out of place. Then, seeing nothing, she checked under the bed, in the wardrobe, peeked in the bathroom. She wasn't exactly sure who or what she was looking for, having just left everyone downstairs.

Satisfied that no one was going to jump out of the wardrobe or from under the bed, she placed the drawer back between the desk and the door. She knew it was an early warning system at best that would only buy her some time should anyone make to come in, but still, it was better than no warning system at all.

She needed to calm down. Gideon was right – there was no proof. It was still quite possible that she was getting carried away with herself.

Lizzy took her laptop from the desk and sat cross-legged on the bed. Opening it on her lap, she tapped on the mail icon and, with tears in her eyes, she typed out a message to her mum. She knew it couldn't be sent, but the act of typing it all out, of getting everything off her chest was very therapeutic. Seeing her mum's name in the address box somehow made her feel less alone – as if they were actually talking. She detailed her whole stay up until this point. Everything that had happened and everything she felt, suspicions included. When she had finished, she sat back relieved. A sudden horrific thought flashed through her mind that this message could one day be viewed by the police – found with her body and used as evidence. Refusing to be drawn by hysteria and tempt fate, she instantly deleted it.

CHAPTER 42

Ellie rose from the bed, flushed and sweaty, and hunted round for her underwear. Evan stayed under the covers and watched her, grinning like the Cheshire cat. She dressed quickly and gave him a peck on the cheek.

'I'd better be going. In case Dad comes looking.'

Evan's face fell and paled instantly at the mention of her father.

Ellie huffed as she brushed through her blonde matted hair with her fingers. 'Ok, what exactly has he said to you? Because he has no right.'

Evan looked away, all his attention towards the window instead of her. Ellie sat on the bed and shuffled until she was close to him. He still wouldn't meet her eye.

'Evan?' She took his chin in her hand and sharply forced him to look at her. 'You better start talking.'

He sat up then, looking at her. Big tear-filled eyes stared back into hers, and her anger evaporated.

'Shit, what is it? What's he done?'

'It's... it...' His face crumbled. 'Oh God, Ellie, I'm so sorry.'

'For what? Evan, you're scaring me.'

'Ellie, your... your mum... she died, she's... dead.'

Dead?

Ellie sat statue-still staring at him, watching as a tear escaped his eye. Her mind whirled as she struggled to process what he had just told her. She looked round the room like the answers were somehow there waiting to unveil themselves. Hoping that someone would spring out and yell 'Gotcha!'. It was a joke. A sick joke, that's all. It had to be. Her heart started beating with increased voracity, and she turned back towards him, her eyebrows knitted and voice weak.

'What do you mean? What are you talking about?'

'I'm so, so sorry, Ellie. She was found in the lake yesterday. She drowned.'

All emotion drained from her face and she looked off into the distance, unblinking. It was as if she had just shut down, broken. Her brain didn't know how to work, her limbs didn't know how to move, and numbness was ruling all other emotions, like a robot who had just been turned off.

'Ellie? Are you ok?'

Evan moved around to face her and took her limp hands in his. A single tear rolled down her cheek as she stared straight through him, and he brushed it away.

'Ellie?'

Her eyes came back into focus, and she saw him then. Saw the guy who'd known her mum was dead and hadn't told her. The guy she had just slept with. Bile rose in her throat, and she fought to swallow it. And then every emotion – grief, rage, physical and mental agony – slammed into her all at once. She wouldn't let him see her like this. He didn't deserve to see her vulnerable.

With a look of pure hatred, she stood and slowly left the room, all thoughts of being discreet gone as she slammed the door behind herself.

CHAPTER 43

Bang.

Lizzy's eyes snapped open from where she lay on the bed. A door slamming shut? It wasn't her business. She closed her eyes again, trying to picture where her story was going, work through a couple of plot holes her current idea would run into.

Bang.

Her eyes snapped open for a second time. That one definitely sounded more like a door banging open into a wall. And then raised voices began to filter in.

She stared at the swirls on the ceiling as she tried to work out who the voices belonged to and what was being said, but she couldn't make out a single word. The bed creaked as she sat up and got off before she tiptoed to the door and removed the drawer so that she could inch the door open.

Ellie and Paul.

So, he had finally told her. Or at least someone had.

Mr Franks' booming voice joined in, making her jump. 'Will you keep it down? Some of us have very important work to do.' It came from the other direction. He must be shouting from his room.

With a frown, Lizzy inched through the doorway and charged out into the corridor to give him a piece of her mind and tell him to leave them to it. Explain the situation if necessary. But as she rounded the corner, his door slammed shut. At the other end of the corridor, Ellie stormed out of Paul's room.

'Just leave me alone. I never want to see you again,' she screamed, going into her own room.

'Ellie, wait…' Paul appeared mid-follow but stopped short when he saw Lizzy standing there.

Ellie's door slammed.

Lizzy wanted in so many ways to tell him 'I told you so' but bit her tongue. She stood unable to move, waiting for the outburst that was sure to come. His face had reddened, turning from concern to anger upon seeing her, and she was certain she was in for a torrent of abuse. Paul clenched his fists and set his jaw, took a deep breath, then returned to his room. He almost looked like a petulant teenager.

Lizzy let out a slow and steady breath of relief and went back down the corridor. She rounded the corner and noticed her door standing open. She stopped and stared, thinking back. Had she shut it? She had left in a hurry. It was possible she'd just charged out in the moment. Even so, she approached cautiously, stepping lightly and listening for movement. She paused as she reached the door, placing her hand on the wooden surface and pushing it further. It banged against the desk, making her heart leap into her throat. Well, she'd lost the element of surprise if anyone was in there.

Taking the continued silence as a good sign, she eased herself round the door and into the room, going through the motions of checking the small space once again. It was clear. No one lurked in her bathroom or wardrobe. No one hid under her bed. Safe, she went back to close and lock the door, then returned to the body of her room.

She stopped before sitting back on the bed. Her phone and laptop had moved. Or had they? They were on the bed where she had left them, but they looked wrong. The angle or the positioning.

Oh, I'm being ridiculous.

The Storm

She threw herself down on the bed next to them. She needed to get out of the hotel. Get some air. Get some exercise. This storm was really giving her cabin fever and playing on her suspicions. She looked towards the window, where the rain was steadily falling. Steady but not torrential. It wouldn't be the most pleasant walk, but it wouldn't be ludicrous either. Not if she dressed appropriately.

Lizzy grabbed her boots and put her waterproof coat on. She made sure the door was firmly shut and locked as she left, then dashed through reception, purposely ignoring Gideon on her way out.

With her hood up, the rain wasn't all that bad. She breathed the fresh air in hungrily and revelled in the openness. Without thinking, she took the nearest path. The layout of the grounds almost favoured this one by guiding her straight to it, and the heather clinging to the banks on the sides of the path gave a beautiful burst of colour that drew her in. She got a few meters in before she realised where it was taking her. This was the path that led down to the lake. She stopped walking with a sharp intake of breath. She shouldn't go down that way. Shouldn't go near the lake. Not alone but also because it may be a possible crime scene. Although Lizzy doubted much evidence could remain after the hammering of the storm. She'd probably already destroyed anything left behind when she'd waded in and pulled her out. There'd be no discernible footprints left at least.

Lizzy changed direction and headed the opposite way round the hotel. The outbuildings were here. Two large stone structures rising from the neatly trimmed lawn. One large with double wooden doors that looked intended for vehicles. The second one smaller and longer. Lizzy could easily imagine it was once stables from the shape of it. If it were, most of the doors had since been bricked in. Detecting faint outlines, it looked as though there had originally been four from what she could see. Now, only one remained on the shorter end of the building. Probably a shed now, she mused. Both buildings had been built to match the house in their colouring and stonework. It was yet another sign that this had once been a grand house.

Lizzy shuddered as she passed by, suddenly imagining poor Fiona lying in one of them. Alone, cold, bloated, and decaying. Images from her dreams floated in her vision and clawed fear down her spine. She swallowed down a gag at the memory and moved quicker.

To the left of the outbuildings lay a small patch of woodland. Though the trees had started shedding, they still held enough leaves to provide some shelter from the weather. Not that the rain was bothering Lizzy. It felt so good to be out here where everything smelt so fresh and alive. Still, her mind wandered to Fiona just a few feet away. Her eyes flicked back to the buildings, and as they did, the air soured. Whether she was really smelling decay or her mind was playing tricks, she wasn't sure, but she moved further away into the woods.

The ground underfoot was spongy, and small waterfalls sprang from all around. Lizzy saw a flash of red ahead of her and paused, tracking with her eyes, looking for movement. The Lake District was one of the few areas left in the country to have red squirrels, and she longed to see one. She approached where she thought the blur had been heading, quietly rounding a large oak and peering ahead. There it was. Sat on a fallen branch, munching away at something. It had seen her, she was sure, but it made no move to go. She was clearly at a distance it deemed safe.

Lizzy slowly removed her phone from her pocket, hoping to get a few photos of it when there came a snap of a twig from behind her. The squirrel shot off, and Lizzy turned, scanning the area. She removed her hood so that she could hear better. Everything was still apart from the steady dipping of the rain through the branches.

Calm down, she thought, this is a woodland full of animals, any one of which could have broken a twig or snapped a stick. She continued through the woods but kept her hood down just in case.

CHAPTER 44

Ellie lay balled up on her bed. She'd cried until she couldn't cry anymore. Then after a few moments' reprise, she'd found reserve stores and started all over again. How could her dad not have told her? He'd known since yesterday morning. A whole twenty-four hours ago. Not only that, but he didn't even seem sad. His wife. The apparent love of his life. Her mother. Dead. Gone. Ellie's heart ached for her with a pain so real she thought she could die herself.

It wasn't real. It couldn't be. How could she compute that she would never see her mother again, never hold her again, be held by her again? And he had been planning all this shit to do together, all father-daughter bonding crap. How could anyone do that at a time like this? She hated him. As soon as they got home and she left for uni, she was never going back. Never seeing or talking to him again. Ever.

There came a soft rap on the door, the fifth or so time since she'd confronted him.

'Ellie? Look, I can explain,' her dad desperately called out. 'Please. Let me in. We need to talk. I'm so sorry, Ellie. Please?'

A few moments of silence stretched while he waited for a response. Then she heard his footsteps retreat and his door close. He would be back. He seemed to be on a half-hour cycle of trying.

Ellie hugged her legs tighter against her body. She wanted to squeeze herself into nothing. To not exist. To not be here. She pulled the cover over her head and started crying all over again.

CHAPTER 45

Lizzy had managed forty minutes in the woods. Her eyes and mind had cleared, and her headache had all but gone. She hadn't even had to pass Gideon on her way back in, which was a bonus. She was still angry with him after their disagreement earlier and had no desire to see him again any time soon. She peeled off her wet jeans and hung them over the radiator, then towelled her hair and changed into something dry.

Feeling a lot calmer for her amble, she took her laptop to the bed, snuggled back against the pillows, and began a read-through of her work. If nothing else, the break had certainly done wonders for her story. It was as if her book mirrored her mind. Back at home, where she was stressed and constantly interrupted, the story had been strained and stuttered. But out here, where she was free and alone, the words flowed. She was now confident that she would have a polished manuscript she could deliver on time.

Lizzy's stomach rumbled as she became aware of the lovely smells wafting up the stairs enticing her down to lunch. She sat back and rubbed her eyes. She'd read for too long without a break and now they felt dry and tired. She shut the laptop, stood and stretched, then placed it on the desk on her way out of the room.

Gideon was standing at the dining room door as she got there – his usual stance as he welcomed the guests in. Her heart sank a little, but she supposed she couldn't put off the inevitable forever. He looked up as she approached. His smile dropped instantly, his mouth setting into a hard thin line.

'I suppose I have you to thank for Ellie finding out,' he whispered harshly.

'Me?'

Gideon looked around, checking that they weren't being overheard.

'Well, if not you, who would have said anything? You made your stance on the matter very clear.'

'I wasn't the only one who knew, Gideon.'

She felt him scan her face. His features and voice softened. 'I heard the ruckus. I'm not happy, but I think what was said probably needed to be.'

Lizzy nodded. She would have appreciated an apology for the accusation, but at least it now felt less awkward with Gideon. 'Have you seen them since?'

'No, no sign. And all has been quiet.'

'Well, at least we can tell everyone now. Now that everything's out in the open.'

'What?' Gideon grabbed her arm, keeping her from moving past. 'No. Nothing's changed, Lizzy. The only fact is she died, but the matters surrounding how are all still just circumstantial speculation, and I will not have my guests terrified on such a flimsy theory.' He looked around again, aware his voice had started to rise. 'I mean it, Lizzy. I don't want you mentioning this to another soul.'

Lizzy frowned. 'But your guests have a right to—'

'Hello.'

Gideon instantly released his grip as Lizzy turned to see the lovebirds arrive. She hadn't heard them approach. From the look on Gideon's face, he hadn't either.

'Hello, and how are we this afternoon?' Gideon said, regaining his composure and plastering on a smile. He didn't wait for them to answer. 'Here, let me show you to your table.'

The Storm

He strode ahead, leading them away and into the dining room. Lizzy followed them and sat at her table, silently fuming. Who was he to tell her what she could and couldn't say?

'Everything alright?' Mr Lovebird asked with a grin as he settled himself at the table. 'No more spiders today?'

Mrs Lovebird sniggered and covered it with her hand.

Lizzy had forgotten about that. A slight blush crept up her neck. 'No, all fine, thank you.' She smiled. She felt as if she were back in school. The geek who couldn't quite make it to the popular table. She rose almost as soon as she had sat and headed for the buffet.

Lizzy spooned some couscous chicken salad onto a plate and returned to her table. The lovebirds hadn't moved. They looked up as she approached and shuffled their chairs closer to her.

'Did you hear the argument earlier?' Mr Lovebird asked, his voice full of so much intrigue that she was surprised he wasn't bouncing up and down in his seat.

'Erm… yeah, a little.'

'Gosh, it was awful, wasn't it? Do you know what it was about? So much shouting, I hope everyone's ok.' Mrs Lovebird managed a more convincing concerned voice. It was the twinkle in her eyes that let her down though. With or without Gideon's warning, Lizzy wouldn't have wanted to say anything to them at this moment in time. Not after the crass show they both were making.

Lizzy caught Gideon looking over at her. His eyes bored into her as a silent warning, and suddenly, her feelings reversed. She swallowed them down.

'No, I'm afraid not. I don't like to get involved.' Casting a glance at Gideon, she turned back to her meal.

The disappointed vultures replaced their chairs and slunk off to the buffet.

Neither Paul nor Ellie came down to lunch. Lizzy stretched out her meal as long as she could in the hope of seeing them. Well, in the hope of seeing Ellie. She didn't much care about Paul, but she wanted to check the girl was ok. She even sat with a tea in the lounge afterwards just in case. Nothing.

Gideon kept passing the doorway or finding something to do that took him through the room. She had no doubt he was checking on her. Eventually though, she grew bored of waiting and went back to her room.

Lizzy unlocked her door and stepped into the room, nerves immediately hitting her again. She wasn't sure if it was her fear or that something was actually wrong, but something just felt off. She quickly scanned the room, looking for the culprit. Everything was where she had left it – laptop on the desk, jeans on the radiator, phone on...

Her mouth opened slightly as her breathing deepened.

Wet footprints on the carpet.

They couldn't have been from her returning from the woods, could they? Surely, that was too long ago; they would have dried by now. There was also an odd smell in the room. Not unpleasant, but one that hadn't been there previously. Although – she sniffed the air – yes, familiar. Familiarity was a good sign though, wasn't it?

She checked the room over for anything missing and for anywhere someone could hide. Nothing untoward. Placing the drawer back on the floor between the desk and door, she settled herself back on the bed with her laptop and opened her work in progress.

She scanned the last few sentences she'd written earlier over and over, desperate for the following words to flow as easily as they had been recently. The sky was such a brilliant blue that— No. She pressed the backspace button. The sky cleared to reveal a day so... Her fingers sat poised above the keyboard, her brain failing to work. She huffed and deleted the sentence completely.

The Storm

Gideon and the lovebirds had rattled her and destroyed her earlier calm. She had come here to finish this book though, and finish this book she would. She just had to concentrate and lose herself in it again. Easier said than done at the moment, but she was determined to give it a damn good try.

CHAPTER 46

Ellie sat on her bed, leaning against the headboard, fully dressed but under the covers, hugging the duvet to her chin. Her eyes kept drifting shut and her stomach continued to growl. She'd missed lunch, though she didn't feel as if she could actually eat anything.

She was exhausted. She had tried to sleep, but it wouldn't come, and though she knew she should probably try to eat something, she hadn't dared go down for lunch in case she had run into her dad. She really wasn't ready to face him yet. She wasn't sure how she ever would again. The only other person she knew in this place was Evan. But finding him involved leaving the room and then she was back to the risk of seeing her dad. He was still knocking every so often, though the time between attempts was getting longer. His last one was over an hour ago now. Ellie really hoped he'd give up soon.

Now and then, she could hear him shuffling around in the next room. She wondered what he could possibly be doing in there now that he was all alone. Her mum wasn't with him. She never would be again. Ellie turned the TV on to drown out the sounds and her own thoughts. She let it play the first thing that appeared. It made no difference what it was; she wouldn't be watching it.

CHAPTER 47

After a slow start, Lizzy found she had actually made good progress. The edits were all but complete, she was nearly halfway through her read-through and the book was flowing with minimal typos. She closed the laptop and sat back, feeling pleased and proud of herself.

She hopped off the bed and ambled over to the kettle, switching it on and noticing that the carpet had dried while she'd been working. It confirmed in her mind that it couldn't have been her. Her skin prickled at the thought of someone being in her room. As the kettle started its low rumble, she made a mental note to ask Gideon, or maybe Poppy, if anyone had been in her room today. It could easily have been a staff member on an innocent visit for something, but she felt uneasy not knowing who it was and why they had been here.

Lizzy reached for a sachet of coffee, then thinking caffeine would probably only exasperate her jitters, switched for a herbal tea and popped a bag into a mug while she waited for the water to boil.

Although the desk was still pushed up by the doorway, the chair remained in the bay window. Lizzy took her tea and settled into it, watching the rain, which had increased in its vigour again. She was pleased she'd managed to get out earlier when she did. Though after an afternoon slouched over her screen, she could have done with another amble. She was really starting to miss her daily runs.

Lizzy arched and stretched the kinks out of her back. She should put the desk back, she thought. At least move it a little to make it useable. Sitting and working on the bed was really not doing her any favours.

She grabbed the remote from the bedside table and flicked the TV on, hoping for a news update on the landslide. The more that time marched on, the more trapped she felt. She could use a weather forecast too; if the storm lifted and she could get out, that would be something. A rerun of an old eighties comedy filled the screen, then stuttered and pixilated. Lizzy tried a few of the other channels to the same effect. Great. She clicked it off and threw the remote onto the bed with a frustrated sigh. Then she took her book back to the chair with the intention of reading until dinner.

After working on the bed all day, she couldn't get comfortable. She shifted in the chair, crossing and uncrossing her legs, pulling them up and then stretching them out. She tried on the bed too, sitting, lying, leaning, but it didn't matter. She put the book down and tried going through her pre-run routine to loosen her up – squats, lunges, and twists. She'd lost interest in the book anyway. After already reading for a long time, her heart wasn't really in it. It wasn't work she was reading now, but it was still reading, nonetheless, and her eyes felt tired and strained.

Irritably, she paced the room like a caged animal, finding her mind wandering to Deidre and Fiona. They couldn't have been more different. One, a glamorous, eccentric old lady; the other, a frumpy, middle-aged mother. Lizzy hadn't seen them speak or interact in any way. They seemed to exist in different orbits and originate from different areas of the country. What could possibly link them? Deidre was way past working age, so it couldn't be that. Unless they'd worked together many years ago? Maybe they were related in some way? An argument over inheritance maybe? Or maybe it was someone they both knew – they didn't know each other but had a common acquaintance? She was conjecturing again. She couldn't help it though. There must be a connection surely. What had made someone want to kill those two ladies?

Unless Deidre really had been natural causes after all. Maybe she couldn't see a link because there really wasn't one. Deidre was quite elderly. It happened. People slipped away in their sleep all the time. That would maybe make more sense.

Fiona could be a standalone incident. Lizzy was still convinced that she was not natural causes. There had been no reason at all for Fiona to be outside in the storm. None that Lizzy could fathom. It had been torrential. Nobody in their right mind would voluntarily go out walking in the night in that. Had someone taken her out or chased her out?

Lizzy stopped her pacing. Fiona had died the night of the argument. And though she hadn't been able to hear what was said, it was clearly a big one. In Lizzy's mind, that put one person top of the suspect list.

Fiona's husband, Paul.

CHAPTER 48

Lizzy was pacing again, her mind spinning with different scenarios and possibilities, making her edgy. She was suddenly aware she was wringing her hands as she walked and threw them down by her sides, scared she was becoming everything Gideon was accusing her of – a hysterical woman jumping to conclusions on nothing but conjecture. She closed her eyes and took a deep breath, then sat on the floor. Continuing the deep breathing, she began to practice a little yoga, starting with the lotus pose – she crossed her feet up onto her thighs in a cross-legged fashion and tried to still her mind. She hadn't done any for a few years now, falling out of the morning practice once Luke moved into the flat, but the moves came back to her. The effort and patience of each stretch were harder than she remembered, but she got there slowly, and with each passing minute, she felt her body give in to it and relax a little more.

After going through the few moves she could remember, Lizzy hopped into the shower to freshen up before dinner, then dressed and went down a little early. She wanted to speak with Gideon to ask him about the wet footprints she'd found in her room earlier. It was all probably very innocent, but she'd feel a lot better about them if she could have the reason explained and confirmed.

As she descended the stairs, trailing her hand down the wooden bannister as she went, she could see the doorway to the dining room ahead was empty. Gideon seemed to take his role as maître d' very seriously, so she was surprised to see he wasn't in his normal position for this time of the day.

Reaching the bottom step, she looked to her right where the big oak reception desk sat. No Gideon. She walked over to it and lay her hands on the smooth polished top, considering what to do and where to check next. She was just about to walk back to the dining room when she heard a noise coming from the office.

Slipping round the desk, she approached the door and was poised ready to knock when she heard him talking within. She lowered her hand, not wanting to interrupt, and waited, although she couldn't work out what was being said. Then she heard the distinct sound of a phone hitting its cradle, and her eyes widened.

She burst into the room to a startled Gideon. 'The phones are working?' It came out half-question and half-statement in her excitement.

'No, still out, I'm afraid.'

'But I just heard you talking on it.'

'No, it was just me talking to myself. I often do on occasion when I'm alone. Always have done.' He gave a small laugh, but it was half-hearted. If she hadn't heard what she'd heard, she could have easily mistaken it for embarrassment.

Lizzy looked at him with a furrowed brow and an accusing eye. 'Can I try?'

'What?'

'The phone. Can I try?'

The smile dropped from his face, and he sighed heavily. 'The lines are down, Lizzy. Have been since yesterday morning. You know that,' he said firmly.

'Do I?'

Lizzy launched and made to grab the handset as Gideon surged forwards and batted her away. Together, they managed to knock the phone, which clattered to the floor.

Gideon shook his head, his palms flat against his desk. 'What is wrong with you? Calm yourself down and get out of my office. Now.'

Lizzy stared back at him with a steely glare, hands on hips, refusing to be intimidated. She knew what she'd heard and didn't trust him one bit. She'd come to ask about the footprints in her room, but she wouldn't believe his answer. Not now. She'd keep it to herself for the time being and ask Poppy later. She eyed the phone one last time before turning and walking from the room.

CHAPTER 49

There was no Ellie at dinner. Paul was there, but he sat alone. He kept his eyes downcast to the table, his face pale and drawn. Lizzy wondered if Ellie would venture down after Paul had returned to his room. When he could tear his eyes away from his table, he glowered at Lizzy and Evan, as if everything that befell him was their fault. Lizzy wasn't in the mood for his petty shenanigans and stared right back at him. She took her seat, never letting her eyes leave his until he looked away, downcast once again. She would not be intimidated by him, same as with Gideon. She would not show any weakness. Evan, on the other hand, skirted him every opportunity he got, making himself scarce and spending most of his time in the kitchen.

Lizzy surveyed the menu as Mr Franks appeared, arriving like a thunderstorm in a cloud of rage. The man was a coronary waiting to happen. With a scowl, he deposited himself heavily in his chair.

'Your menu –'

'I don't need to look,' Mr Franks barked at Evan, waving it away. 'I'll have fish, chips, and a beer.'

Evan took the proffered menu back with an eye roll. 'Of course.'

'And hurry it up, please; your service is abysmal. Much like the rest of this so-called hotel.' He spat this last part out as though it were a bad taste in his mouth.

He continued to hurl a torrent of abuse at poor Evan. A blush of deep red crept up Evan's neck as the list went on, but as he went to open his mouth and respond, Gideon appeared at his side out of nowhere and ushered him away. Lizzy wished Gideon hadn't been quite so quick. Mr Franks could use a good dressing down and someone to stand up to him.

Gideon caught her eye on his way back from Mr Franks' table. Yet another warning look. Another man full of anger. How she wished she could leave this place. At least the lovebirds seemed to be keeping to themselves tonight. They had clearly deemed Lizzy a useless source of gossip and barely given her a second glance since she'd come in. They seemed to have dropped the spider jokes as well, much to Lizzy's relief.

'Can I take your order?'

Lizzy looked up, startled at Poppy's sudden presence. The girl wafted through the hotel like a ghost.

'Oh. Erm, yes, could I have a glass of rosé, please? And I'll have the Caesar salad.'

Poppy turned to leave.

'Poppy? I was wondering if anyone has been in my room today?'

'No, not that I know of.'

'There's been no maintenance or anything?'

'No. Is something broken? I can tell Gideon.'

'No, no, that's fine. Thank you.'

As Poppy left to fetch her order, Lizzy's mind whirled. Nothing had been missing from her room, not that she had anything valuable with her anyway, so what would anyone want? What possible reason could anyone have for being in her room?

A sudden smash lifted Lizzy from her thoughts.

'You imbecile,' roared Mr Franks. 'Well, go on, then, clean it up.' He gave Evan a shove and motioned to the floor where a puddle lay peppered with the remnants of a glass.

Evan's jaw set and his lips became a thin line. He retrieved a dustpan and brush from another room and then

The Storm

silently swept the shards and mopped up what he could with some paper towels. As he went to leave the dining room, Paul stood, absentmindedly bumping into him as he did so. Each man gave the other a steely glare.

'This is all your fault,' Paul hissed at him. 'I hope you're happy.'

Evan was less discreet with the volume of his reply. 'My fault? Her mother died and you kept it a secret from her. Did you really think she'd never find out?'

Cutlery stopped clinking and all conversation stopped. There was a collective gasp as all eyes homed in on the pair and the room fell silent.

'I... you... ' Paul faltered, stuck for words, then left the room.

Gideon was ashen. He looked around dumbstruck now the situation was out in the open and out of his control. His mouth moved, but no words came out, panic washing over him as he decided how best to handle the arising situation. Lizzy, along with the lovebirds, sat mouth agape, not quite believing what she had just heard. Mr Franks was beetroot red. For a moment, Lizzy thought he really was having a heart attack as his hand clutched at his chest. Then he gulped at his beer and Lizzy deduced it was probably just gas or heartburn. Slowly, murmurs started up behind her.

'I thought they were here with her mother?'

'That must be her stepmum.'

'We haven't seen her for a while though.'

'Oh gosh, you don't think someone else has died, do you?'

'No, no, the police would have been back.'

'No, there's been a landslide, did you not see the news?'

'What landslide? No, I missed the news; I was in the shower.'

Lizzy found the voices unbearable. She had wanted it out there, but not the way it had happened.

She looked up to see Gideon wander off in the direction Evan had gone as Poppy appeared with her food. She picked at it half-heartedly, feeling very self-conscious. Even though no one knew the horrible truth yet, she still felt that all eyes were on her. The whispering and speculation continued from the lovebirds behind her, and Lizzy felt that they would try her once again at any moment. She ate mechanically, tasting nothing.

Mr Franks finished the rest of his meal in silence and left.

Lizzy decided to skip dessert. Still nothing had been said to her, but she yearned for the confines of her room out of the spotlight she saw herself under. She ordered a whiskey to take to her room and a sandwich to take for Ellie. As she was waiting, she penned a quick note to accompany the food. She'd leave the food outside the room and slip the note under the door.

CHAPTER 50

Knock, knock.

Lizzy frowned and placed her empty whiskey glass on the bedside table. From what she knew of the people there, there weren't many she'd want a conversation with, so whatever the reason for the knock, she'd keep it short.

She removed the drawer barricade and opened the door as far as the desk allowed.

'Hi.' Ellie's face was red and blotchy and bore no hint of makeup. She looked all of twelve years old.

'Oh, honey.' Lizzy went to reach out to pull Ellie into a hug, then remembered that she didn't know this girl. Her arms dropped to her sides.

Ellie wavered by the door, lips trembling and arms drawn into her body, her hands clasped under her chin.

'Come in.' Lizzy ushered her inside, and Ellie squeezed round the desk. 'Ignore that, I'll explain later,' she added, realising how ridiculous it must look.

Ellie didn't seem to notice. She shuffled to the centre of the room like a lost soul and stood rocking slightly, her eyes roaming the floor. 'I'm not sure why I'm here,' she croaked.

'Come and sit down.' Lizzy sat on the bed and patted the covers next to herself. 'I thought you might want to talk. I didn't know if you'd like me to explain anything.'

'She's really dead?' Slowly, she moved closer and lowered herself to sit on the bed.

'She is. I am so sorry.'

'Where? Where is she?' Her eyes filled with fresh tears that spilled silently down her face. 'Dad's been making excuses for ages now. I knew something wasn't right.'

'Can I explain a little first? Or the answer to that question won't make a lot of sense.'

Ellie nodded.

'I found your mum yesterday morning,' Lizzy said gently. She knew this was going to be a lot to take in. 'She was in the lake. I went to her and pulled her out, but it was too late.'

Ellie closed her eyes against the torrent that poured from them. 'Evan already told me she drowned in the lake, but…' She shook her head. 'It still doesn't feel real.'

Lizzy swallowed hard. 'I left her on the bank and came back to get help. Gideon, the manager; Evan; and Carl, the chef, went back out. We didn't want your mum left out in the storm, and with the landslide out on the road, it could be a while before anyone can get through for her. They brought her back here. She's outside in one of the outbuildings. I'm so, so sorry.'

A haunting moan escaped Ellie's lips, and Lizzy clung to the girl, holding her tight and rocking her. Tears were now pouring from Lizzy's eyes too, and it occurred to her that she probably needed the embrace just as much as Ellie did. Lizzy rubbed Ellie's back as her mother had done hers as a child when she was upset. They stayed like this until Ellie had exhausted herself and run dry.

Eventually, Ellie sat back, but Lizzy kept an arm around her back, not wanting to withdraw all comfort. Her bloodshot eyes looked hollow and the only colour in her complexion came from the darkness underneath them. Lizzy was hesitant about her leaving, not that Ellie had shown any indication of doing so. Watching her eyes grow heavy, she gently encouraged her to lie down and then covered her with a blanket. Then she started to creep towards the door, treading lightly, wanting to give Ellie some peace to sleep.

The Storm

'Lizzy?'

She turned. 'Yeah?'

'Thank you. For being honest with me. No one else has been.'

Lizzy gave her a sad smile and turned.

'Stay with me. Please? I don't want to be alone.'

A lump formed in her throat. 'Of course.'

Lizzy lay next to her as the girl fell instantly asleep. She wept silent tears for her all over again.

CHAPTER 51

Lizzy woke with a start, disorientated and confused. The room was in total darkness. It had been the soft thump of the door that had woken her.

The door.

She sat bolt upright, heart hammering, and fumbled blindly on the bedside table. She needed something that could be used as a weapon. She kept her eyes trained towards the door, looking for any hint of movement. As dark as it was, she was sure she'd notice a shape move if there was one. If it was big enough. There was nothing on the table. Not of any use anyway. Her book, a hair tie, and either a pen or a pencil. She kept hold of the pen, or pencil, thinking that at least she could stab with it. It would do very little damage, but it might buy her some time.

Lizzy slipped silently from the bed into a crouch beside it. If someone was coming for her, she didn't want to make it easy by being in the place they expected her to be. Slowly, she crawled round to the foot of the bed. Her eyes were beginning to adjust, but she still couldn't see the intruder. She could make out the shape of the desk though, and it wasn't far away. If she could get to it and get behind it, it would offer her some protection. She'd also be next to the main light switch and the door.

She made for the desk, slow and steady, not wanting to make a sound and draw attention to herself. The carpet beneath her brushed against her clothes with inordinate volume and she was sure her heartbeat was audible. Eventually, she reached it. She waited a few moments, listening for movement, trying to sense where the presence was. Still nothing. She slowly rose to a standing position and flicked on the light. It stung her eyes, but she forced them to remain open. Scanning and searching. The room was empty. She ran round the bed, then checked the bathroom. That was empty too.

Lizzy sat on the bed, letting her breathing and heart rate return to normal.

Ellie.

It all came back to her. Ellie had been here. They had lain on the bed. Ellie had fallen asleep and Lizzy must have followed soon after. She looked down at her attire – last night's clothes, not PJs. She must have heard Ellie leaving, not someone entering. Relief flooded every vein in her body.

She padded over to the door and locked it, placed the drawer back on the floor, slipped into her PJs, then went back to bed. She didn't notice that the wardrobe door was slightly ajar.

CHAPTER 52

Ellie trailed her hand across the wall as she felt her way down the corridor to her bedroom in the darkness. Unlike other nights, the night lighting hadn't come on. She wasn't afraid of the dark, but it had a way of playing with your head, particularly in unfamiliar places. There were no sounds except for the gentle echo of snoring that she couldn't quite locate. Part of her wanted to retreat to Lizzy's room, back to a person who for some reason made her feel safe amidst the sadness despite being a stranger, but she'd felt uncomfortable in her bed, unable to fall back to sleep, and didn't want to impose. Lizzy had already done more than enough for her.

Still weary from sleep and navigating blindly, there was suddenly a gap where there should have been wall, and Ellie realised she'd taken a wrong turn. She backtracked, then halted. Did she just see someone dart across the corridor she'd just come down? She was sure she had. There was no other way she could account for the large moving shadow she'd just seen. She couldn't tell where they had come from or where they'd gone, but she was suddenly very wide awake. Had they been watching her? Had they actually gone into a room, or were they still there in the shadows?

Ellie felt her throat constrict and a shiver run down her spine as a possibility dawned on her. Lizzy hadn't said it outright, but Ellie was vividly aware of the implications of her mother's death. Someone had potentially killed her and now someone was lurking in the shadows of the hotel late at night.

The Storm

She could suddenly no longer feel anything but threat as a prickling sensation shot up her spine. She looked around wildly, trying to find her bearings, eyes wide, as if they could possibly take in more undetected light. The hotel wasn't that big; her room couldn't be far away.

She pushed her back as soundlessly as she could against the corridor wall, hand over her mouth to try to cover the sound of her breathing, although she was sure her heart could be heard pumping loudly in her chest. She inched across the wall, keeping as close to it as possible so as not to cast any shadows or become a silhouette should anyone still be there. It seemed to take an age, but eventually, she was confident she had the right door. The layout felt right, familiar, walls and doors where they should be. As quickly and quietly as she could, she fished her key out of her pocket, holding it firmly in her hand to stop it rattling against the keyring. She tried to locate the lock with it, but her shaking hand made it skitter across the surface. The sound of scratching metal on metal felt deafening in the small space, making her wince and shake harder.

Come on, come on.

Eventually, it went in and the door flew open. As much as she wanted to slam it shut behind her, she caught herself in time and eased it back into position quietly. She stood panting, back to it as if holding it shut, then flicked the lights on. The sudden illumination was so welcome she could have wept had she any tears left. She locked and checked the door, and all at once, the desk in Lizzy's room made sense. She was scared too. It was a barricade.

Tentatively, Ellie checked her room, peering into the bathroom and under the bed in case whoever it was had slipped in. No one had. She was alone. Then she went to her own desk and leaned against it. She pushed with as much effort as she could muster, but she could only manage to shift it a few meagre inches. Shit.

She looked around, scanning the rest of the room, but there was nothing else in there even remotely heavy enough to work. She went to the bathroom and took the two glasses from the shelf above the sink, then she stacked them by the door. It wouldn't stop anyone coming in, but they would fall should anyone open the door. The clatter would wake her. Nowhere near as good as a barricade, but it was all she could think to do.

Ellie slipped into bed fully dressed and left the light on. She was certain she wouldn't sleep a wink, but the emotion of the day had fully exhausted her and she was fast asleep within half an hour.

CHAPTER 53

Lizzy woke from a surprisingly deep and restful sleep despite the disturbed night. Stretching, she rolled onto her back and rubbed her eyes, letting them adjust to the day. Her mouth was stale and sour with the taste of whiskey. She ran her tongue over furry teeth, realising she had gone to bed without brushing them. She got out of bed and padded to the bathroom to give them a good scrub, then she jumped in the shower.

Towelling herself dry, she took her last clean outfit from the wardrobe and prayed that today was the day the roads would be clear.

As she dressed, Lizzy flicked on the TV. Not even a partial picture this morning. The screen remained blank albeit for a lime green rectangle that danced across it bearing the words 'No Signal'. She sighed and clicked it off again.

The skies outside her window were looking a lot less angry today and all that fell was a light shower. It was grey and miserable, but after the past few days, it filled Lizzy with hope.

Before going down to breakfast, she knocked softly on Ellie's door. If she wasn't going to come down, she would make up a plate for her. There was no answer.

'Ell…' Lizzy stopped, and her eyes flitted to Paul's door. The last thing she wanted was to summon him. She had no desire for another showdown of hatred, and even less to be caught alone in the corridor with him.

She hesitated in the doorway for a while debating and then left, heading down the stairs.

As she entered reception, a ray of sunlight beamed in through the glass of the door. Oh hallelujah, she thought as she walked towards it and soaked it in. She stepped out of the front doors and took a deep savouring breath in. The light shower was barely a drizzle and the clouds had parted just enough for a fleeting sunbeam to shine through. As she released the breath and opened her eyes, she saw a flicker of movement to the side of the hotel. Her trainers crunched on the gravel as she wandered the path, and as she rounded the corner, she found Gideon with an aerial in his hands.

'Oh, so that's why there's no signal this morning?'

'Yeah, came down last night.'

Lizzy looked him over and the ladder that was laid in the grass. He followed her line of vision.

'If the weather holds, I can have a go at putting it back up. I'm no expert though; can't guarantee anything.'

Lizzy stiffened slightly, suddenly feeling uncomfortable in his presence. Putting it up or taking it down? she wondered uneasily.

'Well, I'll leave you to it,' she said, backing away slowly as she spoke. 'I'd better get to breakfast before it's all gone.'

She maintained a smile, only letting it drop when she rounded the corner and turned, trying to walk with composure but managing to kick up loose stones as she hurried away. She ran up the few steps to the entrance, only feeling better once she was inside the hotel. The door normally stood open during the day, but she found herself closing it behind her as she let out a breath. She stood and composed herself before crossing the empty reception, then entered the dining room and sat at her table. Poppy was by her side almost as soon as she was seated, wavering with the coffee pot.

'Yes, please, Poppy, thank you,' Lizzy said.

Poppy poured the coffee and wandered away to another table.

The Storm

Lizzy lifted the cup, staring into it as if it contained all the answers. Whatever happened today, whether they could leave or not, she decided she was telling everyone. Gideon be damned.

Lizzy took a moment savouring her coffee and tried to order her thoughts. She bounced between Deidre being natural causes or murdered and eyed everyone with suspicion as she evaluated the possibility of them being the culprit – how they could have done it and for what possible reason. Every time she formed a theory, some piece of information would discount them or throw up more unanswered questions to set the confusion swirling again. But the part she did keep coming back to was if Deidre had indeed died in her sleep, why hadn't she been undressed and under the covers? It wasn't exactly warm enough to sleep on top of the bedding.

Lizzy sighed. She had the beginnings of a headache. She really hoped the weather held today. She was going stir-crazy and the need to get out was overwhelming, even if the furthest she could venture was the hotel grounds.

Suddenly, Poppy was by her side, topping up the coffee in her cup.

'Thanks, Poppy.'

Lizzy looked up, her focus shifting to the door as a movement there caught her focus. Ellie hurried into the room. Lizzy smiled, pleased she felt able to come down, but her face fell and her gut clenched as Ellie drew nearer. She was in last night's clothes, her hair dishevelled and her face puffy, her eyes wildly searching. They locked on Lizzy, and she rushed over.

Lizzy half-rose, leaning forwards towards her and feeling her heart quicken. 'Ellie, what is it? Are you ok?'

Ellie's eyes started darting around again as soon as she reached the table, flicking between the other guests and glancing over her shoulder. 'Yeah… erm… can we talk?'

'Of course. Here or—'

'Not here.' Ellie hurried from the room, leaving Lizzy trailing after until they reached the lounge. With everyone either eating breakfast or still in bed, they had their pick of seats.

'Honey you're shaking, come here.' Lizzy wrapped an arm around her as they sat on one of the big sofas. Ellie fell into the embrace and looked up at her with big glassy eyes.

'She was killed, wasn't she? Why else would she be dead? It's not like she would have gone out there swimming in a storm. She didn't even like swimming in a pool.'

This further confirmed Lizzy's fears, not that she'd ever thought she would have gone swimming out there. Lizzy considered her answer before speaking. She didn't want to scare Ellie, but she didn't want to lie to her either. It wasn't fair. And if she was planning to tell the others later, then Ellie definitely had a right to know.

'I think so, yes. And I think Deidre probably was too.'

'What?' Ellie sat up straight and stared.

'It's just, well, I know Deidre was old and all, but two deaths in two days in the same hotel. It is a bit suspicious, isn't it?'

Gideon passed by the entrance to the lounge and doubled back. He stood in the doorway, his face flushed with anger. Seeing the two of them sitting together, she could just guess what he was thinking, but it was all out there now, Ellie knew, so he could just back down and leave her alone.

'Lizzy, a word, please?'

'No.' She stood and faced him, moving so fast that Ellie flinched a little. 'No more words. And no more secrets either.'

He looked between the two women, his mouth working but no sound coming out. He huffed as his eyes narrowed.

'And I'd appreciate it if you don't talk to me like I'm one of your staff,' Lizzy added, crossing her arms.

Gideon clamped his mouth shut and stormed away, although they heard his footsteps slowing pretty quickly, ready to put on a fake smile for the guests, ever the professional.

'What was that about? What secrets?' Ellie asked, her eyes searching under knitted brows.

Lizzy sat. 'It doesn't matter. There aren't any anymore.'

'But—'

Lizzy ran her hand through her hair, not knowing how to get out of the situation in any way apart from with the truth. Plus, why would she protect Gideon? And she had just said no more secrets, hadn't she?

'Evan and I were sworn to secrecy.'

'To keep your mouths shut? But if there's a killer, people need to know.' Ellie's eyes, already wide, blinked rapidly.

'My argument exactly.'

Ellie suddenly sagged and sat back, realisation dawning. 'It wasn't just him that wanted you to keep quiet, was it? It was my dad too?'

Lizzy winced but nodded. That wasn't a point she had been going to reveal. 'Your dad didn't want to upset you. I know it doesn't make a whole lot of sense and I did try and reason with him, but, well, he just wanted you to have a few more days of happiness. Of normal life. Before it all came crashing down.' She put a reassuring hand on Ellie's shoulder and gave a squeeze. 'It may have been a stupid idea, but I think it came out of love.'

She didn't owe Paul this explanation and part of her hated that she'd given it so nicely such was her fury for the man, but Ellie was her priority and the last thing she needed was Lizzy's pure negativity towards her dad.

'As for Gideon, he thinks there is no evidence and I am getting carried away with myself. I am not to "worry the guests unnecessarily".' Lizzy made the air quotes and rolled her eyes.

Lizzy watched as Ellie processed it. She looked down at her hands as she fiddled and picked away at some loose skin around her fingernail.

'Someone was lurking in the corridor last night,' she said quietly, as if she were scared to say the words out loud.

Lizzy's stomach dropped. 'What? Where?' She leaned closer, trying to get Ellie to look at her.

'When I left your room. It was dark and I couldn't find my way. Made a wrong turn. When I looked back, someone ran across the corridor.'

'Where were they? Did you see which room they went into or came out of?'

'Not really. I couldn't tell. The lights were off and...' She took a deep shuddering breath, her voice trembling. 'God, I was so scared.'

'Sshhh, ok, it's ok.'

Lizzy brought her into a hug again and thought about what this meant. It was surely evidence, wasn't it? No, she thought, thinking about it rationally. It was evidence to Lizzy. Someone lurking about in dark corridors at night was definitely suspicious and they were no doubt up to no good. But she could also see it how Gideon would – a guest trying to find their room in the dark, just as Ellie had been. She gave Ellie's arm a reassuring squeeze and offered her a wan smile.

'Come on. Let's get some food and then we can decide what to do.'

They went back into the dining room and headed straight for the buffet table. Lizzy noticed the lovebirds' gazes fix on them and follow them round the room, their heads bowed together, their mouths working in quick whispers. She saw Ellie notice them too.

'Just ignore them. Nosy gossips with nothing better to do,' Lizzy said.

They filled their plates and took them to Lizzy's table. Ellie was clearly famished, but after a few mouthfuls, she

The Storm

started pushing the food round her plate. Lizzy ate steadily, aware of the whispering but unable to pick any of it out.

CHAPTER 54

Mr Franks entered the dining room in his usual gruff manner but faltered when he saw Ellie. He stood just shy of their table, as if he were hesitant to pass them. He looked clammy and dabbed at his forehead with a handkerchief. As Ellie looked up at him, he opened his mouth to speak but instead lowered his head and carried on to his table. Lizzy guessed it was as close to a show of respect as he could manage. To be fair, it was more than any of the other guests had offered so far.

'Everyone's looking at me. I feel like a freak,' Ellie whispered.

Lizzy gazed around the room. They were looking – snatching glances between forkfuls. They looked away when they saw Lizzy. 'It'll get better. Let them look and get it out of their systems.'

Ellie picked her fork back up, speared a piece of bacon, and put it down again without eating. 'What about if Dad comes down? I'm not sure I can face…'

On cue, Paul appeared in the doorway. His clothes looked slept in and his hair stuck up at odds. He immediately spotted Ellie and came rushing over. His face flashed through a full range of emotions as he decided how to broach the pair. He settled on tactile.

'Ellie, I'm so happy to see you've come down.'

She didn't look at him. Her body had gone rigid and she kept her eyes firmly fixed on her plate.

The Storm

'Why don't you come over to our table? I think we should talk.'

'I'm ok here, thanks.'

'It's times like these we need to be together, as a family,' he coaxed, reaching down to gently rub her arm.

She ripped her arm away before he could get close. 'We're not a family, not anymore,' she shot back, looking him dead in the eye. All the emotion she'd felt that morning – sadness, fear, shock – had been completely pushed aside by anger.

Paul's face turned beetroot and his nostrils flared. His hands balled into fists as he glared at Lizzy.

'Don't go blaming Lizzy; this is all your fault.'

'But, Ellie, you have to understand—'

'No, you have to understand. The moment you decided to keep this from me, the moment you decided to lie to my face, you destroyed everything. I hate you. And the less time we have to spend together, the better.' With that, she rose and left the room with slow dignity.

Paul watched her go, his mouth open. The fight and tension had left his body. He seemed to have sagged under the weight of his daughter's words, going from the big, strong man spoiling for a fight with Lizzy to the rounded-shoulders shell that was now left behind. He seemed to waver, his movements stuttering, almost as if unsure whether to stay or follow her.

'Just give her some time,' Lizzy offered in place of 'I told you this was a bad idea'. 'It's a lot to take in.'

Paul's body tensed at her words, but he kept staring on through the doorway and the place his daughter had just vacated. His hands clenched back into fists and it seemed to take all his strength to walk away to his own table.

His gaze drifted back to Lizzy as he slowly sat, silently seething, not taking his eyes off her until Evan came in with a tea tray. They locked eyes, and Evan froze, turned heel, and left again without setting it down, back into the kitchen.

Moments later, Poppy emerged through the same door holding the tray. She walked over and placed it in front of Paul, then backed off and hurried away. The silence in the room was suddenly deafening. Eventually, Paul poured his tea, the clinking of the spoon as he stirred breaking the spell as chatter began once again and people turned their attention back to their own table.

CHAPTER 55

Lizzy kept her head down for the remainder of her meal. As she set her knife and fork down, Mr and Mrs Lovebird sidled up to her table from their own. It had taken them longer than Lizzy had expected.

'Is she ok?' the woman asked.

'No, not really, she's just found out her mother was found dead.' Lizzy looked up at her and instantly regretted snapping. Her forehead was furrowed and her jaw tense. The poor woman did actually look genuinely concerned.

'Sorry,' she offered. 'It's been a very long couple of days. It was me who found her.'

'Oh gosh.'

They both took this insight as an invitation to sit and pulled out chairs from Lizzy's table. Though hesitant at first, Lizzy soon poured out all the gruesome details, explaining how and when everything had happened and all that had gone on since. She only left out the part about the person Ellie saw lurking in the corridor last night, though she wasn't exactly sure why. She sat back feeling two-stone lighter for unburdening it all.

'Jesus,' was all Mr Lovebird could manage. His girlfriend sat in stunned silence. Her hand had moved to his arm and she clung tightly to it.

'Alex, what do we do?' she asked, pulling on his arm and drawing him closer. He looked to her, mouth working, but nothing came out. He had nothing to offer.

'I think I'm going to take a drive down the road today,' Lizzy said. 'See if the landslide has been cleared and I can get through to get help. If not, maybe I can pass on foot, just far enough to get the message out. There has to be people there, workmen at least.'

'I think that's a really good idea. Is there anything we can do? I'm Alex, by the way, and this is Jenny.'

'Thanks, Alex. I'll let you know. And I'm Lizzy, by the way. Nice to properly meet you.'

While Alex looked a little wary, Jenny looked positively terrified. There were no sappy smiles and puppy-dog eyes anymore. No, now she held on to Alex for dear life with a pale face and darting eyes.

CHAPTER 56

Ellie had finally faced her dad, seen him for the first time since their argument, and she felt so much better for it. She didn't know what she had been so scared of. He was the one in the wrong, not her. He was the one who should be scared to see her. Embarrassed and guilt-ridden. She had meant what she'd said to him too. Right now, she did hate him.

She sat in her room all alone. The TV wasn't working, her phone was all but useless here, she had no one to talk to and nothing to do. She realised again just how alone she was. She missed her mum so badly it was like a physical pain. Lizzy had said she was in one of the outbuildings. She understood why, she really did, but it was just so awful – the thought of her lying out there cold and all alone, rotting away. Alone, just like her. Cold. Was she covered with a blanket at least? Ellie knew if she were, it would be to hide her body, but she couldn't help but think of her still alive, still needing warmth and comfort. Or was she in a bin bag? No, Ellie couldn't handle that idea. She needed to check she was... some version of ok. She needed to be with her.

She slipped a coat on, peered out from her door to check the corridor was empty, then snuck to the back staircase.

Outside, the rain fell in a hazy drizzle that almost floated through the air. Like when the first flakes of snowfall come and it wafts around in a half-hearted attempt.

Ellie barely noticed it as she descended the steps, then stopped by the hotel's back entrance.

Two stone buildings lay a few hundred metres to her left. A large one with double doors was nearest, a low long one running behind it. Ellie wondered suddenly if they'd be locked. She hadn't even considered this before.

After a quick check of her surroundings to make sure no one was around or watching, she darted over to the first building. She aimed for the far side and disappeared around the back. The double doors were in full view of the hotel windows, so she was hoping to scope out a side door that would be less obvious. Nothing on this side, but there was a single wooden door at the back. It was old and worn, the vegetation around it overgrown but trampled in places. Ellie tried the handle, but it didn't budge. She looked at the lock, wondering if she could try to pick it. She'd never picked a lock before, but it always looked fairly easy in the movies. As she considered this though, she noticed the gap to the side of the handle. The lock wasn't engaged. She tried the handle again, this time giving the door a good shove. It rattled in the frame, but it still didn't open. She stood back and took a deep breath before giving the door a good kick by the handle, as if she were a policewoman on a drugs bust. The jarring rippled up her leg into her body, and she collapsed on the ground in tears. She rubbed at her throbbing leg and tried to calm her breathing.

'Stupid fucking door,' she hissed.

She sat for a few minutes composing herself. Gingerly, she stood on her sore leg and took the handle again. Taking all her pent-up rage, she yanked the handle back and forth. At least, she had intended to. The first pull on it had the door flying open, knocking her to the ground.

'Oh, you stupid twat, Ellie.' She pounded her fists into the sodden earth, stood, then limped through the open doorway, damp soil still stuck to the sides of her hands.

There were no windows in the building, so the only light was what flooded in behind her. It smelt dank and oily.

The Storm

There was a ride-on lawn mower parked to one side and various gardening tools and equipment stacked, hung, and shelved. A section of the front was a dedicated wood store stacked full of seasoning logs.

Ellie shuffled her way round, looking at all the various gardening paraphernalia. She had almost done a lap when her foot kicked at something that clattered away from her. She looked down at a discarded Coke can and nudged it with her toe. She noticed several others along with other litter – tin cans and empty packets.

Scruffy buggers, she thought.

She wondered who did the gardening – if there was a dedicated gardener, or if the manager roped in one of the staff. Probably Evan if anyone.

Her mind wandered to their little encounter the other day, and she smiled. Jeez, had that only been yesterday? She felt as if she'd lived a thousand lives since then.

She pictured the two of them here in the workshop. Evan all muscular in dirty overalls – her bit of rough. She shook it from her head. Shut it down as quickly as it had appeared. How could she be thinking such things at a time like this? What kind of a person, of a daughter, did that make her? She brushed a hot tear that had escaped her eye and left the building as shame burned on her face.

Ellie hobbled over to the second outbuilding. This one was slightly obscured by the bigger one she'd just left, so she felt less inclined to hide herself. There appeared to be only one door. She braced herself, taking deep shaky breaths, mentally preparing for what she would see on the other side of the door. She reached out to try the handle but stopped before she touched it. Her hand was shaking. She closed her eyes, shook her hands out, and tried again. This time, she held it firmly, then turned, but nothing happened. Whichever way she tried, pushing or pulling, all it did was rattle in its hinges. This one was definitely locked. Made sense, she thought, if her mother was in there, they wouldn't want anyone to stumble in on her.

The door was solid wood – no glass she could break. She had nothing on her to try the lock with either. She walked the perimeter, looking for a window, but there were none. The door was the only point of entry.

With a huff, she slammed her hands against the weathered wood, then turned and leaned her back against it. She would have to find something she could use to pick the lock. She wouldn't be getting in any other way. With another huff, she limped back the way she'd come and slipped into the back door. Unless she could sweet talk Evan into letting her in… He must have access to the key.

CHAPTER 57

The gravel crunched under Lizzy's car as she manoeuvred it to face the car park exit. She was just about to pull off when she saw Gideon appear at the door. He waved a hand aloft as he ran towards her, his face a confused frown. Lizzy sighed, her raincoat letting off a crinkling sound as she leaned back in her seat. She briefly considered driving off and ignoring him, but instead, she put the window down, steeling herself for whatever rant he was going to unload on her this time. He leaned in.

'I'm going to drive up to the blockage, see if I can get a message out,' she said before he could talk. 'It may be futile, but I can't sit around here just waiting and doing nothing.'

'Well, I think it likely a fool's errand. Carl's lived here all his life, and if he says there's no way through, then there's no way through. But I do understand your need. Anything's worth a try, I suppose.'

She sat back, speechless. He had been so against everything she had said so far that she had been fully expecting a rampage of why she shouldn't and couldn't go. He nodded and backed away from the car, allowing her to drive off. He even gave her a little wave as she pulled out of the car park.

The single-lane track wound back up towards the main road. It was darker under the trees today, and the fallen leaves, wet from the storm, made the road feel greasy under her wheels. After about half a mile, something came into view up ahead. She pulled slowly closer to take a look and then let out a frustrated and irritated growl. She was about ninety per cent sure she was witnessing the reason Gideon had allowed her to leave so easily.

Dickhead.

A large tree lay across the road, blocking her path, and in its descent to the ground, it had landed on and taken out a small stone bridge. The stones from the structure, along with the tree itself, had created a damming effect to the stream. The whole area was flooded and completely unpassable.

Lizzy's heart sank. She vacated the car and stood staring at the scene, her eyes roaming the area while her brain processed what she was seeing and how she could overcome it. She couldn't remember how far this track went before it hit the road, but she had a feeling it was a long way. She was a runner though. Fit and able. If she could just find a way to cross the stream, it may be doable to reach the road on foot.

She shut the car door, not bothering to lock it, and started trekking to the left, following the path of the stream. She had no idea of its usual state but guessed it had been exacerbated by the storm. It was wide and deep and not one she wished to cross. She hoped that it would thin out away from the flood or at least get shallower. Wet feet were one thing, but at its current level, she imagined there being a good chance of being submerged or swept downstream.

The ground was spongy underfoot and seemed to climb the further from the track she got. It didn't take long for her to realise her path was headed for a peak and therefore not crossable. She turned and headed back towards the car, disheartened but still determined. If her current path rose, she deduced that the opposite direction must fall.

By the time she got back to the car, her feet were sodden from the undergrowth. The drizzle in the air was turning into a shower, but she pressed on and followed the stream in the other direction. She was right – this path fell into a valley. But that didn't help her either. Water flows down after all and so the whole area was flooded.

Lizzy trudged back to her car. That was it. There was no way out. Tears prickled at her eyes, threatening to fall, but she wouldn't let them. She opened the door and slowly lowered herself back into the driver's seat, shutting it with a soft clunk. Breathing hot air through her nose she suddenly pounded the steering wheel with her fists, letting out a scream. A few steadying breaths later, she put the car into reverse. The track wasn't wide enough to turn there, so she started creeping it backwards to the hotel in a steady crawl.

CHAPTER 58

'Hi.' Ellie gave a small smile, the door having finally opened after multiple knocks. She hadn't found anything in her room worthy of being a lockpick – she didn't wear hair clips and there were no complimentary tweezers or sewing kit – which meant she'd had no option but to go to her last resort.

'Are you ok?' Evan took the buds out of his ears, chucked them towards the bed, then enveloped her in an awkward hug.

'Well, my mum's dead and my dad hid it from me, so I've been better.'

'Shit, sorry, stupid question.'

He shut the door behind her and led her to the bed. She sat next to him at the bottom of it. He looked searchingly at her face, lost for words but knowing he should offer some, taking in her watery eyes.

'Could you just hold me for a moment? Please.'

Fat tears rolled down her cheeks as Evan wrapped his arms tightly around her. He held her until the sobbing stopped.

'I wanted to ask you something.' She pulled out of the embrace so that she could look him in his eyes.

'Sure, anything.'

'I want to see her.'

'Who?'

'My mum. I want to see her. I need to see her.'

The Storm

Evan stood and started pacing the room, running his hand through his chestnut hair as his eyes bulged. 'No, Ellie, you really don't, you—'

'Look,' she interrupted, 'I realise she's not going to look the same. I'm not a child. But she's my mum and she's all alone.'

Evan paused his pacing and looked away. She thought he'd want to help her, but she also knew she was probably asking a lot of him.

He sat back down and sighed. 'Ellie, look, seeing your mum like that… it was, I mean, it's not…' He trailed off, breathing out another sigh. 'She's not your mum anymore, Ellie, not really. Please don't see her like that.'

Ellie held back the retort that sat on her lips. Of course she was still her mum. She couldn't get cross with him, couldn't risk him walking away and not helping her. And so she just stared into his eyes pleadingly until he broke eye contact.

'I can get the key,' he said eventually, his voice barely more than a whisper.

'Really?'

Evan swallowed hard, clearly not thrilled by the idea. 'I'll have to wait until Gideon isn't around. He can't know what we're doing. It may take a little while, but yeah, I'll get it.'

'Thank you,' she said, jumping up and planting a kiss on his cheek.

'I'm not sure I can come with you though. When you go. It's just—'

'I'm not asking you to,' Ellie said quickly.

He nodded, his whole body visibly relaxing. 'I'll come by your room when I have it.'

CHAPTER 59

It had taken an agonisingly long time considering the distance, but Lizzy had finally made it back to the hotel driveway. She parked up and hurried inside, eager to change out of her wet footwear. Her feet squelched with every step through reception, and Gideon looked up with a hint of smugness on his face as she passed.

'How did you get on?' he asked, his face full of fake concern.

Lizzy didn't look up, choosing to carry on walking as she spoke. 'Flooded. There's a tree down. It's totally unpassable even on foot.'

She hurried past and up the stairs to her room. Tosser, she thought. She couldn't understand why he was so against them getting a message out. Surely, it was in his interest too. Maybe he was just against her. Maybe he liked being in control and her disagreeing with him had done something to his ego. She had gone against his wishes in speaking out and he'd lost control of the situation. But now they were trapped, he was back in charge. Could it really be that simple? A power play?

When it came down to it, he was just like Luke. The method of controlling was different, but they were both controlling all the same. She stopped walking suddenly at that thought, the realisation dawning on her. Luke was controlling. How had she not seen it before? It was masked as love, but that 'love' was used as a weapon.

The Storm

She let herself into her room and locked the door. God, she'd been so blind. Her sweet, loving Luke. The man who would do anything for her. The man who worshipped the ground she walked on. The man who texted her constantly throughout the day. The man who couldn't leave her alone. Always touching, hugging, being right there, always there, too close there. No wonder she had felt so trapped.

She took her shoes and socks off and placed them on the radiator to dry. It wasn't on, but it would be at some point. She rummaged through her bag for another pair of socks. All she had left were worn ones, but at least they were dry.

Lizzy sat down heavily on the bed. Luke could wait for another day. Right now, she needed to consider her next move. The road out was blocked and there was a mountain range behind them, so leaving for help was out of the question. Was their only option really to just sit and wait to be rescued? It couldn't be. It felt too helpless. They couldn't call... or could they? Gideon had been so cagey about the phone lines, but Lizzy was still convinced she'd heard him using the phone in his office. Whatever bond they'd once briefly had was broken though. There was no trust going either way and she knew he'd never let her anywhere near the phone now. But when he wasn't in his office, did he lock the door?

She grabbed her book, made her way downstairs, and settled herself in the lounge by the fire. From her seat, she could just see through the door into the reception. The desk was partially in view, but more importantly, the route that Gideon would have to take to leave his post was also in view. He would have to walk past the doorway to go to the dining room or up the stairs. Either way, she would see him.

He was currently busy with some paperwork. He had noticed her, but she was obviously of no concern to him right now. He'd paid her no attention as she'd passed through – no pleasantries, no offer of a drink – his hosting duties were slipping, at least to her. What had she done to offend him so much? Or maybe the better question was, what was he hiding?

She sat idly scanning the pages of her book, her concentration all through that doorway as she kept up the pretence of reading. Lunch was surely being prepped about now, and she wondered if Gideon had any hand in it or if he would need to visit the kitchen to liaise with Carl.

The minutes passed slowly and the tedium of the task and warmth from the fire made Lizzy's eyes grow heavy. She sat herself up straighter in the chair as she felt her lids droop. She had to stay alert. She kept the book open but stopped scanning the pages; instead, she started to run through scenarios she could create that would take Gideon away and speed things up. She'd thought of and discounted two when movement caught her eye. Restraining herself from looking up, she watched out of her peripheral vision as he left the desk. Slowly, she crept to the doorway and risked a peek. He was at the foot of the stairs and moving up. Perfect. That would give her more time than a kitchen run.

She hurried over to the desk, slipped round, and silently entered the office. It felt like breaking and entering and her heart thudded in her chest. She moved round to the desk, grabbed the phone and froze as the door suddenly swung open.

'I was just... oh, Evan,' she said with a sigh, sagging with relief.

Evan stopped midstance, wide-eyed. He shifted nervously from one foot to the other. 'Just need to grab something,' he said at last.

He went behind the desk and took a key from one of the drawers. He didn't seem at all bothered or interested by her presence in the office.

'Listen, Evan,' she began, but key found, he darted from the room. She put the phone down and followed him out. He was quick, already on the stairs by the time she'd rounded

The Storm

the reception desk. On the stairs though, he slowed to his usual lumber, and Lizzy saw Gideon coming the other way.

He was doing something he didn't want Gideon to know about, she realised.

Evan maintained this slower pace until Gideon had passed, then quickened his step again once he was out of view. Lizzy did the same, trying to catch up with him. She reached the landing, a little breathless, just in time to see Evan disappear towards the back of the hotel. She started to jog, determined to reach him, as he turned to the left. There were only two rooms down that way: Ellie's and Paul's. Lizzy could guess which one he was heading to. As she rounded the corridor herself, she saw him knock quietly and enter. Lizzy reached the room just as the door was shutting. She caught it and stepped inside to two shocked faces.

'I'm sorry, sorry for barging in, I just really need to talk to you, Evan.'

'Lizzy, what's going on?' Ellie asked. She looked confused. Evan looked scared.

'Evan, I need you to forget seeing me in the office. Please don't tell Gideon.'

He didn't move or speak. Ellie looked back and forth between them.

'What's going on? Evan? Lizzy?'

'I just wanted to see if the phone in his office works. Gideon says the line is down, but I swear I heard him talking on it yesterday. Please don't say anything.'

Evan didn't respond. He looked nervously at Ellie, as if working out what or how much to tell her.

'We won't if you don't,' Ellie suddenly said, arms folded.

'Ellie,' Evan hissed, his eyes wide and pleading.

'I want to see my mum. Evan was getting me the key for the outbuilding.' She looked down at her feet.

Lizzy paled as her head filled with the images from the lake. Fiona's bloated and marbled face. How her skin appeared to be sloughing off. Ellie shouldn't see that. It would destroy her.

'Oh, sweetie, no. Don't see her like that.'

'I have to. It's not real until I see her, and… and she's all alone. I just want to be with her. To say goodbye.' Tears spilled down her cheeks in a silent sob.

Lizzy rushed over and sat with her on the edge of the bed. She wrapped an arm around her and pulled her close as Evan stood hovering to the side.

'I understand that, I really do. But, Ellie, she doesn't look like your mum anymore. It's much better to remember her in life. The water… well, water does things to a body.'

'I need to see her,' Ellie said firmly.

Lizzy knew it was a terrible idea, but she also knew Ellie didn't exactly need her approval either. She'd made up her mind and she would make it happen one way or another. So, she made the only choice she felt she was able to do considering the situation.

'I'm coming with you, then.'

CHAPTER 60

Ellie held the keys so tightly they pressed into her skin. She didn't feel it though. She didn't feel much of anything right now. The first, larger outbuilding provided cover for the rear one, so, as before, they headed over to that one and round the side, out of sight. Pain flared up Ellie's leg with each step, leaving Lizzy to pull ahead, not that the pain bothered Ellie much other than the frustration that she couldn't reach her mum quicker. Lizzy noticed Ellie wasn't next to her and stopped and turned, looking back.

'What have you done to your foot?'

'It's my leg. I... well, I tried to kick the door in,' she said, a blush colouring her pale cheeks.

They looked at each other, and Lizzy burst out laughing.

'You muppet.'

It broke the tension, and Ellie couldn't help but join in.

Now they were shielded, they didn't need to rush. They ambled along the length of both the outbuildings to the door Ellie had found before.

'Are you sure about this? Like, really sure? Because once you've seen her, you can't unsee.' Lizzy took Ellie gently by the shoulders. 'I know you feel the need to be with her and say goodbye, but... well, I think you should remember her how she was. And you'll have the chance to say your goodbye at the funeral.'

Ellie had never been more and less sure of something in her whole life. She needed to know her mum was safe and had been looked after, and she needed to know that this was real, that it really was her, because until she'd seen it with her own eyes, then this could all be a big mistake.

God, please let it be a mistake.

She nodded and stepped forwards, took a moment to steady herself, then put the key in the lock.

It had only opened a crack when the smell hit them. They both immediately gagged and turned away, bringing hands and sleeves up to cover their noses and mouths. It may have been cold for the time of year, but it was still August. Nowhere near cold enough to preserve a body. Ellie pushed the door wider, hoping to let some fresh air in and to dissipate the smell. The space was a hum of flies.

She breathed slowly and shallowly until her stomach settled, then moved warily into the room. It was a big space, long and thin and mostly empty. There were a few stacked boxes, some old wooden barrels, and some lengths of timber and rope, but that was all. Ellie saw none of it though; her eyes were drawn immediately to the form lying in the centre of the space.

Her mother... because damn, it really was her mother, had been laid on her back on the concrete floor, her dress and hair arranged with care. This was part of what she needed to see – that her mother hadn't just been dumped, that she'd been treated with decency and respect in the aftermath of such an awful situation, that she hadn't been tied up in a bin bag and stuffed into a dusty corner. Cautiously, she edged nearer as Lizzy waited in the doorway. As she caught sight of her face, she had to turn away. She swallowed down the bile that had risen in the back of her throat.

Lizzy came over and put a reassuring hand on Ellie's back. 'Do you want to leave now?' she whispered.

The Storm

Ellie took a few moments trying to steady her breathing. To concentrate on taking the air through her mouth and not her nose. 'No,' she finally managed.

Shakily, she turned and approached the body... her mother – or what had once been her mother. She looked all wrong. The wrong shape, the wrong colour. Her skin looked waxy and shiny and somehow fell loose on her bloated face, which was so pale it was almost translucent.

Ellie knelt next to her, feeling such love and heartbreak for the woman she'd been and now would never be again. She ached to hold her one more time and reached for her hand, stopping just short as she noticed the loose wrinkled skin looked ready to fall off. She gagged again, bringing a hand to her mouth and turning her face.

She bowed her head, unable to look but also not ready to leave. 'I'm sorry,' she repeated over and over. 'I'm so sorry.' How could she not have noticed her mother wasn't in the room next door? Investigated the fact she hadn't come for food multiple times in a row? Even if her mother had been alive through all that and in the room, what sort of daughter didn't even check in for a conversation? Then her mouth set in a thin line. Was her father not more to blame than she was? But this wasn't about him right now.

'I miss you, Mum,' she said, her anger subsiding to sadness, tears beginning to fall. 'And I love you. I love you so, so much.'

She continued to kneel silently by her side, her tears streaking her face and landing on the dusty concrete. After a while, Lizzy walked over, helped Ellie to her feet and led her to the door. Once outside, Ellie ran to the bushes and immediately threw up. Lizzy took her time locking up to give her some space and privacy.

'Thank you for coming with me,' Ellie said without turning, still leaning over in the bushes as her body tensed, although nothing was now coming up. 'I'm sorry you had to go through that again. You didn't need to come.'

'It was the least I could do. Come on. Let's have a little walk before we go back. I think a bit of fresh air would do us both some good.'

CHAPTER 61

It had been bad enough when she'd found Fiona in the lake, but two days later, well, Lizzy was shocked at what forty-eight hours could do to a body. It had taken all of her strength and will not to join Ellie in the bushes. The suggestion of a walk had not just been for Ellie's benefit. The stench of death clung to her nostrils and crept over her skin, making her grateful for the cleansing drizzle that was falling.

Lizzy opted for the small woods, making sure to avoid going anywhere near the lake. There was no destination, just aimless walking, putting physical and mental distance to what they had both just witnessed. After a while, they came to a small clearing that had a patch of rocks. They sat in companionable silence side by side, each with their own thoughts.

What a bloody mess. There were no words. She couldn't imagine what Ellie was going through.

Lizzy thought back to everyone in the hotel and why anyone would want to do this. It didn't make sense. She could find reason for Deidre. She could find reason for Fiona. But not for both together. Nothing linked them no matter how hard she tried to fathom it.

After a while, the two girls stood in unison, as though some telepathic agreement had been reached, and started back towards the hotel.

As they entered the rear doors, they were met with the smells of lunch from the kitchen and had to pass the half-filled buffet table on the way to the rear staircase. Lizzy looked away as her stomach rolled and lurched, and she was suddenly very glad they had chosen to do this before lunch. They slipped quickly into the stairwell.

'I know you may not feel like eating, but I think we should at least have a sweet tea.'

Ellie's pale face looked back at her.

'Something to settle our stomachs and for the shock.'

'Ok, but can we have it in the lounge? I don't think I could stomach sitting in there around all the food.'

'Fine with me. Let's meet back in the lounge in ten minutes.'

Lizzy dashed up the stairs to her room before Ellie could respond as her stomach rolled again. She inched quickly through her partially open door and threw herself to her knees on her tiled bathroom floor, only just getting her head over the toilet bowl in time. Afterwards, she rinsed her face and stripped off her death-tainted clothes. She dug around for one of her previous outfits. It was crumpled at the bottom of her bag, but it was much more preferable. She took a carrier bag she had been using for dirty underwear, dumped the contents on the floor, and stuffed the death clothes inside. She didn't want to risk them touching any of her other things. Contaminating them.

'Thank you,' Lizzy said to Poppy as Poppy placed the tray in front of them and left.

Lizzy poured tea from the steaming pot into two cups, then heaped a generous spoonful of sugar in each. She splashed in milk and gave them both a good stir. As she handed one to Ellie, Lizzy noticed that she too had changed clothes.

'How are you doing?' she asked.

'Ok,' Ellie said despite looking utterly drained of all energy and emotion. She still looked peaky, but some colour

The Storm

had returned to her face. She lifted her tea and sipped. Lizzy did the same.

Evan passed by and looked over. Lizzy nodded. He acknowledged with a nod of his own and continued.

'What do we do now?' Ellie said, looking up. 'Someone did that to her. Someone killed my mum, I know they did.'

'I'm not sure. I tried to get a message out this morning. Drove as far as I could, but the road is unpassable. By car or foot.'

'What about the phone?'

The phone. Shit, she'd forgotten all about the phone. In her panic at being interrupted and silencing Evan, she had never listened to the handset.

'We'll ask Evan to try. When he returns the keys.'

They sat in silence for a while sipping their drinks.

'Tell me about her, your mum.'

Ellie's face brightened at her memory, and her pained features softened. 'She was wonderful. So kind and lovely. Always there for me, you know? Stopped work when I was born just so she could be with me, like, all the time.'

'Wow, and she never went back?'

'When I was older. Worked her way up in an office. Started as a part-time secretary so she could still do the school run, ended up head of HR. She was amazing.'

'She really sounds it. I'm sorry I never got to know her.'

'She'd have liked you.'

'Yeah?'

'Yeah. Pleased that I've made a friend that stops me moping and being a stroppy bitch.' Ellie laughed, and Lizzy smiled at the comment.

'She was always supportive. Even when I was being a stroppy bitch. And I was. A lot.' Ellie's face clouded over, her expression solemn again, pain held in her eyes. 'I was horrible to her on this trip. And before we came. I didn't want to come, moaned about it the whole way here and every day since. That's her last memory of me. I can't remember my last words to her, but I bet they were spiteful.' Ellie erupted into fresh tears, and Lizzy took the cup from her shaky hands and placed it back on the table.

'That will not be her last memory. I guarantee it.'

The tears continued, but she looked up.

'From everything you just told me, it's clear just how much you meant to your mum and what she thought of you. She'll have known deep down how you felt. I promise.'

Ellie took a napkin from the tray, wiped her eyes, and sniffed loudly. Lizzy didn't know if Ellie really believed her or not, but she hoped so.

They lapsed into silence as they sipped the remainder of their tea. A few minutes later, Evan came for their tray. Lizzy placed the key onto it just before he lifted it. He nodded and slipped it into his palm, discreetly pocketing it.

'Evan, I never checked the phone line. When I was in the office before. When you take it back, could you?'

He paused before answering, his gaze firmly on the tray in his hands. 'Sure.'

Ellie rose and put a hand on his arm, forcing him to look at her. 'Thank you,' she said, kissing his cheek. She looked deep into his eyes. Nothing else needed to be said. It was obvious how much it meant to her. Evan relaxed into a small smile, clearly glad of his decision to help.

As he turned, they became aware of Paul standing in the doorway. Lizzy wondered just how long he'd been there and how much he'd seen or heard. He strode purposefully over, glaring at Evan as he left the room.

'How are you doing, sweetheart?' he said, going for a hand on her shoulder but getting shrugged off.

'Fine.'

'What are you doing with that boy Evan?' As he said it, he looked back the way Evan had gone, clearly unhappy with his daughter having anything to do with him.

'Nothing.' She rolled her eyes. 'For God's sake, he just brought us tea.'

The Storm

'Really, cause I've seen how he looks at you, and—'

'Dad, just stop. I'm a big girl now.'

Ellie turned to Lizzy. 'Come on,' she said, all but dragging her out into the dining room.

CHAPTER 62

'I think I may be ready to eat something now. Would you like anything?' Lizzy asked, pausing by her table without sitting.

Ellie considered but shook her head. Her sole reason for coming in here was to get away from her dad.

Lizzy went to the buffet table and plated up a snacking plate that she could just pick at. When she returned, Jenny and Alex were sitting at her table either side of Ellie. They were close, leaning into her while she shrank away, looking small and younger than her years. They really were like vultures.

'Ahh, Lizzy,' Alex said, looking up. 'Did you get out to the road? How did it go?'

'Not good, I'm afraid. There's a tree down. It's taken out the bridge and the whole area's flooded. You can't get across. I tried on foot too. It's impassable.' Lizzy sat.

Alex's face fell from hopeful to concerned. 'Shit. What do we do now, then?'

Jenny was hanging on to his arm again, her face pale, her eyes wide. She reminded Lizzy of a frightened toddler. If they'd have been standing, she could imagine her hiding behind Alex's legs and peeking out.

'I don't know.'

'We can't just sit here,' Jenny blurted out.

'I saw her today. My mum. I saw her.' Ellie stared ahead into nothing as she spoke. 'Someone here did that to her.'

The Storm

Though she had spoken quietly, even Mr Franks at the furthest table had heard and lowered his cutlery, mouth open slightly, eyes fixed on them. Her words had cut through everything and silenced everyone.

'Oh, Alex,' Jenny said through trembling lips.

'It's ok, Jenny, we'll think of something.' Alex put a reassuring arm round her.

Lizzy doubted his words of comfort even convinced himself though. If phone lines really were down, they were utterly stuck. Looking at everyone else's faces, they all knew it too.

Alex gave Jenny's hand a squeeze. 'Let's go back up to the room, shall we?'

Silently, they rose and left, Jenny leaning on Alex like she needed the support as he led her away and out of the dining room. Lizzy picked at the food on her plate and Ellie reached over for a samosa. Lizzy smiled and pushed the plate into the middle of the table.

'What are we going to do?' Ellie asked. Her voice was small, and it pained Lizzy that she had no answers.

'We're going to stay safe, and we're going to get through this.'

It was all she had to offer, but it seemed to appease Ellie for the moment. She continued to pick at Lizzy's plate until it was empty, then with a sigh, she put her head in her hands, leaning her elbows on the table.

'I'm so tired. I just want to sleep and sleep, and when I wake up, I'm back home lying in my own bed and we never came here.' She pushed her hands into her hair, staring off into the distance, then brought them back down to the table. The shadows under her eyes were pronounced and they were so baggy that the skin had almost dimpled.

'I know, I know.' Lizzy held one of her hands over the table. 'Why don't you go for a lie-down, see if you can sleep for a bit?'

Ellie nodded, pushed her chair back, and left the dining room. Lizzy watched her go, then returned to the buffet to restock her plate. As she reached the end of the table, Evan entered the room and came over.

'It's done, there's no phone line,' he whispered.

'Shit.' Lizzy's heart sank. So that was it. They really were on their own. 'We need to come up with something, Evan. Ellie saw someone lurking in the corridor.'

'Lurking in the corridor?' He shot back from her wide-eyed, his voice suddenly loud.

'Sshhh.' Lizzy ushered him to the other side of the room, realising that they were in Mr Franks' earshot. He seemed oblivious and continued to plough through his meal.

'Last night, there was someone in the corridor. The lights were all out, so she couldn't see who, but it spooked her. Spooked me too, to be fair.'

'The lights shouldn't be out. They don't go out; they're on a motion sensor at night.'

'I know. Which is why it's a bit suspect, don't you think? Someone turned them off so they wouldn't be seen.'

'But nothing happened last night. Did it?'

'Not that I'm aware of. Maybe Ellie stopped them... scared them away.'

Evan seemed to consider, then shrugged, back to his nonchalant attitude. 'Could have just been a power cut. Happens here.'

He wandered off, leaving Lizzy wondering if she'd made a mistake in confiding in him. She had trusted Gideon once, and look how that had turned out. Still, Evan had hidden things from his boss to help them. If there were sides to be taken, he was definitely on theirs, at least for the moment.

CHAPTER 63

It had been a couple of days now since the autopsy results had come in, and Blackwell had been right in her assumptions. Even though they had done everything by the book, their every move and decision had been questioned. She had felt as if she were back on probation and had stumbled her way through the questions put to her by their sergeant. No doubt Myers had taken his in his stride, she thought, though she imagined that being her senior in time served meant that they had come down harder on him. He had said little about it to her since, but he seemed unfazed.

Attempts to visit the hotel had been made again, but the landslide had stopped them getting anywhere close. Still, if they couldn't get in, then at least none of the guests could get out. Highway maintenance was working hard to clear a path through, but it could still be a while yet. They would be the first to hear when it was passable.

Blackwell finished entering the report onto the ancient computer in front of her and picked up the next case file to attend to. Now that it was being classed as a murder, Briar's Crag had been passed on to CID. While she was glad to be rid of it, it still bothered her that they hadn't seen the signs. What had they missed?

CHAPTER 64

Ellie didn't even have the energy to undress. The climb up the stairs and walk to her room had sapped what little she had left and so she climbed into bed fully clothed and pulled the covers over her head, blotting out the world, craving what little comfort they could give.

She was just drifting off when there was a knock at her door. Begrudgingly, she threw back the covers and dragged herself to the door. Her dad stood before her. He looked smaller than when they had arrived, but he stood taller when he saw her, his sagging body perking up. Ellie considered slamming the door in his face, but she didn't have the strength for him right now, knowing he'd only keep bothering her if she did.

'What?' she barked, getting back into bed.

He came slowly into the room, shutting the door gently behind him. 'We need to talk. I… I want to explain.'

'There's nothing to say. You're a piece of shit of a dad who lied and kept Mum's death from me.'

He sat on the edge of the bed and put a hand on her shoulder. 'I did it for you.'

'For me?' Ellie sat up, shoving him off. 'How exactly did that benefit me? This was all for you.'

Paul wiped at his glassy eyes and struggled to keep the emotion from his voice. 'You mean everything to me, Ellie. I would do anything for you.'

The Storm

The tears were freely spilling down his face now, and Ellie couldn't help but feel sorry for him. She had never seen him cry before and she couldn't help the lump that formed in her throat. Her heart hurt for him. She shuffled her legs round so that she could sit next to him and moved in for a hug but stopped herself short. No. This didn't change anything. She was still mad. Still hadn't forgiven him.

'You were always a daddy's girl. I wanted to protect that. Keep hold of it for just a little longer. How could I tell you your mother had died? How could I hurt you like that?' He shook his head. 'I couldn't find the words, I couldn't say it. I didn't even understand it myself.'

She stayed silent, not trusting herself to speak. The ice was thawing, but it hadn't melted yet.

'I don't even know why or what happened. I mean, what was she doing out there? It's no excuse though, Ellie. I was a coward and I'm sorry.' He placed a hand over hers, and she let him.

A soft rap on the door broke the moment, causing them both to look up. Before either of them could answer it, it opened, and Evan sauntered in.

Paul was instantly on his feet and walking over to him. 'What are you doing here?' he snapped, jabbing a finger at Evan.

'Dad.'

'No, you can't just walk in here, into a teenage girl's room uninvited.'

'For God's sake, Dad, it's fine.'

He swung round to face Ellie. 'How can that be fine? It's unprofessional and it's sick. I've seen the way he looks at you, Ellie.' He turned back to a panic-stricken Evan. 'You need to stay away from my daughter.'

'Dad. Get out.'

'What?' He turned, open-mouthed, as the anger fell from his face.

'Get out!'

He stumbled away from Evan back towards Ellie. 'But, Ellie, we still need to—'

'Evan's staying and you're leaving,' she hissed, her words laced with the venom she was feeling inside. She could and would see and talk to whomever she wanted.

Evan hovered, his gaze flicking between the two of them.

Paul strode back over to Evan. 'This isn't over,' he said through gritted teeth as he left, slamming the door behind him.

Evan's mouth fell open as he looked at Ellie. 'Shit, Ellie, I'm so sorry, I shouldn't have just walked in, I should—'

'It's ok. Fuck him.'

'But he's your dad and—'

'And I don't care.'

Ellie stood up from the bed, walked up to him, and kissed him hard, pulling him back towards the bed as she did so. Her hands went to his belt, and she started fumbling with the buckle.

'Ellie, I don't think this is a good idea.'

'Shut up.'

She kissed him again and continued with the buckle, working his trousers loose and letting them slip to the floor. He didn't need much convincing, and Ellie smiled in delight as she realised she was getting her way. She quickly removed her clothes before he started getting second thoughts, then slipped beneath the covers.

She didn't exactly exaggerate her moans of pleasure, but she also made no effort to conceal or muffle them. Let him hear, she thought. That would teach him to meddle in her life.

CHAPTER 65

Lizzy sat on the edge of her bed mulling over the last few days. Everything that had happened and the possible reasons behind it. Ways that they could get themselves or word out. She sighed, still none the wiser. Today was supposed to be her last day here. She should have been on the road back home by now. Luke would be going spare. She wondered how many calls and messages were waiting to ping to her phone.

Luke. That was it. He would surely raise the alarm when she didn't come home. He probably had her trip worked out to the last second – he'd know when she had to check out, how long her journey would take, what time to expect her back. He'd phone the police when she didn't show. Oh, hallelujah.

She worked it out herself. 10 a.m. check out. Two-hour drive, two and a half if she stopped, 1 p.m. home latest. It was 1.10 p.m. now. He would be panicking. How long would he give it? An hour? Two? By dinner time, he would have phoned, she was sure of it. Help would be coming. No, wait. Didn't there need to be at least twenty-four hours before an adult was considered missing? Shit. Ok, so this time tomorrow, then. They only had to get through one more day before help would be coming.

It was all going to be fine. Her work was all but finished, she was pretty sure she had come to a conclusion about Luke, and help would very shortly be on the way. Maybe Gideon had been right. Maybe there had been no need to panic; after all, nothing else had happened. Everyone was fine.

She suddenly felt bad. Maybe her stressed-out mind had blown everything up and out of proportion after all. Had she terrified Ellie and that poor couple for no reason? If so, she had also been a right bitch to Gideon, who had only been trying to calm her down and prevent the panic that was now rising thanks to her.

But one more day and then she'd never have to see him again, never have to feel awkward and uncomfortable around him. It was time to apologise. To go and be an adult. She at least owed him that.

Lizzy got up, eased herself round the desk, and locked her room before going downstairs. She found Gideon shuffling papers, organising, and stapling them at the reception desk.

'Gideon,' she began.

He looked up, wary and on edge.

'I'm sorry. I've come to apologise. I don't think I've been all that nice to you, and I'm sorry.'

He narrowed his eyes and went to speak, but she raised a hand to indicate that she wasn't done.

'I don't think I realised just how stressed I've been recently, and I think I may have let things run away with me a little.'

He relaxed a little and his whole face softened. 'That's... quite alright.'

'No, it's not. I was bossy and rude, and you were only trying to help, to calm me down. I can see that now.'

'Well, it was all very understandable. Trauma can play havoc. Let's say no more about it.' He resumed his shuffling and stapling.

'Great, thank you for understanding.' She stepped from the desk, relieved that was over, then turned back. 'Oh, Gideon, today was supposed to be my last day.'

'Don't worry,' he said, laughing. 'I won't be throwing you out. We're all here for the foreseeable, I'm afraid.'

The Storm

She smiled at his misunderstanding. 'No, what I mean is… I'll be missed. My boyfriend will be asking questions. People on the outside will know something's wrong. Help will be coming.'

'Oh, I see. Oh, that's great news.'

Lizzy thought he might have been a bit more enthusiastic or relieved, but his words sounded hollow. Maybe he knew it wasn't going to be as easy as she was hoping.

She needed a minute before talking to the others, so she stepped out for a breath of air. There was a break in the rain and weak sunlight shone through a chink in the clouds. Maybe she could get a run in this afternoon. Today was looking up. She would have to find Jenny and Alex first, confess that she may have gotten a little ahead of herself and reassure them that help would be coming very shortly.

She still couldn't explain the lurker in the corridor though. Although she supposed it had more than likely been a drunk guest trying to find their room, or even a sober one if the lights were out.

She headed back upstairs and knocked on Jenny and Alex's room. They had the one opposite hers – she'd seen them coming and going from it a few times. Lizzy could hear shuffling from inside the room and then saw the peephole blacken as they checked out who was knocking.

'Just a minute,' came Alex's voice.

Their door opened slowly, as if they were checking it really was her and that she was alone. Wow, she'd really scared them. It revealed Alex standing ready and alert. Jenny was at the furthest side of the room on the other side of the bed. Practically as far away from the door as she could get without leaving the room. She wore a worried expression and held her arms up and close to her body, one hand over the other.

'Sorry to bother you,' Lizzy said.

'Is there news?' Alex, suddenly animated, pushed the door wide and eagerly let her in.

Lizzy smiled her thanks and wandered into their room. It was slightly smaller than hers, with not having the benefit of the bay window, and looked out to the front of the hotel. It must have been directly above the reception.

'Kind of. Firstly, I wanted to apologise for scaring you. There have been two deaths, but there isn't actually any evidence that says they weren't accidents. I don't know if I was being over-cautious or if I just scared myself. I feel bad for passing that on to you guys.' She bit on her lip as she flicked between the two of them, watching for a reaction.

'What do you mean?' Jenny edged closer, doubt and confusion in her voice.

'I mean, it's horrific obviously and it looks very suspicious, but we don't know for sure. I don't want to ruin your holiday by terrifying you.'

'But we don't know that it was an accident either?'

'No. Until the police get here, we don't know either way.'

Alex exhaled loudly and ran a hand over his face. Lizzy couldn't tell if he was relieved or frustrated.

'Either way though, the alarm will be raised. Today was supposed to be my last day. I should have been home by now, and when I'm not, my boyfriend will phone the police. I know for sure he won't rest until contact has been made and he knows I'm ok.'

'Oh, thank Christ for that.' Alex's whole body visibly relaxed.

Jenny beamed and practically skipped over to Alex. She hugged his arm. 'So, they'll be coming today, then?'

'Well, no.'

'An adult has to be missing twenty-four hours before they're missing,' Alex cut in.

'Yes, and there's still the landslide and flood to negotiate. We don't know how far they've got with that and if the road's open yet. But they'll have to check on us. It's something at least.'

The Storm

They passed a look between themselves, and Jenny sagged. Lizzy wondered if coming here had been as good an idea as it had initially seemed. It had filled her with such hope earlier, but now, saying it out loud and talking it through, she wasn't quite sure. It all sounded so weak.

'Well, I just wanted to let you know. Something is happening. It won't be long.' She gave them a half-smile that she hoped was reassuring.

Neither of them spoke.

'I'll... leave you both to it, then.'

Lizzy let herself out. As the door shut behind her, she heard the shuffling again, presumably some sort of homemade security as she had been doing. She hadn't convinced them at all.

CHAPTER 66

Lizzy quickly changed into some running gear before the weather had second thoughts and headed out. She decided to brave the lake but was careful to take a different path that would lead her away from the potential crime scene and skirt the edge off to the side instead of leading directly to it. It was overcast but pleasant enough. At least it was dry. Well, the weather was. The ground was saturated and her footing constantly slipped. She tried to keep off the path and run on the grass to the side, but that was equally treacherous in places.

After twenty minutes, she slowed to a brisk walk. As she approached the foot of the mountain, the ground started steadily rising, water from the past few days cascading down its gravel trail. Her running shoes would be no match for it. She took a few moments to stretch out her muscles and take a drink, using some of the rocks as leverage to pull her hamstrings and calve muscles. It felt good to get them working again, to feel the stretch and pull as they worked, to feel the cool fresh air fill her lungs.

She looked out onto the expanse of water in front of her. Even reflecting back the grey skies, it was a stunning sight. The light rippled the surface where it managed to break through the clouds and twinkled, dancing as the clouds shifted overhead. The rest was a collection of greys and blacks in varying shades. She stared as the dark water drew her in and pulled her down. The beauty was gone. Shattered. Tainted. Fiona had been floating in that water. Dead in that water. Lizzy

The Storm

shivered. The surrounding peaks suddenly crowded rather than enhanced, the clouds low enough to obscure the tops as though they were pressing down on her.

Lizzy looked away. Broke the spell and looked back to the track. Without the sound of her pounding feet or her panting breath, everything was eerily quiet.

A sixth sense of being watched suddenly prickled at the nape of her neck, and she stood straighter, alert, surveying the area around her. She could see no one and nothing looked out of place. No movement. Paranoid again. She tutted yet only half-believed.

Keeping alert, she began her walk back, scolding herself for getting carried away again. So what if someone else was out there? They had every right to be, just as she did. She didn't own the lake. Still, she felt uncomfortable being alone and so far away from the hotel. It seemed her prison had now become her sanctuary.

Lizzy was halfway back when the feeling overtook her again. Someone out there. Someone watching. She heard a twig snap to her left and whipped her head round. She glimpsed a flash of movement before it disappeared behind a tree, and her breath caught in her throat. She stood still, watching and waiting with a racing heart. If one of the other guests was out for a walk, they would continue, they would have passed the tree by now, but there was no one. No sign. She waited for an undeterminably long time. No one emerged. If it had been a guest she'd seen, they were hiding. Were they watching her?

Lizzy picked up her pace and ran the last stretch, only slowing when the hotel was in sight, although not stopping until she was on the driveway, facing the path she'd just come down, panting and trying to slow her heart rate. Still, no one emerged and no one followed. Was she losing it? She was sure she had seen someone. Think back, Lizzy – someone or something? Could it have been an animal? She had all but been convinced at the time that it was a person, but now she wasn't so sure.

She started a few cool-down stretches using the hotel's wall as support as she balanced on one leg, pulling the other one backwards by her foot to touch her rear. She needed a good night's sleep. A good night's sleep in her own bed.

She released her foot and repeated the stretch on the other leg, then stepped forwards into a lunge, straightened her leg, and bent forwards over it. Her lace was undone, she noticed, and she knelt to tie it. As she did so, her gaze caught on the wall in front of her. A wire came out of the building and was clipped along the stonework. It wasn't the wire as such that had caught her attention though, more the clear slice through it. The phone lines weren't working because they had been cut.

CHAPTER 67

Ellie lay in bed, her insides churning with guilt and shame. She had used Evan to get back at her dad and she had hurt her dad in the most spiteful way she could think of. She was a horrible, horrible person. Evan lay next to her, arms behind his head, staring at the ceiling. Neither of them spoke. She wondered what he was thinking. What he must think of her. She cringed inside. At least it hadn't been their first time together – that had to count for something at least. She hoped. She desperately wanted him to leave, but there was no way of saying it without making it all worse.

'I better get going,' he said, as if reading her mind. 'Gideon will wonder where I've got to.'

She still couldn't speak. Just watched him dress and leave. No kiss goodbye. No peck on the cheek. Shit. He knew what this was, what it had been. She curled into a ball, totally ashamed of herself, and wept.

CHAPTER 68

Lizzy stared at the wire for a good few minutes, not trusting her eyes. Icy tendrils tickled her spine as she stood. She hadn't been wrong. Someone was doing this. Someone at this hotel had killed Deidre and Fiona, then cut the lines so nobody could call for help.

Lizzy raced through reception and took the stairs two at a time. She had to get back to her room, had to think this through. Should she tell anyone? She didn't know who she could trust. Ok, well, Ellie – it clearly hadn't been her. But who else? Help would be on the way tomorrow. Should she just try and wait it out?

Once inside her room, she sat down on the edge of the bed to think, her mind a whirlwind of thoughts she couldn't quite grasp. Someone at the hotel had killed two people, and maybe that same someone was still stalking the corridors at night.

Enough, she decided. She leapt up, snatched her phone from the bedside table, then hurried back out, letting the door slam behind her. She couldn't sit around and wait; she had to do something.

She bounded back down the stairs and out the front door. They only had Gideon's word that the phone signal couldn't be reached at all at the hotel. And she sure as hell didn't trust his word.

The Storm

Lizzy trailed the footpaths, checking her phone every few paces. She had to get a signal. But it didn't seem to matter which direction she went in or how high she climbed, she was always met with the same. Nothing. The signal bars remained empty. 'No service' displayed on the screen like a taunt.

Her legs burned as she climbed yet another track. She wouldn't give up until every option had been exhausted. She ploughed on, determination driving her onwards.

Lizzy looked at her muddy clothes on the tiled bathroom floor as she stepped into the bathtub and pulled the shower curtain closed around herself. The warm water from the overhead shower attempted but failed to ease her aching muscles. There had been nothing. The phone hadn't even shown a flicker of signal. Gideon had been telling the truth. About this at least.

Despite knowing – as she'd checked multiple times – that she'd locked and barricaded her door, she couldn't help but try to listen for any unexpected noises nearby, but she couldn't hear above the steady stream of water. The shower curtain was navy and heavy, and it left her feeling uneasy that she couldn't see even shapes and shadows beyond it. Although she knew her brain would probably work any shadows into human shapes even if this weren't the case.

She quickly cleaned her body, emerging two minutes after she'd gone in, not even allowing herself the time to wash her hair.

Lizzy dried and dressed, eyes constantly flitting to the barricade and locked door, then made her way to Ellie's room.

She knocked gently on the door. Then a little louder when there was no response. Lizzy had begun walking away when the door finally opened. She heard the click of the lock and turned back, seeing two very red and puffy eyes peering out from the small opening. Seeing it was Lizzy, Ellie swung the door wider. Her clothes were rumpled and her hair unbrushed.

As Lizzy approached, she burst into tears and threw her arms around her. Lizzy embraced her and walked her into the room, kicking the door closed behind them.

'Hey, it's ok.' She shushed, stroking her hair. They went over to the bed and sat down.

'I've made such a mess of things. I don't know what to do,' Ellie said.

'What's happened?'

'Dad came by, we talked. I didn't forgive him, but we were kinda making peace. Talking at least. Then Evan turned up and Dad got angry, shouted at him, which made me angry. I mean, how dare he, right? And anyway, I kicked Dad out and let Evan in and we... well, I made it obvious what we were doing.'

'Oh, Ellie.'

'I know, it was a stupid thing to do and I hate myself. Now Dad's gonna know and hate me, and Evan knows I've used him, so he's gonna hate me too.' She erupted into fresh sobs and buried her face in her hands. 'I have no one left.'

Lizzy pulled her close. She remembered what it was like being a teenager, how her hormones had thrown her emotions all over the place. She couldn't imagine navigating that with all Ellie was going through.

'Look, your dad is your dad. He's never going to hate you no matter what you do, ok? And, Evan, well, I'm pretty sure Evan was getting something out of the situation as well, wasn't he? I bet he wasn't exactly complaining.

'If it makes you feel any better, you can apologise, but I wouldn't worry about it. It'll blow over and work its way out. These things always do.'

The Storm

'Urgh, thank you.' Ellie rubbed away the tears from her red and puffy face. 'I can't wait to be out of this place.'

'You and me both. But I was meant to be leaving today and my partner, Luke, will raise the alarm when I don't go home. Just hang tight, it won't be much longer.' Lizzy spoke with more conviction than she felt, offering her a comforting smile. She knew it wouldn't be right for her to add any more to Ellie's plate by mentioning the phone lines.

CHAPTER 69

Ellie ran a brush through her hair and sighed, though she didn't know whether it was with relief or frustration towards herself. She felt better after speaking to Lizzy and she agreed that her dad was maybe obliged not to hate her, but she knew Evan could. Irrelevant of if he'd received something out of the deal, it didn't change the fact that what she'd done was shitty. And, in her own way, she cared about him. He'd been the first to disclose about her mum, showed her real concern, and even temporarily stole the key to the outhouse for her. She had to make amends and check he was ok.

She quietly closed her door and padded over to Evan's room, hoping he hadn't left for dinner prep yet. She didn't want her dad to hear her leave her room after what she'd already made him listen to. Now she was out of that moment, the thought truly made her feel sick. But she'd deal with that another time.

Evan's door was slightly ajar. She knocked gently. 'Evan?'

Nothing.

She knocked harder, and this time, the door swung open. A blur rushed at her and knocked her flying. She landed awkwardly on her arm and bashed her head on the door frame. Her vision blurred as she watched the figure round the corner and disappear from sight.

She touched her head and winced. No blood, but there was already a lump forming and it hurt like hell. Her arm was sore too, but she could move it and wriggle her fingers. Not broken, then.

'Evan?' Ellie quickly got to her feet and stumbled into his room, eyes quickly scanning.

She gasped when she spotted him, her feet rooting to the spot. Blood. It was all she could see. All she could focus on. Blood glistening in the light, blood all over Evan as he lay sprawled on his back. There was a roaring in her ears and the room span a little.

Is he...? She trembled as she stepped closer. Then she noticed he was clutching at his arm and panting hard.

'Shit.' She rushed over to him. 'Evan. What happened? Where are you hurt?'

With shaking hands, she frantically scoured his body for wounds, pulling and tugging at his uniform until he threw her off.

'I'm ok, I'm ok. It's just my arm.'

He winced, sucking in breath as he pulled himself into a sitting position. His shirt was torn and blood oozed from a four-inch slash on his right forearm. His face didn't look too good either – blood was pouring from his nose.

Ellie ran to the bathroom and came back with the hand towel. She wound it tightly round his arm to stop the flow. 'What the hell happened? Who was that?'

'I don't know. I never saw their face.' He winced again as she finished knotting the makeshift bandage around his arm, the white towel already soaking in the deep red blood. 'Someone knocked on the door. When I answered, they shoved it back in my face before I could see anything.'

Ellie examined his face and wondered if he'd broken his nose. He sniffed at the blood that continued to drip from it. At least it seemed to be slowing.

'They had a knife, Ellie. They got me to the bed. They were so strong... If you hadn't come in when you did...' His voice wobbled and caught.

She'd saved his life, but at what cost? She'd seen the killer. Not enough to identify who it was, but they didn't know that. Would they now be coming for her? The thought terrified her, and she didn't know what to do. She did know that Evan needed medical attention though. That cut was going to need more than a plaster.

'We need to get you some help.'

'From where exactly?'

There was only one person she trusted.

'I'll get Lizzy. She'll know what to do.'

CHAPTER 70

'You're very lucky Ellie came in when she did,' Lizzy said as she bandaged Evan's wound with a dressing she had got from the first aid kit she had found in reception. The cut to his arm was thankfully not deep and she'd washed and cleaned it. She wasn't sure if it needed stitches or not, but it was the best they could do under the circumstances.

Ellie appeared to be in more shock than Evan, gently rocking herself on the only chair in the room as she watched, wide-eyed and voiceless.

'I know, it wasn't exactly my arm they were aiming for.'

'And you didn't see them at all? Build? Hair colour? Anything to help tell us who they are?'

'No, it all happened so quickly. The bash to my face made my eyes blur. They were wearing something over their face anyway. Some kind of hat and face mask.'

'What about you, Ellie? Did you see them?'

'Hmm?' She slowly raised her head and her eyes came back into focus. 'No, not really. They were pushing into me before I knew what was happening and then I hit my head. Their clothes were dark, that's all. I only saw their back.'

'Let's take a look at that.'

She motioned Ellie over to the bed. Ellie stood, looking a little unsteady on her feet as she walked over, and perched next to Evan. Lizzy parted her hair as gently as she could. Ellie winced. There was a nasty lump, but it hadn't cut.

'No bandages for you, but I'm betting it's going to hurt for a few days. I've got paracetamol back in my room if you need some.'

Lizzy packed up the first aid kit and sat on the chair Ellie had vacated. What a mess. It further confirmed her suspicions though. She should have trusted her instincts.

'I think we need to let everyone know. It's only fair we can all be on guard,' she said.

Ellie and Evan sat in numb silence but didn't disagree.

They were still in a state of stunned silence when a loud rap at the door made them all jump. Three heads snapped up to look at one another, panic in their eyes.

'Wait here.' Lizzy started slowly inching towards the door as another round of knocking began and Gideon's booming voice was heard. She sagged with relief.

'Evan. You should have been downstairs half an hour ago.'

Lizzy opened the door to him. He stood with his hands on his hips, scowling.

'Look, you can't—' The frown dropped and he cocked his head to the side. 'Lizzy?'

'There's been an incident. You should come in.'

Lizzy moved to the side to allow Gideon to enter. He walked in slowly as she shut the door behind him.

'Jesus, what happened?' His eyes grew impossibly wide as he took in the scene before him.

'It looks worse than it is, but it's not good,' Lizzy said. 'Evan was attacked this afternoon. He's lucky it was interrupted and he escaped with only a slash.'

'Jesus.'

'I've dressed and bandaged it as best as I can, but I'm no nurse. It may need stitches. I don't think he should use it much if he can avoid it.'

'No, yes, I suppose not.'

'These aren't accidents, Gideon; someone in the hotel is doing this.'

The Storm

Gideon stood staring at Evan, his mind whirling. Slowly, he seemed to register Ellie sitting next to him and gestured at her to Lizzy with a cock of his head.

'Ellie was the one who interrupted the attack. She's had a bump to the head.'

Lizzy gave Ellie a warm smile, but it didn't seem to register. She looked in shock. So sad and small.

Gideon rubbed at his chin. 'Right, well, I'll take over your duties for a while, Evan, ok?' He bent to catch his eye. 'Don't you worry.'

'We need to tell the others, Gideon,' said Lizzy.

He whipped round to face her, panic written all over his face. Was he still going to fight it after this?

'I think we have the proof now,' she pushed, gesturing back towards Evan.

He opened his mouth to respond, then shut it again before seemingly coming to some internal decision. His face softened and looked almost sad. 'Ok. Ok, yes. I know you're right, but let me handle it. Please?'

He held her eyes for a moment and then left. It didn't fill her with any confidence, but at least he had agreed. Not that she'd have listened if he'd fought her over it again. It had gone way too far for that now.

CHAPTER 71

Ellie swallowed as she stood facing her dad's door.

Lizzy gave her arm a little squeeze. 'You'll be fine. Are you sure you don't want me to stay?'

'No, thank you. I think I have to do this alone.' She was afraid to face her dad after her earlier performance, but after having spoken with Lizzy, she knew she had to swallow her pride.

'Ok. I'll be in my room if you need me. I'm going to go down to dinner as soon as it opens. I need to make sure Gideon doesn't back out.' She gave Ellie one final smile before turning and wandering back off down the corridor.

Ellie raised her hand to knock but paused as nerves flooded her system. She lowered her hand as second thoughts took root. She couldn't do it. Should she have asked Lizzy to stay? She turned her head, but Lizzy had already disappeared. And then she heard a slow and quiet creak as a door opened.

'Ellie?' a weak voice asked.

She turned to face a shell of a man who had arrived here just four days ago. If you'd have passed her dad on the street, you would have tossed him some change. She wasn't the only one grieving, she realised, they were just grieving differently. She suddenly felt selfish and callous.

'Dad?' The word came out sorrowful and hung in the air between them.

He rushed forwards and pulled her into a hug, tears flowing down his face.

The Storm

'I'm sorry, Dad.'

'It's me that needs to be sorry. I misjudged the situation so badly. I'll never forgive myself for hurting you. It was never my intention.'

'I know.'

He squeezed her tight, catching the injury on her arm. She winced, and he pulled away.

'What's wrong? Who's hurt you?' He frantically scoured her.

Ellie walked into the room and sat on the edge of the bed. Her dad sat beside her, still not taking his eyes off her.

'Dad, I think someone killed Mum. Evan was just attacked with a knife.'

'What?' He was up on his feet again, his hands clenched into fists and his face thunderous. 'And they hurt you too?'

'Not on purpose, no, I interrupted them. They ran past and knocked me over. I landed on my arm funny and banged my head.'

'You could have been killed. I told you to stay away from that boy.'

He couldn't drop it, could he? Ellie's face flushed hot, and she stood to leave.

'I knew it was a mistake to come here.'

'No, no.' His voice softened, and he held his hands out to her. 'Ellie, wait, I'm sorry, I'm sorry, please.'

'I'm not a little girl anymore. You don't get to say how I run my life. I will see and talk to whoever I want.'

'I know, I'm sorry, it's just hard, ok? You're growing up so quickly and I'm not ready.'

Ellie rolled her eyes.

'Yes, I know how pathetic that sounds. I get it, ok? But it's true. And I will get there, but I'm going to need a little patience from you. A bit of understanding.'

Had this talk happened at home, she probably wouldn't have still been standing in front of him to reach this point, but things had changed irreversibly over the past few days. And with that, she had changed too. She'd had to grow up. She understood and she felt for him. Right now though, she had a bigger issue in her mind. The reality of their present situation came crashing back to her, enveloping her like a weight.

'Dad, whoever's doing this is in the hotel. They killed Mum and Deidre, and now they've tried to kill Evan.' Her lips trembled. 'Why would anyone want to kill Mum?'

She collapsed into her father's arms and wept. Whatever he had or hadn't done in the past few days could be forgotten for now.

CHAPTER 72

Lizzy felt shaky. Just a short while ago, she had been apologising and trying to convince people that there was no threat. She had all but convinced herself. And now this. Poor Evan. She paced the room, trying to get her head round it. Trying to work out what to do. What can we do?

She sat and opened her laptop, but the words had no meaning. She shut it again and tried her book, but she couldn't concentrate, her mind continually being drawn into their reality. Then there was Ellie. She really wasn't sure how understanding Paul would be to her or how tolerant of him Ellie would be in return. She expected a knock at any time. Still, half an hour crawled by and not a peep. She didn't particularly like Paul or approve of his behaviour and how he had treated Ellie this week, but the girl needed her father now more than ever.

Lizzy once again found herself mulling over the events that had happened over the past few days. It always went back to the link. What could possibly link Deidre, Fiona, and Evan? She supposed Evan may have inadvertently overheard something due to working in the hotel, maybe seen something. The other two though, as far as Lizzy had seen, were opposites. Deidre had been an over-the-top eccentric, while Fiona had appeared quite timid. It was highly unlikely they'd been in the same circles or had even been aware of each other before coming here.

Had something happened at the hotel? Evan had got cross at Deidre on the first night, she remembered, but he hadn't attacked himself. Mr Franks had been furious with her too for ruining his papers, but neither incident warranted an attack and neither included Fiona. The only person who had been upset with Fiona was Paul as far as she knew, but that argument had happened after Deidre's death.

Maybe Deidre wasn't part of this. What if Deidre was actually natural causes? But no, the police had rung and asked that no one leave. That didn't scream natural causes, did it? And Paul definitely had reason to be angry with Evan. He had already been angry with him before this afternoon, but after Ellie's little stunt, after hearing him having sex with his daughter, Lizzy could only imagine his rage.

But Ellie had been hurt too. He wouldn't hurt her, surely. Unless he hadn't realised it was her. He would have been leaving the room in a hurry, panicked. He might not have seen who it was, or realised. It was accidental anyway – not another attack. But Lizzy still couldn't place Deidre in this. She was the piece that wouldn't work. So maybe not Paul.

Lizzy was going round in circles. Her headache from earlier had returned and was pulsing behind her eyes. She rubbed at her temples and took a few deep breaths.

Come on, Luke, don't let me down. Raise the alarm and get me out of here.

The dining room was deserted. Only the fresh linen on the tables and newly laid cutlery showed Lizzy that she was there at the right time. She went to her table, pulled out her chair, and sat nervously awaiting the others. Everything was too still. Being the only one in the room made her feel vulnerable and exposed, and her eyes darted back and forth between each door.

'Can I get y—'

The Storm

Lizzy spun around to face the voice, took a sharp intake of breath, and jumped back in her chair. Despite trying to be alert to her surroundings, she'd still managed to miss Poppy's silent approach from behind her. 'Shit, sorry, Poppy.' She gave a nervous laugh. 'Sorry, you startled me.'

Lizzy put a hand to her chest. She really needed to calm down and get a hold of herself. Easier said than done though when there was a confirmed killer in the hotel. One she was quite possibly about to share dinner with. This is ludicrous, she thought. What am I doing down here? I should be locked in my room waiting for help.

But that didn't change the fact she still needed to eat.

'I'll, er... I'll have a white wine, please.'

Poppy slowly backed away and then scurried off to the kitchen.

Lizzy held the bridge of her nose as she tried to compose herself, looking up as she sensed movement. It was Paul and Ellie. She watched them silently enter the room. They were together though, which was surely a good sign, and Ellie sat next to Paul at their table. Lizzy eyed Paul with suspicion, not really knowing what she was looking for, when Ellie looked over and gave Lizzy a smile and a nod. It had gone well, then. Lizzy smiled back. Ellie would really need her dad, so she was relieved to see that they had patched things up. Well, at least for now. She imagined it may be a bumpy road ahead for them. She really hoped that all of this had nothing to do with Paul. Ellie had already lost one parent and that would destroy her.

The wine came, and Lizzy took a gratefully long sip. God, she'd needed that. She made a mental note to limit herself to two glasses. Enough to take the edge off but not enough to dull her senses. She needed to keep her wits about her.

Gideon waltzed over to Ellie and Paul, then returned a few minutes later with a couple of drinks. It seemed he was keeping to his word and taking over Evan's duties. Good. The poor boy needed to rest that arm of his. Lizzy hoped her bandaging skills were up to the task. She hadn't bandaged anything since getting her first aider badge at Brownies and that was too many years ago to think about.

Jenny and Alex were the next to enter. Although enter may have been pushing it. Alex entered, then briefly left to drag a reluctant Jenny through from reception. She gripped his hand in a painful-looking fashion while her eyes darted around the room. She had clearly got herself into a state while they'd been upstairs, and Lizzy felt immediately guilty. It was all going to get a lot worse before it got better though.

'You ok?' Lizzy mouthed to Alex.

He made a point of looking away.

She sighed and returned to her menu, not feeling particularly hungry but knowing she must eat something. Half of the options had been crossed out now. With no deliveries coming in, stock was running low.

She looked again to Alex and briefly thought of him as the possible killer but soon dismissed him. There was not a chance in hell he had managed to go anywhere this week without Jenny. So, unless she was in on it too, Alex was pretty much ruled out in Lizzy's mind.

After an interminably long time, Mr Franks arrived. He blustered in, red-faced, and sat down heavily. He had his newspaper with him again, which must have been a good few days old by now, and eyed everyone over before seemingly immersing himself in it. Lizzy assumed he must have read it end to end several times already and wondered what he could possibly be finding in there to entertain himself.

Where were you this afternoon, Mr Franks? she wondered, looking him over. But again, what motive?

Mr Franks caught Lizzy's eye and began a harsh stare just as a clink of a glass sounded harshly and high in the silent space. Everyone's eyes averted to Gideon, who was standing at the centre of the room looking as though he were about to raise a toast. Only this was no celebration.

The Storm

'Sorry to interrupt your evening, but if I could just have everybody's attention, please.' He paused, waiting for what little conversation there was to quieten. His face was solemn and grey. 'This isn't an easy thing to say, but I'm afraid I have some rather troubling and upsetting news to share with you all. It appears we may have a rather unsavoury character in our midst. As you are all aware, we lost poor Deidre earlier this week, and some of you will be aware that a second guest, Fiona, was found dead on Wednesday afternoon.'

Ellie gasped at the mention of her mother's name, and Paul pulled her into a hug. All eyes briefly flicked to their table, then back to Gideon.

'It now seems likely that these unfortunate deaths were not accidental. This afternoon, Evan was attacked in his room. Luckily, he escaped with just cuts and bruises. But I'm sure you can all appreciate how troubling this is.' He paused to clear his throat. 'Now, as far as I'm aware, the road from the hotel remains blocked for the time being, but we think it highly likely that the alarm has been raised, so hopefully it won't be too much longer before help can get through.'

Behind Lizzy, Jenny burst into tears.

'Where's Evan?' Alex shouted out. 'If he was attacked, then he knows who's doing this.'

'He didn't see,' Lizzy offered. 'He was hit in the face and it was all over too quickly.'

'So we just sit and wait to be picked off one by one?'

'We don't know that that's what's happening,' Gideon said. 'I think if we all remain calm and vigilant—'

'Calm and vigilant?' Alex stood and slammed his hands palms down onto the table, his voice rising as he spoke. 'You tell us there's a killer among us and then tell us to be calm. Are you having a laugh?'

Jenny wailed louder, which snapped Alex back to his doting-boyfriend role. He took the chair next to her and held and shushed her, rubbing her back and her hair in a futile attempt to calm her down.

'Load of bullshit,' Mr Franks boomed. 'The old cow's time was up and that other one was either stupid enough to fall in or unhinged enough to go voluntarily. As for Evan, he probably fell and just wanted in on the action.'

'Excuse me.' Paul was up on his feet. He stormed across the room to stand at Mr Franks' table and jabbed a finger at him. 'My wife was neither stupid nor unhinged.'

Mr Franks remained seated, looking pleased with himself and the upset he was causing.

'Well, if she was in fact killed, we all know where to look, don't we?' He crossed his arms over his chest in a triumphant manner. 'We all heard the barney you two had the other night. Get a bit physical, did it?'

Paul took a swing, but Mr Franks, moving with surprising speed, ducked to the side and deflected it with a sweeping arm.

'Bit of a temper, have we? I think we've found our killer. Did you all see how quick he went to attack me?'

Paul lunged again, both arms flying towards his throat this time, but Gideon was there to yank him by the back of the jumper until he had pulled him far enough away to get between them. Then, with an arm across his body, he wrestled him back to his seat and a terrified-looking Ellie.

'You and Mum were arguing?' she said weakly, her eyes glassy.

'It was nothing, sweetheart.'

Mr Franks snorted out a laugh. 'Ha. It was "nothing" that the whole hotel heard. Proper going at it they were. Well, your dad was at least. To be honest, your mum was a bit quiet. I suppose now we know why.'

Gideon held Paul in his seat from behind with a restraining arm across him and one on his shoulder as he tried to get to the man once again. Ellie sat trembling in tears beside him, watching him struggle. Alex, Jenny, and Lizzy sat in stunned silence watching the exchange. Finally, Paul exhausted his attempt and sat back in resignation.

The Storm

'Ellie, honestly, it was nothing. Married couples fight sometimes. Silly really. Just a stupid fight.'

'And how did this "fight" end exactly?' Alex was back on the warpath.

Paul gave him a not-you-too look and gritted his teeth. 'Not that I have to explain myself to anyone, but we argued, both said some things we didn't mean, and she left the room alive and well. That was the last time I saw her.'

'Right, so did anybody else see her after this argument?' Alex scanned the room, but no one spoke up. 'No. So you were the last one to see her alive.'

'That doesn't mean I killed her,' he spat, his face a flush of red. 'I-I loved my wife.'

The room fell silent as everyone processed all of this. Jenny had stopped crying but sat with a trembling lip. Alex and Paul still looked furious. Ellie looked horrified, and Mr Franks looked mightily pleased with the chaos he'd caused. Gideon remained close to Paul, poised and ready to jump in again if needed.

Lizzy wasn't sure what to think, but she had to admit the situation suddenly felt a lot more dangerous now it was all officially out in the open. Maybe this was the panic Gideon had tried to warn her about. At least nothing could happen with everyone here and in view.

'I think we should stay all together until help comes,' she suggested. 'Keep everyone in sight at all times. Safety in numbers.'

She had no desire to be alone in her room tonight. Would the killer panic now they knew everyone was on to them? The thought terrified her and prickled her skin. Her gaze kept flickering around the room, on the lookout for any signs. What exactly she was looking for she didn't know.

'You lot can do what you like, but I'm not going to trap myself with a killer.' Mr Franks made a show of shuffling his paper and opened it. 'As soon as I've eaten, that's me done for the night.'

Gideon cautiously left Paul's side and started distributing steaming plates. Poppy, Lizzy noticed, had gone AWOL. She tried to think back but couldn't pinpoint when she'd last seen her.

CHAPTER 73

Cutlery scraped against plates as people attempted to eat meals nobody had an appetite for. Ellie moved food around her plate, but none of it made it to her mouth. She couldn't believe her parents had fought the night before her mother was killed... maybe the very night she was killed. They never fought. Not that she had seen or heard anyway. Sure, they had the odd row, everybody did, but they were only little tiffs – a disagreement over the washing or cleaning usually. Never a full-blown argument like it appeared that had been. Where had she been when that had happened? Why hadn't she heard it? Or had she?

She thought back. She had been in the bar with Evan that night. They had been chatting and drinking, flirting. She felt the pit of her stomach drop. They had heard raised voices, only she hadn't realised at the time who it was. If she hadn't been so wrapped up in trying to score with Evan, maybe she could have done something. Would she have done something though? Now, after knowing how it ended, she liked to think she would have stepped in. Saved her. In reality though, she knew deep down that she would have turned up the TV or put her earphones in. Drowned them out. Been upset and worried but only communicated it the following day through snide bitchy comments. Even, ashamedly, used it as an arsenal to her advantage. Hindsight was 20/20. But it wouldn't have made a difference.

She gave a sideways glance to her dad, wondering just what had been going on. They had been all happy before this trip, but something changed. When? She had been in too much of a mood to notice, furious at being dragged here against her will. The whole holiday had been spent under a cloud with none of them talking. Her dad couldn't have done it though, could he? Certainly not on purpose. He loved her mum. He loved her, loved his family. He had never once raised a finger to either of them before, not even got close to it. But what if there had been an accident? A heat of the moment thing. Something that he'd instantly regretted and couldn't take back. Something he had to hide. Was that why he hadn't been able to bring himself to tell her? Why he'd tried to keep it a secret?

Ellie pushed her plate away and rose. 'I'm just nipping to the loo.'

She had to get away for a few minutes to think clearly, get some space. She needed a bit of air, truth be told, but she knew she wouldn't be allowed to head outside. Not alone. Not after what had happened tonight. Her head was spinning with too many ideas and fears that she couldn't make sense of. She felt as if she were swirling round a sink, about to be sucked down into the drain.

Her dad opened his mouth, but she walked away before he could speak or object. She only went to the toilets at the other end of the room, but she could feel his eyes on her the whole way there.

Once through that door, the toilets were refreshingly cool. Ellie stood at the basin and splashed cold water on her face. The door opened seconds later, and she half-expected it to be her dad. Her breath caught as she spun around, but it was only Lizzy. The tension left her body as she breathed out a sigh of relief.

'You ok?' Lizzy asked.

Ellie wanted to scream no. Her mum was dead and her dad might be the killer. She wanted to hit out and run away. Instead, she just shrugged and in a wobbly voice said, 'What if

The Storm

it was him? They argued, Lizzy. He wouldn't have meant to hurt her but... what if it was him?'

Lizzy held her gaze with eyes full of concern and compassion. Ellie knew it must have crossed her mind too. Everyone out there had thought it, was thinking it.

'Look, Ellie, it could be anyone in that room. You know your dad better than anyone. Do you think it was him?'

'No... I don't know. I don't think so. I mean, he's strict, but he's never been violent. He's never even come close.'

'Well, there you go, then.'

'But they argued. They never argued. And something was going on; they hadn't spoken all trip.'

'I guess it's possible. An accident maybe? But what reason would he have to hurt Deidre?'

Ellie looked at Lizzy blankly. She couldn't answer that one. Although she did notice Lizzy hadn't mentioned Evan.

CLANG.

Ellie grabbed Lizzy's arm as they both turned suddenly at the sound. It had come from one of the cubicles and was followed by sniffing. They weren't alone.

'Hello?' Lizzy called.

No one answered.

Slowly and cautiously, Lizzy crouched to peer beneath the cubicles. The floor was bare – no feet. She stood and used an outstretched leg to nudge open the first door as Ellie stood back against the sinks. It swung open easily and banged softly on the wall. Same with the second. Only one left. Lizzy moved in front of it, and there came a whimper and a small, stifled scream from within.

'Who's in there?' Lizzy nudged at the door, but it didn't budge. 'It's Lizzy... and Ellie's here too. Are you ok?'

There came the sound of the lock being retracted, but the door remained closed. This time, Lizzy stepped closer and pushed it gently with her hand, revealing Poppy crouched on the closed toilet seat.

'Jesus, Poppy. What are you doing in here? Are you ok?'

Her eyes were red from crying and she was trembling. 'I can't, I just can't. I... I can't do it anymore. I want to go home.' Her words tumbled out in a terrified rush.

'I know, we all do. It'll be over soon,' Lizzy said with a small smile, trying to sound reassuring.

'Lizzy's boyfriend will have phoned the police by now,' Ellie coaxed. 'She should have been home ages ago. Help is coming.'

'Really?' Her tears stopped, and she looked at them with such hope.

'Really.'

Lizzy held a hand out towards Poppy. She took it and slowly lowered her feet to the floor, then stood and came out on shaky legs.

'You don't have to be alone,' Lizzy said. 'To be honest, it's probably worse if you are – your mind starts conjuring all sorts and playing tricks on you. I know mine does. If it helps, you can always come and find me.'

'Or me,' Ellie added with a smile.

Poppy returned the smile and wiped her face.

'Look, I don't fancy being alone tonight,' Lizzy admitted. 'If you want a bit of company, I plan to sit in the lounge for a while after dinner. I'm trying to get us all to stick together, to be honest. But, well, whatever happens, you're both very welcome to join me.'

CHAPTER 74

Lizzy returned to the dining room, almost colliding with Gideon on her way back to her table. They both stopped short, and Gideon swept his hand out in an 'after you' gesture.

'Thank you. Listen, thanks for talking to everyone. For explaining. I know it must have been hard,' she said.

'I'm not sure it's helped, it quite possibly made things worse, but it was only fair in the circumstances.'

'It was what needed to be said and you said it well.'

'Thank you. I—'

'Gideon.' Mr Franks' booming voice had sounded far more times than Lizzy would have liked that evening.

Gideon rolled his eyes and let out a sigh. 'I keep trying to go and talk to Evan, check he's ok, but duty always seems to beckon.'

'I'll nip up if you like?'

'Would you?'

'Of course.'

'Thank you. Please would you ask him if he wants to come down? Not to work, I just thought he may feel a bit better being around people. I know one of us is…' He stopped himself. Lizzy knew what he'd been about to say. A killer. 'Well, safety in numbers, like you said,' he finished.

The lights were on throughout the entire hotel, but that didn't stop fear from taking hold of Lizzy as she stood in the empty reception area. It had been natural to offer to help, but now she was doing it, she realised how she had managed to separate herself from the crowd and how easily she could become the next victim. Her eyes flitted to each potential hiding place as she slowly made her way to the bottom of the stairs. It wasn't exactly a stretch that someone could be hiding behind the reception desk or waiting behind any one of the corners upstairs. She took a deep breath and reminded herself she just had to get up to Evan's room and down again. It would take a couple of minutes at most. Hopefully, she could convince him to come down too and then she only had the up part to do alone.

She darted up the stairs, the feeling of being chased quickly taking hold and landed at the top in a panting heap. She scrabbled to get her back up against the wall quickly so she could check all around her. Idiot, she cursed.

A couple of deep breaths brought her breathing back under control as she surveyed her surroundings. Two corridors led off from her in different directions. She had used the main staircase, which brought her out furthest from his room, but it was the bigger and best-lit of the two. It may have made for a longer route, but it felt the safest. Keeping her senses alert, she moved quickly but quietly along the corridor. She wanted to be able to hear if anyone tried to approach her.

She knocked on his door and waited. When he didn't answer, she knocked again louder.

'Evan?'

Still nothing. She called and knocked again louder still, then tried the handle. Locked. He was surely asleep or in the shower. He'd had a traumatic experience and was most likely exhausted from it. She'd let Gideon know and try again later. Maybe next time, she'd bring someone up with her. She decided to risk the back stairs and skipped down them eager to return to other people.

Back in the dining room, plates were being cleared and coffees were being poured. Lizzy's half-eaten dinner remained at her table. She pushed the cold, congealed remnants into the middle of the table, signalling she was done. Poppy cleared the plate and returned with the coffee pot.

'I meant what I said.' Lizzy smiled. 'If you'd ever like to join me, please do. Whenever you want and when you can. I'd be glad of the company.'

For the first time in the whole trip, Poppy made eye contact with her. She gave a quick smile and scurried off to be replaced with Gideon.

'Well?'

'He didn't answer. I guess he's in the shower or asleep. I'll try again later if you…'

They looked at each other as the other more sinister potential reason for his absence occurred to them both simultaneously.

'Shit.'

With a scraping of Lizzy's chair, she followed Gideon as they hustled back up the rear staircase she had just come down. Gideon had his keys out and jangling by the time they reached the top.

'Evan.'

Lizzy pounded on the door as Gideon found the master. With a shaky hand, Gideon inserted and turned the key. It opened with a soft click, then ricocheted off the wall with the force of his eagerness.

The room was in darkness, the only light spilling in from behind them, and eerily quiet. Lizzy could just make out a form on the bed, and she hoped beyond hope that he was just sleeping.

'Evan?' This time, it came out slowly, hesitant, barely more than a whisper.

Gideon's eagerness had suddenly dissipated, and they stood in the doorway reluctant to move forwards, the only sounds their breathing and the softening jangle of the keys. With Gideon's authoritative nature gone, Lizzy found herself taking control and moving to the light switch. She flicked it on, bathing the room in a soft, warm luminescence. The normally romantic and cosy lighting did nothing to hide or even blur the horrific scene that confronted them.

Lizzy put a hand to her mouth and gasped. Gideon remained a few steps back near the doorway, shock rooting him to the spot, clearly unable to take in what his eyes were showing him.

Evan lay on the bed face up. His shirt and much of the bedclothes around him were covered in blood. It had soaked and spread, eventually finding its way to the floor, where it had dripped and pooled beneath his dangling feet. His hands and arms, which lay limp at his sides, were littered with defensive nicks and cuts, and his bandage was unravelled and torn.

'Oh my God, Evan,' Lizzy cried. 'How didn't we hear anything?' She wasn't sure if she was speaking to Gideon or out loud to herself, but Gideon was in no position to respond.

Where had they all been when this was happening? Had they been eating? Enjoying their dinner while Evan was suffering?

Lizzy moved closer, careful not to step in any of the blood and contaminate the scene. Most of the blood seemed to have originated from Evan's central mass. She was no doctor, but she could safely determine that he had been stabbed in the chest. Repeatedly. There was also an angry slash to his neck, but that seemed insubstantial compared to the rest. When her eyes met Evan's – open in shock and horror, looking but no

The Storm

longer seeing – she squealed and closed her own, a tear rolling down her cheek as she stepped backwards, straight into Gideon.

She jumped at the sudden unexpected contact and whipped her head round to look at him. They stared at each other deeply, neither saying a word, then through some unspoken understanding, they silently left the room and locked the door.

'How?' Lizzy began, bewildered. 'We were all together.'

Gideon's eyes cleared as he snapped back to reality. Colour flooded his face, and he stormed off down the corridor toward the staircase. Lizzy had to follow down the stairs at a jog to keep up with him. He reached the door and crashed into the dining room with the force of a raging bull.

'I need everyone in the lounge. Now!'

Everyone froze and the room descended into complete silence at his interruption. Even the people who had been halfway to standing from their chairs stopped midstance. Glances flickered anxiously between themselves. Then nervously, they began to move, filing through to the other room like a class in front of the headmaster. Nobody dared speak, but confused and questioning looks continued to be thrown.

No one sat. Some people perched, but most stood, waiting in nervous anticipation. Even Carl, the chef, had been summoned in. He stood to the side, arms crossed, looking like an annoyed bouncer. Gideon took a moment to look around the room. To scan each and everyone's face in turn slowly and purposely before speaking.

'Evan is dead,' he began with no preamble, barely holding his anger in check.

Gasps erupted. Ellie broke down and was comforted by her father.

'This happened tonight, not long ago, and someone here did this. Someone in this room.' Gideon went round the room for a second time, looking at every face in turn, scrutinising each and every person.

'Now, I don't know how or why this is happening. But it stops tonight. Enough. No one is to leave this room, no one goes anywhere unattended. We are not losing anyone else. Do you understand?'

Jenny whimpered and collapsed into a chair. Alex sat on the arm next to her and rubbed her back. Poppy peered around wild-eyed and backed herself into a corner, lips trembling.

'You can't keep us here,' Mr Franks objected.

'At some point tonight, one of you slipped off and killed Evan. We are going to stay here, where we can all watch one another until the police arrive.'

'And how exactly are we supposed to have done that, then? None of us left the room. We've been here all night.'

Everyone went quiet, seemingly thinking back through the evening. Lizzy cast her mind back too. They had all arrived. Poppy and Gideon had been in and out of the kitchen, Ellie and Poppy had gone to the toilets in the dining room. Lizzy had followed. She could have missed someone leaving while she was in there, but everyone was still there when she returned. But it was possible someone could have slipped out in that time, wasn't it? How long had they been in there? Five minutes maybe? Was that enough? The person who did this would have no doubt been covered in blood afterwards. They would've needed time to change and clean themselves before coming back down again. That wasn't long enough – five minutes to get upstairs, gain access to Evan's room, have a struggle and kill him, shower, change, and then return. Lizzy didn't think that was doable. Then it hit her.

'It happened before everyone came down.'

'What?' Mr Franks' face was flushed, and he stood hands on hips, having none of it.

The Storm

'You're right, no one left the dining room during the meal. Since everyone came down, no one has left. Well, except me and Gideon when we went to talk to Evan.'

Mr Franks snorted and gave a flick of his wrist. 'Oh, well, there you go, then, accusing us. The only people it could have been were you two.'

'No. No, think about it. When did any of us last see Evan?'

'When we left him in his room after he was attacked. The first time, I mean,' Ellie offered.

'Yes, exactly. That leaves quite a window of time between then and coming down to dinner. Two hours maybe? Evan must have been killed before we all came down.'

People slowly began to sit as they thought about this.

Mr Franks remained standing, arms crossed defiantly. 'And what? We all sat around in our rooms mere feet from him and heard nothing?' he said with a raised eyebrow. 'I think that's unlikely.'

Lizzy went to speak but found she didn't have an answer.

'You don't always scream with fear.' Ellie looked up briefly and then away, speaking quietly. 'He might not have screamed or shouted. Sometimes, you freeze.'

Mr Franks rolled his eyes. 'Well, you all know my views,' he said with a huff.

'Oh, here we go again,' Paul retorted. 'And why exactly would I want to kill Evan?'

'Ha. Why indeed. Like you even need to ask. You're not the only loudmouth, are you? It would seem that volume runs in your family. It's not just the argument we heard, was it?' He sneered at Ellie, and Lizzy gritted her teeth, knowing exactly what was coming next. 'We could all hear your little tramp of a daughter getting it on with him. I'm betting you didn't approve of the hook-up? Lovely performance it was though, my dear, I enjoyed it immensely.'

He winked at Ellie, who had gone a shade of beetroot and shrunk in the sofa as if she were hoping it could swallow her up. Paul was up and out of his seat in a shot as Carl launched to intercept him. Mr Franks didn't even flinch.

'There goes that temper again. And I'm just here spouting a few words. I'm not the one who was pounding his daughter.'

Paul's eyes bulged in their sockets and his face had turned so puce it was as if all his blood had rushed there, where Lizzy could see it throbbing through a vein in his forehead. He tried to scramble free, pulling and tugging to get out of Carl's grip, muttering obscenities as Carl remained latched to his legs. The intercept had resulted in a rugby tackle that had pushed Paul into a luckily vacant chair.

'Well, I think I've proven my point. Look no further, ladies and gentlemen,' he spoke and gestured as if he were the ringmaster at a circus. 'And now, if you'll all excuse me, I shall take my leave. I'm not about to share my evening with a killer.'

And with that, he barrelled out of the room, head held high.

Ellie looked around at everyone with skittish eyes. 'It couldn't have been Dad,' she said in a meek voice, swallowing her pride enough to stand up for him. 'When Lizzy and I left Evan's room, I went straight to Dad's. I was with him until we came down.'

Not everyone looked convinced, but those who didn't chose to remain quiet. No one wanted to shout at a girl who had just lost her mother. Paul did present as a neat suspect though. He fit. All apart from Deidre. It was Deidre who snagged Lizzy every time.

'It might not be a man,' Jenny suddenly said. 'We've all just assumed, but we shouldn't just be looking at the men. A woman could just as easily have done it. And let's face it, Lizzy has been present at every death scene. All these people here and all this land and somehow she's the one to discover all of them.'

The Storm

She had been casting her gaze around the room as she spoke, but she ended up staring directly at Lizzy. Lizzy felt herself grow hot and sweat prickle the nape of her neck. She didn't know how to stand or hold herself under everyone's stare. How could they think it was her? The accusation hung in the air. She shifted uncomfortably.

'I…'

'No one thinks it was you,' Gideon said, his voice now weaker. His fury had burnt out with no one to direct his anger at. He seemed tired, beaten.

Lizzy felt her face cool and her body relax from the relief that he had stepped in to defend her. That someone had. Looking round the room though, at the glances coming her way, she wasn't quite so sure anyone else shared his opinion. She could feel the suspicion like a weight in every look. Everyone's look apart from Ellie's. Lizzy sat then, lost for words. How could she prove that she hadn't done any of it?

'Maybe a drink to calm everyone's nerves?' Gideon announced.

He looked over in Poppy's direction, but she didn't see him. Lizzy wasn't sure she was seeing anything. Not anymore. She had slumped in her corner against the wall and was staring fixedly at her shoes. She may as well have been rocking.

'I'll get us all some tea,' Gideon continued, making to leave the room.

'Wait a minute.' Alex stood. 'What if it's you?'

'What?' Gideon turned and fixed him an incredulous look.

'The killer. What if it's you? I'm not having a drink that you've prepared. And all this "no one goes anywhere unattended" bullshit. You were gonna leave alone just now.'

Gideon's mouth fell slack as he stood floundering. 'Well, I would have asked somebody to accompany me.'

'Like hell, you were leaving. Who can account for your movements, hey?'

Everyone looked to one another, but no one spoke. Gideon's mouth moved but produced nothing.

'Aha,' Alex exclaimed.

'Look, I doubt none of us travelling alone or working here will have had someone with us the whole time.' Lizzy retorted. She was growing tired of all the accusations. She wasn't exactly sure why she had leapt to defend Gideon. For all she knew, it could be him. Maybe because he had defended her first. Plus, it didn't hurt that her statement included herself. If she thought about it though, she'd seen the look in his eyes when they'd found Evan. Either he was a very good actor, or he had been genuinely deeply disturbed and upset by what he'd seen.

'Oh, I see. In it together, are we?' Alex continued.

'Oh for God's sake.' Lizzy tutted. 'We can go round the room all night accusing each other. I highly doubt it'll do any good. I'm sure there's not a single one of us with a rock-solid alibi.'

'And there speaks a guilty conscience.'

Lizzy rolled her eyes and looked away. 'Well, I would have gone with you to fetch tea, Gideon, but seeing as Alex is trying to push some silly narrative, how about something from the bar? Something sealed or bottled.'

No one threw out any objections, so Gideon went over and busied himself with the drinks. Lizzy watched everyone else in the room following his every move behind the bar at the end of the lounge and realised just how much he, and potentially she, were true potential killers in their minds. He returned with a few soft drinks and a bottle of wine and whiskey for those needing something stronger, all still sealed.

The men pounced on the whiskey, while Jenny went straight to the wine. Lizzy hesitated. She could really do with a whiskey herself, to steady her nerves and calm her mind, but she also wanted a clear head just in case. In the end, she took a very small measure of whiskey and a bottle of Sprite. Ellie hadn't moved and neither had Poppy.

CHAPTER 75

Jenny was drinking far too much for the state she was in. It had been a crutch to begin with, something to get her through. Now, she was swigging like a raging drunk, her words slurred and actions clumsy. She had loudly accused each and every one of them in turn. Even Alex. Alex had attempted several times to get her a coffee or even persuade a Sprite into her hands, but she was having none of it. In between bouts of accusations, she swung wildly from tears to laughter. Alex looked both horrified and embarrassed.

'I should probably get her to bed.'

'I'm not a child, y'know,' she spat before dissolving into another crying fit.

'Normally, I'd agree,' Lizzy said to Alex, 'but don't you think we should be sticking together?'

Alex looked round the room like a helpless child, at a loss at what to do.

'Maybe it would be best. I think she needs to sleep it off,' Gideon said, agreeing with Alex. 'Plus, there are two of them, so neither would be alone.'

'Oh, trying to separate us from the group now?' Alex turned to Gideon in full and sudden fury. 'It's not as if she'd be an asset fighting against a murderer in her state.'

'What?' Gideon's brow puckered. 'It was your idea.'

'Yeah, and you soon jumped on it, didn't you?'

'I was just trying to be helpful. I mean, look at the state of her.'

'Hey, don't talk about her like that.' He pointed a finger in Gideon's direction. 'And helpful for who exactly? You or the killer? Or are they one and the same, hey, Gideon?'

Lizzy rubbed her eyes. This was exhausting. Deep down, she believed that they should all stick together, but Alex and Jenny had become so disruptive she really did want them to leave. Ellie and Poppy winced every time one of them spoke, each trying to shrink smaller in the hope that they weren't on the receiving end of the abuse. At some point, Ellie had joined Poppy in the corner of the room and they now sat huddled together. It was both painful and comforting to see.

Jenny's crying petered out and she hiccupped. 'Alex, I feel sick.'

'Maybe you should take her to bed,' Lizzy conceded.

With no argument, Alex hooked his arm around Jenny, scooping her off the sofa, taking her weight. She had no fight left. She trudged and stumbled along as he dragged her out of the room. Lizzy wondered how long their relationship would last after the events of this holiday. They'd certainly seen another side to one another this week, and she doubted they would come out stronger for it.

A lot of the tension in the room left with Jenny and Alex. The silence that ensued felt like a relief.

Paul shifted in his seat. 'With three of us gone now, is there any point to us staying together? It kinda feels like that ship has sailed.'

'It just feels a bit dangerous to peel off and separate ourselves, don't you think?' Lizzy looked to the three men.

'How do you suppose we sleep, then? We can't just sit here all night.'

Paul had a point there. It wasn't even midnight and already Lizzy was struggling. The events of the last few days weighed heavily and had taken their toll. They had a good idea that help would be coming tomorrow, but they had no idea how long it would take. They didn't even know if the road was passable yet.

The Storm

As if in answer, Ellie yawned, and Lizzy could feel them slipping away. She really had no desire to be on her own. It felt like that turning point in a movie when someone suggests they all split up and you're yelling at the screen to stop them. Splitting up felt like becoming sitting ducks; it would be far too easy for someone to creep around the hotel unnoticed, picking them off one by one should they want. What could she say though? Paul was right – half of the group had already gone.

Paul stood and went over to Ellie. She looked to Poppy before taking his hand and standing.

'Do you want to share a room?'

Poppy didn't acknowledge her, just sat trance-like.

Ellie crouched down to look her in the face. 'Poppy? Wanna share a room?' she repeated.

Poppy didn't answer, but she did take Ellie's outstretched hand. Paul led them both out of the room, and they slowly disappeared up the stairs. That just left Lizzy, Gideon, and Carl.

Carl sat legs splayed, with his hands clasped between them. His head was bowed, but his gaze was up, alert, watching the room without being obvious. Gideon was hovering by an armchair. That he had chosen to remain standing throughout made Lizzy think he was trying to maintain some authority. She wasn't sure it much mattered anymore.

The two men seemed to be waiting for Lizzy to make a decision. Truth be told, she had no desire to be alone with them. She hadn't exactly been getting on well with Gideon lately and she had barely even met Carl. The thought that in the sanctuary she'd built, she may be trapping herself with the killer. It could very easily be one of them. Or both, come to think about it. Sticking together only worked if it was everyone.

'I guess that's it, then, we'd better go to bed too.' She sighed. 'Night, both.'

Somewhat reluctantly, she stood, not knowing whether she was making the right decision or not. The walk through the lounge to the staircase felt one of the longest of her life, and she could feel Gideon and Carl's eyes on her the whole way. It took a lot of composure not to break into a run.

CHAPTER 76

Every turn was a potential ambush, every shadow was a hidden killer. Lizzy's movements became quicker as she climbed the stairs, and she struggled to control them and keep quiet in her haste to get to her room as quickly as possible. She arrived at her door panting, her heart hammering. She fumbled to get her key in the lock and dropped it. Sweat prickled her brow as she scrabbled on the floor to retrieve it. A sound emanated from behind her, and she suddenly became aware of a presence growing closer. She turned too quickly and fell backwards into the wall with a gasp.

'Jeez, calm down, will you?'

Alex towered above her. Their doorway opposite hers was open. She was fine. Everything was fine. Just Alex.

'I thought I'd better check out all of this commotion. Turns out, I was wrong to ever consider you, Lizzy; you'd make a shit killer with your level of stealth.'

Laughing at his own joke, he turned and went back to his room, his door closing with a soft thunk behind him. Lizzy picked up her key and went into her room.

Once inside, she immediately placed the drawer between the door and the desk. She sat back on her bed and kicked off her trainers. Should she bother with the rigmarole of preparing for bed properly or just sleep fully dressed? If she could sleep at all.

Out of habit, she reached for her phone. Her hand met with nothing on the bedside table. She looked over at the empty space quizzically, then searched the floor in case it had been knocked off, moved the pillow, and pulled back the bedding. Nothing. Her phone had sat on that table all week, so where was it?

Lizzy set about searching the rest of the room and eventually found it by the window on the floor. Had she dropped it? She bent to pick it up. The back of the case felt damp against her hand. She turned it over in her hands, not quite understanding, then she touched the carpet where she had found it. Someone had been in her room again. It had dried enough that it wasn't visible to the eye, but there were clear wet patches to her touch.

She scoured the floor on hands and knees, following the trail. There was a path from the door into the room and round the bed. Lizzy quickly went through all her belongings. Nothing was missing. What would someone want in her room if they weren't there to take anything? And maybe more importantly, how had they got in?

CHAPTER 77

Poppy stood in the middle of the room almost limp, waiting to be moved or dictated to, with a face devoid of emotion. It reminded Ellie of dealing with some of her drunk friends after a night out, only with a lot less singing and swaying. She wasn't sure how much use Poppy would be should anything actually happen, but it felt nice having someone with her for a change. She'd felt so utterly alone the past few days.

Her dad had been reluctant to leave them. He had insisted on staying at first, and Ellie had been relieved at the thought of having him with them. Despite her trance-like state though, Poppy was clearly unhappy with him being in the room. She flinched when he was near, and when he locked them all in together and started setting up a bed for himself by dragging his mattress from his room into hers, she had rocked and wailed, summoning several of the others, who came to check on them.

In the end, they decided it was best for him to leave. Ellie felt torn, but they couldn't exactly leave Poppy on her own, not in the state she was in. Though they were only going to be separated by a wall, it may as well have been another place entirely to Ellie. She'd given him a big hug at the door while biting her lip to stop herself from crying. She could do this. She'd got through this far on her own, so what was another night?

Ellie put a gentle hand on Poppy's back to guide her to the bed. 'It's ok, it's just us now.'

Ellie removed Poppy's shoes and got her to lie down. She set the glasses by the door, as she had done previously as an early warning system, then, after a quick visit to the bathroom, she got into bed herself.

She lay looking at Poppy, trying to see beyond the blank exterior to what she was feeling. Nothing. It was as if her eyes held no life. Poppy blinked and her brow creased slightly. Then she blinked again in rapid succession and the light came back on as she slowly became aware of Ellie's presence. She took a shuddering breath in.

'It's just me, Ellie, we're all alone, you're ok.'

Poppy quietened and looked searchingly into her eyes. 'Why is this happening?' she whispered. It was the first thing she had said all night since meeting her in the toilets.

'I don't know. I keep asking myself the same question.'

'I just want to go home.'

'Me too. Help should be coming tomorrow. We just have to get through tonight.'

Poppy accepted that with a wan smile and took hold of Ellie. They kept one of the side lights on, both scared of the dark for the first time since being children. Holding each other and hoping for sleep, they prayed for the morning to come.

CHAPTER 78

Lizzy's spine tingled with fear at the thought of someone being in her room and going through her things. It made her feel dirty and vulnerable. And then it made her feel terrified. She wondered if that was how it started – examining your life before the kill. Was she next? She couldn't fathom why anyone would go to the trouble of rummaging through everything and not take anything. Were they searching for something they thought she had, or did they get a sick kick out of touching their victims' things?

She looked to the door. The drawer that had filled her with such confidence and security now looked flimsy. Lizzy hurried over to remove it. She placed it on the desk and set about heaving the desk against the door. There was no way she would feel safe enough to sleep without being totally barricaded in. It hurt her shoulder to push and it was hard for her feet to find purchase on the carpet. Determination eventually won though, and she managed to get it close enough to prevent anyone entering.

She leaned back panting, eyes still scouring the room, unable to remove the fear that clung to every part of her despite the new and improved barricade. Who the hell was doing this? She mentally ran through the options again. Immediately, she dismissed Ellie and Poppy. There was no reason she could find for either girl to do this and both had seemed genuinely distraught and distressed. She also doubted either girl had the strength required for the attacks unless they had used the element of surprise. No, their reactions had seemed too genuine. And why would Ellie want to kill her own mother? Though, she supposed, she'd not known her very long and hadn't particularly witnessed their relationship.

Ellie's dad, Paul. He'd had no reason for hurting Deidre that Lizzy could fathom. There had been the big argument with his wife, Fiona, though. Heat of the moment? Crime of passion? And he also had clear reason to be upset with Evan. Paul only made sense if Deidre was natural causes. But the police had been suspicious – if Gideon could be believed, that was.

That brought her to Gideon. There was something definitely off about him, but Lizzy couldn't quite put her finger on it. She couldn't think of why he would want to do any of this, but he had been so keen to shush everything up, to prevent her reaching out for help or even trying. Was it him who had cut the phone lines? And what was that business with the TV aerial? Was he really hoping to put it back up, or had he actually just taken it down? But why take a TV aerial down? Unless he just wanted to stop them seeing the news? The only reason for that would be if the roads were open again.

Lizzy's optimism lifted slightly at that thought. But if the roads were open again, surely the police would have been back. If, that was, they really did intend to and that wasn't something Gideon had made up. But once again, the thought of Gideon's reaction to Evan pushed him away as a suspect despite her confusion over him.

She moved on. Mr Franks certainly had the temperament. He'd had an altercation with Deidre that first night, but that was hardly worth killing over. There wasn't anything that would have upset him about Evan that she could think of, unless something had happened before she'd arrived. But then why wait? And Fiona? Lizzy hadn't ever seen them speak or even acknowledge each other. There was no link.

Jenny and Alex, well, they were too self-absorbed. And Jenny was either genuinely terrified or an incredibly good actress. Lizzy highly doubted Jenny would have left Alex's side long enough for him to be doing this alone either. Unless he was drugging her at night. Sleeping pills? Maybe that was why the killings happened at night. But then Evan hadn't died at night. Unless they were in it together? But then what possible reason did they have?

That just left her with Carl. Lizzy didn't know anything about the man, having only met him twice. Once when he returned from driving out to get help and then again tonight. He hadn't said much either time, so it was difficult to form an impression. He definitely had the strength required though. She had seen that when he had intercepted Paul tonight – he had moved with lightning speed and held him with ease. As the chef, he had little interaction with the guests though. Almost certainly not enough to form a grudge.

If she was next – if scoping out her room was a sign of things to come – why? Why her? She didn't know anyone here. Hadn't upset anyone as far as she was aware. Well, maybe Gideon, which put him back on top of her list. But again, why? She was no threat to anyone.

And then she thought of another scarier possibility... that these killings were random. A serial killer amongst them who wasn't able to keep their murderous needs under control. And if that was the case, no amount of thinking would find a link between the victims other than the fact they were all in the wrong place at the wrong time. And that meant any of them could be next. Herself included.

Lizzy's head hurt. She massaged her temples and closed her gritty eyes. God, she was tired. She got up and lay on the bed fully dressed, leaving the light on.

The light was worsening her headache, so she switched it for a side lamp. Tried to get comfortable and drift off. It was going to be a long night.

CHAPTER 79

Ellie heard Poppy's breathing change and deepen as she slipped under, watched the gentle rise and fall of her chest. Her own mind still whirled, too busy to submit itself to slumber, on high alert for any sound. And there were plenty of those. The hotel was old and creaked in the wind. Every time she started to drift off, another sound would snap her back. She was exhausted. The light wasn't helping either. She liked her bedroom dark, but the possible threat kept her from switching the light off. There were too many shadows without it.

Ellie slipped out of the covers and padded to the bathroom. She relieved herself and splashed her face with cold water, then checked the glasses were still set by the door. A slip of light came on under the door, then extinguished. The communal lights were on a motion sensor after 10 p.m. Someone had tripped them, which meant someone was moving in the corridor.

Ellie dropped to the floor and scooted backwards away from the door as if it had burned her, staring at the strip beneath it, listening for footsteps, searching for the light. The light had been too quick, she realised. Either it had come from an open doorway – from someone looking but not stepping out – or the lights had been tripped and switched off. The

The Storm

second thought scared her, and she sat hugging her knees, staring, waiting.

Eventually, she scurried back into bed and buried herself in the covers, trying to be quiet and calm her breathing so as not to wake Poppy. She had never wanted her mum so much in her life.

CHAPTER 80

Lizzy woke with a start. She immediately sat, looking round the dimly lit room, looking for threats. Something had woken her. But what? There came a soft thunk that she recognised as the door closing, and she shot out of bed, switching the main light on. The desk was undisturbed and still in position. It must have been the sound of the door hitting the desk that had woken her. Someone had tried to get into her room.

Lizzy ran to the desk and clambered on top. In a crouch, she peered through the spyhole. The corridor was in darkness. With no windows to offer even moonlight, it was pitch black. If someone was out there, she had no chance of seeing them.

She sat back on her heels. The light hadn't come on, she realised. Someone must have disabled the sensor again. Or was she imagining things? Could it just as easily, if not more likely, have been a noise from another room?

She was all but ready to put it down to her imagination when her gaze travelled down the door, and more importantly, to the mark on it. She trailed a finger along the groove in the wood. It was only slight, but it was definitely there. The door had hit the desk. She struggled to keep her thumping heart under control as she tried the handle. It opened; the door was unlocked. Not only that, but the mark lined up perfectly with the edge of the desk. A wave of fear rolled in her stomach. She quickly shut and relocked it. Though the latter seemed a little futile given someone had

The Storm

clearly managed to open it before. She sat back against it, shaking, a hard, quick pulse in her veins. Thank God she had created a barricade.

Staff would have access to a key. Although it was easy enough for anyone else to get hold of a key, she realised. They were just there for the taking, hanging out in the open. Anyone could have helped themselves... or picked the lock. Lizzy had never picked a lock before, but she didn't imagine it being too hard with these old doors. The locks were old and worn and the key turned lightly, barely meeting with any resistance each time she used it. It was hardly Fort Knox.

Satisfied that no one could get into the room with the desk in place, Lizzy went back to bed. She sat half propped up with the covers to her chin, far too wired and scared to sleep. Longing for daybreak and praying on Luke. Please come soon.

CHAPTER 81

Ellie had eventually succumbed and slept a dream-filled sleep. In it, she was trying to hide in an empty room adorned with windows. Everyone could see her and there was no exit – no escape. People were throwing stones, trying to break the windows, trying to get to her. Someone threw a rock, and the window smashed. She woke with a jolt. Panting. Just a dream.

She reached out in the darkness, seeking some comfort, some reassurance, but the space beside her was empty. She sat up to reach further, her hand skittering over bare sheets until she reached the edge of the bed. Poppy had gone. It was then she noticed the darkness – someone had turned the light out. An unease bubbled in her stomach. Cautiously, Ellie slipped from the covers. Poppy was more than likely in the bathroom; still, Ellie wasn't about to take any chances.

She got into a crouch by the side of the bed, using it as a physical and visual shield to anyone who may be in the room with her. She waited for her eyes to adjust to the dark, using the time to listen for sounds. There were none other than the hotel shifting and settling. Satisfied, she made her way to the bathroom door. It was open a crack, but no light or sound came from within. She eased it open.

'Poppy? You in here?' she whispered. There was no response and she couldn't see any shadowy figures. Where had she gone?

The Storm

Ellie crept back out of the room and walked towards the door. She stifled a cry as her foot met with something sharp.

'Ow, shit.'

Stealth forgotten, Ellie switched on the light. The glasses she had stacked by the door lay in a scattering of shards amongst droplets of blood. Her blood. Her chest constricted in fear. Someone had opened the door. Someone had been in her room. The breaking glass. It hadn't just been a dream.

She turned and flipped on the light quickly in the bathroom to check she really was alone – that whoever had opened the door wasn't still in the room with her, waiting. The light hummed softly, illuminating an empty space.

She turned back to the main room, edged around it so that she could check behind the bed, then slowly and steadily, holding her breath, she forced herself to the floor to check underneath it. She was alone, safe. She scooted back to the wall and leaned against it, letting her panting subside.

Gradually, she became aware of the pain radiating from the sole of her foot. She lifted and bent her leg to turn it up towards her. A shard of glass protruded from the sole. With gritted teeth, she gingerly tried to pull it out. She gave a muffled yelp from the sharp pain as her fingers slipped on the blood.

Breathe, she told herself. Slowly. In, out, in, out.

She tried again, yelped and slipped once more.

Third time lucky.

She gripped it once more and pulled, stifling a cry of pain as it finally came out. Blood streamed from the gash it left behind. It looked nasty. No doubt it needed stitches, but that wasn't an option right now.

She stood and hobbled back to the bathroom, being careful not to put too much pressure on her injured foot or to step on any more glass. A bloody trail led around the room where she had walked, and now the shard was out, it flowed faster, spreading further. She rinsed her foot in the bath, then sat on the toilet lid, drying it off with a towel and binding it with toilet roll.

She wasn't sure what to do next. Should she try and find Poppy, or should she stay put? Poppy could have left of her own free will and just returned to her own room. In which case, the safest thing to do would be to stay put. But what if Poppy had been taken? No, she would have felt a struggle, surely. Ellie had woken when the glass broke, which didn't leave enough time to come in and take someone. Still, it didn't sit right that Poppy had just left without saying anything. And why had she turned out the light? Swallowing down her fear, Ellie made her mind up. She would go to Poppy's room and check on her. It was the right thing to do. At least, she hoped it was.

She turned her lights off and got herself accustomed to the dark, ready for leaving her room. The blackness instantly enveloped her and made her want to crawl back into bed, safe under the covers. She wouldn't do it though; she couldn't leave Poppy out there alone. Trying to still the tremors that shook her body, she reached out and turned the door handle as silently as she could, easing open the door. Carefully, she peered out into the gloom. Nothing but darkness.

Moving slowly, she inched her way into the corridor, all the while keeping hold of the door handle should she need to dart back inside. She paused. Waited. Listened. No sound. No one rushing her. Safe. The light hadn't come on, she noticed. Her earlier assumption had been correct – someone had disabled it, switched the sensor off. She had been right to turn her own off and avoid becoming a beacon.

The blackness seemed to stretch on for an eternity before her, and she paused, debating her actions and the stupidity of continuing to Poppy's room. No, she needed to know she was ok, especially after Evan. She eased her door shut, trying to soften the click as it latched and still her hand as it shook and clattered the key in the lock.

The Storm

With her back hugging the wall so as not to make an obvious target moving down the corridor, she crept on. It really was pitch black and she had to navigate entirely through touch. Her dad's room was next to hers to her right. To her left, there was just flat wall that ran along until open corridor that then splintered off. Follow to the left for the main staircase, Lizzy's room and Alex and Jenny's. Follow to the right to the back stairs and the other bedrooms – Evan next to the stairs, Deidre's old room in the corner, and curving back round towards the left was Mr Franks' and Poppy's. She would have to cross the corridor to get to Poppy's, but at least it was the closest.

She paused at the end of the wall to her room, braced herself, strained to hear or see anything out of the ordinary. She detected nothing. Hurried across what felt like the biggest void in the world and instantly flattened herself against the wall she met, panting. Still no sound. Still no one rushed her. She inched round the contours until she found the door. A door that was open.

CHAPTER 82

A sound in the room jolted Lizzy awake, and she scrambled into a sitting position, back against the headboard, covers pulled to her chest. She listened intently for what had woken her. There came the soft squeak of the handle being depressed, then a rattle as the door moved in its frame. All the breath instantly left her body and a cold sensation trickled down her spine. They were coming for her.

Lizzy threw the covers off and knelt on the bed, frantically scanning the room for something she could use to defend herself. Anything. The sounds at the door remained insistent as whoever it was continued to try and gain entry. They were struggling; they couldn't open it, she realised. The need for a weapon suddenly felt irrelevant.

Lizzy clambered up onto the desk and put her eye to the peephole. She saw only darkness. Then the handle moved again, and Lizzy shot away from it. Sitting with her legs brought up in front of her and her arms supporting her from behind, she braced herself ready to kick back at the door if it opened.

'Lizzy?' a loud whisper came.

'Who... Ellie, is that you?'

'Let me in, please.'

'What's wrong? Are you ok?'

'Please, just let me in.' Her voice grew higher and the words came faster as she spoke.

'Give me a moment.'

The Storm

Lizzy jumped down from the desk and hurried to the end furthest from the door. She crouched, took hold of the edges in a bear hug, and pulled with all the strength she could muster. In her exhausted state, it seemed to have gained fifty pounds. She shifted her position, trying to get a better grip or a better foothold, and pulled again. It inched painfully across the carpet at a pitiful pace. She tried again and again, hoping that Ellie wasn't in immediate danger. Eventually, sweating and panting, Lizzy determined the gap was big enough. Almost immediately, the door banged open and Ellie squeezed through. She quickly shut and locked it behind her, then came further into the room, where she stood trembling.

'What's happened? Are you ok?'

'It... it's Poppy, she's missing.' Ellie's eyes were tear-filled and frantic.

'What do you mean missing?' Lizzy frowned, then gasped as she caught sight of the floor. 'Oh my God, what's happened to your foot?'

The toilet paper bandage was blood-soaked and soggy. Trails of it hung limply behind, making for a very grotesque sight. Ellie looked down like she was noticing it for the first time.

'I stepped on some glass.' She waved it away as if it were nothing. 'We need to find Poppy though. I woke up and she'd gone.'

'Ok, don't worry, we'll find her, but we can't have you walking round like that. Come with me; that needs sorting.'

Lizzy led Ellie into the bathroom. There were some dressings and plasters on the counter that she'd kept back from the first aid box earlier. She sat Ellie on the side of the bath and washed the wound as gently as she could. She dabbed it dry, then pulled it closed with plasters and applied a proper dressing. She finished it off with one of her own socks in an attempt to hold it all in place.

'Go easy on it,' she warned. 'It'll need stitches as soon as we can get you to a hospital.'

Ellie frowned, her mind still far from her foot. 'Poppy was gone when I woke up. I went to her room and she's not there either. Her door was open, Lizzy. Something's not right.'

Lizzy could see the concern etched in the girl's face. She felt it too. A gnawing sensation in the pit of her stomach. A tingle of anticipation on her scalp. Something definitely felt off. It was the open door that bothered her. No one left their hotel door open even at the best of times – especially not in the middle of the night when there's a killer on the loose.

'I'll come and look with you. I'm sure there's a reasonable explanation.'

Lizzy hoped she had said that with more confidence than she was currently feeling. She also hoped that if there was a body to be found, it was her who found it before Ellie did. The poor girl had gone through so much already that Lizzy didn't know how she was still holding it all together. She slipped her trainers on and grabbed her phone, thinking the torch feature may come in useful. With that, they approached the door.

Using Ellie's wall-hugging method, they inched their way slowly down the corridor, navigating by memory and touch. Ellie led the way, her injured foot setting the pace. She scoured the corridor in front of them, while Lizzy scoured the corridor behind them. Every so often, usually when they came to a door or other obstacle in the wall, they would stop to listen. Choosing to communicate with hand grabs and gentle pushes so as not to risk speaking and making a targetable noise.

What was a minute's walk in the light took the girls five in their stealth mode. Poppy's door was still open just as Ellie had left it. They slipped inside and eased it closed behind them. Only when it clicked shut did they risk the light. After straining in the dark for so long, it was blinding, and they took a good few moments to blink through it and readjust.

The room was a clone of all the others – the same décor, same bedding, similar hardwood furniture. Though being the

The Storm

central bedroom of the hotel, this one had no windows. The bed was unmade, rumpled but with no signs of a struggle. No furniture was upturned, no marks or signs of blood. Lizzy went into the bathroom. Miniature hotel bottles of toiletries and nothing more. Poppy hadn't known she would be staying when she'd clocked on to her shift and ended up stuck here, so it wasn't surprising. There was little else to see. Certainly no Poppy. They sat on the bed at a loss at what to do next.

'Start from the beginning. What happened after you left the lounge?' Lizzy asked.

'We came up to my room, said night to Dad. He was going to stay, but Poppy got upset.'

'Upset? How do you mean?'

'I don't know. She seemed to be in shock mostly. She was pretty out of it. Just... blank. But when Dad mentioned staying and started making a bed, she got really agitated, so he left.'

'What about after? How was she when he left? Did she say anything?'

'Trance-like again. I'm not sure she ever came out of it, to be fair. Even when she got upset at Dad, it was like she wasn't really seeing. I practically had to tuck her in.'

'And then?'

'After we'd been in bed a while, she started to come out of it. She said something about wanting to go home, then fell asleep.'

It seemed consistent with how she had been downstairs – shocked, traumatised, frightened. Would she have risked leaving the hotel though? Tried to get home? It was quite a leap for someone in that state; however, it was also in that state that she wouldn't be thinking clearly. Had fear made her run?

'She didn't say anything else? And you never heard anything?'

'I woke up to the glasses breaking hours later.'

'What glasses?'

'I couldn't move anything to block the door, so I set a couple of glasses up instead so I would hear if anyone came in. They smashed and woke me. Poppy was gone.'

'And you trod on one, I'm guessing?'

Ellie nodded. 'I was awake as soon as I heard it break though, so I don't think anyone took her then – there wasn't time. She left but never made it to her room or was taken from here.'

'The door being open doesn't necessarily mean she came here. Anyone could have opened it. Maybe looking for her.'

'Then where is she? Where did she go?'

Lizzy had no answer for that. There was no reason to suspect foul play though. Not yet anyway. They had found no evidence to suggest anything untoward had happened to her, but at the same time, there was every reason to be worried. She was young, she was vulnerable, and she was wandering the hotel or grounds alone in the dark.

CHAPTER 83

'I need to find Poppy.' Given Poppy's current state, it wasn't only the potential threat of a killer that worried Lizzy. She feared Poppy had left the hotel in an attempt to make it back home. Even properly dressed for the weather, that wasn't a good idea, and Poppy only had the clothes on her back. Fine for waitressing but useless outdoors. At least at this time of year and in the current weather conditions.

'We,' Ellie corrected.

Lizzy shook her head. 'I think you should go to your dad. Stay with him.'

Ellie looked hurt, her lips pulling down at the corners and mouth falling open slightly. 'What? Why? I want to come with you.'

'You shouldn't be walking on that foot. Plus, there's every chance Poppy might come back. Maybe she just left to get something. Hopefully, she's already there.'

Ellie pouted and gave a small huff. She obviously wasn't convinced. Her foot was clearly bothering her, however, as she didn't argue.

'I'll come back with you, make sure you get back safe, then I'll search the rest of the hotel. I'll come back up before looking outside to check in. It'd be pointless trying to search outside until daybreak anyway.'

They rose from the bed. Ellie winced as she put pressure back on her injured foot but waved Lizzy away as she moved to help her. Nothing more was said. They moved to the door and switched off the light. With ears pressed against the wood, they listened for any hint of a presence in the corridor. Hearing none, they eased the door open, paused, then cautiously stepped out. Backs once again against the wall, they shimmied down the corridor towards Ellie and Paul's rooms.

Standing outside both rooms, they gently rapped on Paul's door. They even tried the handle, but the door was locked. Lizzy was hesitant to make any more noise than they already were, but she equally didn't want to leave Ellie all alone. Sweat prickled at her brow. Swallowing down her fear, she raised her hand again to try one more time, but as she did, there came the click and unmistakable sound of a door opening. It sounded close.

Lizzy's heart stopped and she groped for Ellie in the dark, but she didn't need prompting - she already had the key to the lock and was fumbling to get it open. The sound seemed too loud in the space and it took far too long, but eventually, Ellie got it open and they slipped inside the room as quickly as they could. Ellie grabbed the door behind them and started to push it shut, but Lizzy shot a hand out to stop it from fully closing at the last minute. She didn't want to risk it making any noise, any more noise, plus she also wanted to be able to hear what was happening out there.

They stood still, breaths held, listening and waiting. Someone was clearly shuffling around out there, but it was difficult to ascertain in which direction they moved. The sound seemed to move closer at first, but then it receded and drifted away. Whoever it was had come past Poppy's room and then gone either towards the back or main staircase. Unless the sound had originated from the direction of the main stairs, then they would have gone towards the back stairs or Poppy's room. Either way, Lizzy felt confident enough to click the door closed and switch the light on.

'Shit, that was close.' Despite the bright light, Ellie's eyes were wide. She released a breath and stood panting, then hobbled over to the bed and sat down.

The Storm

'Could you tell where they came from? Where they went?'

'No. Too busy shitting myself. They came closer for a while though. I thought they were headed straight for us.'

'I think they've gone downstairs.'

'Are you still going? Now that they're out there?'

Lizzy paused, then nodded. 'Yes, I have to. We can't leave Poppy out there. Even more so now we know there's someone out there roaming around.'

'Please be careful.' Ellie grabbed Lizzy's hand and squeezed.

'I'll be fine.' Lizzy squeezed back. 'Stay here and lock the door. Keep your light on and find something to use as a weapon.'

Ellie's eyes hadn't left Lizzy's face. At the suggestion of finding a weapon, her face paled, the realisation suddenly dawning on her that someone might actually come into her room to hurt her.

'It's just in case. Better to be prepared. Anything you can find that's heavy or sharp. Something you can swing.' Lizzy hurried over to the door. 'I'm going to turn the light off while I go outside. Turn it back on after I've left.'

With that, she flipped the switch and slipped back out into the corridor before either of them could change their minds.

CHAPTER 84

Ellie switched the light on as soon as Lizzy had cleared the door. Half of her was pleased that Lizzy had gone alone. She wanted to find Poppy, she really did, but being out there was terrifying, especially now there was definitely someone out there sneaking around and not just fragments of their imagination.

The other half, however, missed being in Lizzy's presence. She felt safe with Lizzy and now that safety was gone. Ellie debated going back to her dad's room and trying again. She really didn't want to be alone right now. She stood by the door, her hand hovering over the door handle, but she couldn't make herself touch it. She let out a breath, shook her hands out, and tried again. No, she'd stay put. She locked the door, turned, and went back into the room. Even if she could rouse him, her dad would only fuss and drive her crazy.

Ellie looked around the room, trying to find a suitable weapon. Most of what was there was soft – the bedding, her discarded clothes. Her suitcase was too big; all her knickknacks, her makeup, and hairbrush were too small. It was slim pickings. She debated the kettle but decided upon her hair straighteners and one of the bedside lamps she'd unplugged from the wall. She reckoned the lamp would be a good blunt object to hit with, preferably over the head, and she could use the straighteners to both attack and defend.

She placed them on the bed within easy reach and sat back. Her heart ached for her mum so badly, but there was no

The Storm

time for tears. Not yet. There would be plenty of time for those after tonight. Survive the night, make it to morning, survive the night, make it to morning. She felt that if she could just get through tonight, then everything would be ok. With her eyes never leaving the door, she repeated the mantra and longed for the sunrise.

CHAPTER 85

Lizzy stood outside Ellie's room not quite believing what she was doing. It was a crazy idea sneaking around a dark hotel trying to find someone who may or may not be in there. Crazier still to do so with a killer on the loose. Still, she couldn't let it go. Couldn't let Poppy go. Not if there was a chance she could help her. Possibly even save her.

Gathering her courage once more, she started her shimmy down the walls, pausing every so often to listen. At the end of Ellie's wall came the decision. Left to the main staircase or right to the back one? The main stairs were bigger and would bring her out in reception. She would be quite exposed and it was a big area to find cover in. The back stairs led to the rear of the dining room. This route would be more enclosed, but she'd be trapped if anyone else should be there. She chose left.

The light was a little better at the top of the stairs. Reception had windows, and though it was still night, the sky offered enough that shapes were discernible. This was both a help and a hindrance, she realised. It would greatly ease her passage and help with the search for Poppy; however, if she could see, albeit only vague shapes, then so could the other roamer. And she didn't like her chances that it was just a sleepwalker.

Keeping to the edge of the staircase, Lizzy made her way down as quickly as she dared, hoping that none of the steps were creaky. Halfway down, she found one and froze mid-step. The noise seemed deafening in the silence. She daren't breathe let alone move. Her heartbeat pounded in her ears and her eyes darted around the space around her. Nothing came. No sound, no movement. Slowly, she eased off the step, internally cringing as the sound resonated once more on its release. Hurrying down the last few steps, she turned to the left at the foot and pressed herself into the corner of the room.

Lizzy waited, trying to hear over her heartbeat, until she was sure no one was coming and she felt some of her confidence return. Not that she felt much of that at the moment. She was just steeling herself to move off from her spot when she heard a clinking sound, and her blood froze. Metal on metal. It came from behind her – the dining room or kitchen. Cutlery or pots and pans, she thought. She wasn't sure what to do for the best. If she stayed where she was and they came out this way, for the main staircase, they would pass right by her. Would the dark be enough to hide her? She was just debating whether to make a run for the reception desk when the noise stopped. It was soon replaced with footsteps. Slowly and steady. She was too late.

Cursing her indecision, she pressed herself back as far as she could, trying to meld with the wall behind her, her body tensed against whatever was coming. A dark shape emerged from the doorway to her left, crossed in front of her, and headed for the stairs. Lizzy went instantly weak, her legs turning to jelly. She couldn't make out who it was, as the light wasn't enough to get more than a moving shape, but it was enough to glint off the object they grasped in their hand. Lizzy's breath caught in her throat. Definitely not a sleepwalker. This person was holding a knife.

CHAPTER 86

A creak resonated in the corridor. It was soft but discernible. Someone moving slowly and quietly over old floorboards. Ellie was on full alert, her fear seeming to heighten her senses. She hoped it was Lizzy but doubted it was – she had not long left. Unless she had forgotten something. Shuffling feet. The click of doors. Were they looking for something? Or looking for someone?

Ellie debated what to do. Remain sitting on the bed poised for an attack or hide. She glanced around the small space. Her options amounted to the wardrobe or under the bed. Neither was exactly original. The wardrobe would give her the option of bursting out and catching an attacker unaware. Under the bed, she would be more vulnerable, but at least she would be able to see.

She was starting to wish she'd gone back to her dad's room. She could have knocked a bit louder knowing they were downstairs. Done more to rouse him. She'd have felt safer with him and it would be two against one if it came to it. Too late now. There was no way she was going back out there now she knew someone was prowling.

Hurry up, Lizzy.

Ellie grabbed the straighteners and got off the bed. Lying on her front, she commando-crawled her way under the frame. The space only just cleared her body, and although she could see, she felt as if she were in a coffin.

The Storm

Panic gripped and restricted her throat, and she felt as though the entire weight of the bed was pressing down on her. This was a stupid idea. She had to get out – she couldn't breathe. She started backing out the way she'd crawled in when there came a noise from the door. The creak of a spring. Was it the handle? Ellie froze. She tried to steady her breathing, to make it silent even though the panic still coursed through her veins. More so now as she watched her door opening.

CHAPTER 87

As soon as the figure had cleared the stairs, Lizzy darted into the dining room and out of sight. It was the closest room to her and one that had multiple exits and hiding places should she need them. She stood for a few seconds, trembling, wanting to turn back and follow, to finally see who was doing this and stop them from hurting anybody else, but fear rooted her to the spot. Everyone upstairs was on alert, with their doors locked. As long as they stayed put, they should be safe, she reasoned. What use would she be out in the open in the dark? An easy target. No, she needed to find Poppy. Poppy was the one out here and vulnerable… unless she was already too late.

As the roamer had only just left, Lizzy figured she had a good few minutes before they might need or want to return. Switching the torch app on, she made a quick sweep at various heights to see above and below the tables. Nothing.

'Poppy?' she whispered.

Nothing but silence.

Multiple exits to the room also meant multiple entrances, and Lizzy didn't want to hang around any longer than she needed to. She swiped the torch off and headed for the kitchen on her right – presumably where the roamer had just come from.

The kitchen was accessed through a swing door. Lizzy took her time steadying it to a stilled position once she'd passed through, cautious of any noise it should make. Her skin prickled being in this unfamiliar environment, and an unease

The Storm

grew in the pit of her stomach like a radiating heat. Strange shapes loomed out of the darkest recesses and crowded her. She'd have to put a light on, she realised. With so many things to potentially bump into and clang, it would be dangerous not to. She switched her phone torch back on and looked around. Everything looked how she imagined a hotel kitchen to look. No blood smears, no disarray suggesting a struggle of any sort.

A small room led off to the left, so Lizzy dipped inside. Sinks and shiny, large aluminium equipment. It looked like a pot wash room. Two industrial-sized pump bottles of cleaner sat on a worktop that was otherwise bare and meticulously scrubbed clean. A couple of racks hung above, empty and in wait of soapy pots. The main event in the room was the large commercial dishwasher. At least that's what Lizzy assumed it to be. Apart from that and some coat pegs that held only chefs' whites, the room was bare. Nowhere to hide. Nothing to see.

Lizzy went back into the main kitchen. Prep areas of worktops lined the walls with a central island of hobs sitting above large ovens. Pots and pans hung from above the island, while utensils hung off the walls. Everything gleamed silver and bounced the torchlight around the room. Two doors led from the furthest corners of the space, which Lizzy assumed to be cupboards of some sort.

Slowly, she walked around the central island, sweeping the floor and surfaces for anything out of place. It was spotlessly clean. She took the door off to the left corner. A food store. Dry goods arranged and organised in perfect unison.

The door in the opposite corner turned out to be a refrigerated room with two large chest freezers. She grabbed a chopping board from the countertop and leaned it against the door frame, preventing the door from shutting. She was eager and hesitant to see in the freezers, but she'd seen enough horror films to not risk getting trapped in one of these.

Walking over to the nearest one, she took hold of the handle. Bracing herself against what she might find inside, she hefted the lid up. Labelled and dated meat packets stared up at her. She breathed a sigh of relief and passed to the next one, where she found more of the same.

Careful to secure them correctly, Lizzy closed the lids and shut the door.

CHAPTER 88

Black shoes and black trousers grew closer to Ellie. The feet drew level with the bed and halted.

This is it, she thought.

Ellie gripped the straighteners and screwed her eyes shut. Her whole body tensed as she waited to be grabbed. Surely they could hear her pounding heartbeat – to Ellie, it was deafening. She held her breath, trying to stop herself from breathing loudly with panic. It was as if she were in bed with one foot hanging off the side, waiting for a monster to grab it. Except this time, the monster was real.

She couldn't work out if the killer's silence was worse than if she could have heard them. All her mind could focus on was them peeking under the bed, grinning. She daren't open her eyes.

Shuffling. Finally, a sound other than her beating heart. And the shuffling sounded as if it were feet moving away. She risked a glance. They walked back towards the door, ducked into the bathroom, and then left. They had come for her and not found her.

CHAPTER 89

Lizzy left the kitchen the way she had come in. Apart from an external door leading to the grounds at the rear of the hotel, it was her only option. Sticking to the shadows, she edged herself around the walls to the toilets opposite. They contained only a couple of cubicles, which were shared with the bar – having an entrance from there and the dining room. It was a very enclosed space, but at least there were two exits.

With the torch app ready, she cracked open the door, swiped the light on and scanned around the small space from the perceived safety of the dining room. All clear as far as she could tell. She went inside to conduct a more thorough search. Lizzy nudged each stall door open in turn with an outstretched leg, pushing with enough force to open it fully but not to bang it or hurt anyone inside. No Poppy.

Where are you, Poppy?

Lizzy paused to weigh her options, turning her torch off. She imagined hands reaching to grab her in the darkness, somehow felt the air behind the movements, and leaned back against the sink to at least get rid of the vulnerability from one direction. Darkness had a way of conjuring the worst of thoughts in the best of times, and she focused her whole mind to Poppy to try to push away her fear or at least take the edge off it.

The Storm

She couldn't help but really begin to think she had left the hotel to try and make her way back home. As well as Poppy might know the area, the nearest village was miles away and on the other side of a flood. Lizzy had seen how dangerous it was in daylight – to attempt it in the dark would be madness.

She slowly eased the door to the bar area open, listening for any movement from inside the room. Hearing nothing, she moved into the bar and shut the door silently behind her.

The bar was open-plan, but whilst the lounge boasted comfortable armchairs and sofas, the bar area had hard wooden tables and chairs. To her left lay the actual bar. An oak-panelled affair that would make any English pub proud. Lizzy was yet to use it and doubted now that she ever would. She approached the bar and peered over the countertop, checking the area behind. Her light illuminated a door off to the left, presumably a storeroom of some sort. She lifted the hatch to allow her entry behind the bar and set about checking it out. It was locked with a keypad entry. Not somewhere she could check, then.

'Poppy?' She knocked gently and called out in a whisper. 'Poppy, are you in there? It's me, Lizzy.'

Silence. She doubted that Poppy was hiding in there. She doubted that she was hiding full stop. If Poppy wasn't in her room or Ellie's, the only other logical place for her to go was home. Or to attempt to.

Lizzy turned to go back into the bar area when she heard the steady soft drum of approaching feet. Her heart leapt into her throat, and she fumbled with her phone, trying to switch the torch off, suddenly all fingers and thumbs in her haste, her breathing growing rapid as she failed again and again. In a panic, she covered the light with one hand as she furiously swiped at the screen with the other. It must have only taken a few seconds, but it had felt like hours. It was finally off though.

Lizzy let the dark surround her once again and strained to hear the footsteps. Someone was in reception and coming her way, their feet tapping against the wooden parquet floor.

With no time to find a proper hiding place, she ducked and crouched behind the bar. Silently, she cursed herself for not finding a weapon while the light was on. She should have taken a knife from the kitchen or a bottle from the bar. She could feel shelves around her, but she daren't explore them in the dark. She imagined them stacked with glasses, which would be of little use to her and only tinkle against one another and give her position away if she tried to grab one.

The footsteps were slow and steady. They became softer as they reached the carpet of the lounge, but the room remained shrouded in darkness. No flickering or sweeping torchlight.

She could hear them shuffling about, searching blindly. She desperately wanted to look. Just a quick peek to see if she could see who it was and what they were doing. She couldn't even see her hand in front of her face. She knew it was darker back here, crouched in her hiding spot, but she also knew there wouldn't be much more light out there. No. It wasn't worth it. She needed to stay put. Stay still. Not risk any movement that could make a sound.

The air grew heavy as they drew nearer. They were definitely close to her now. She instinctively pushed herself backwards, shrinking further from the threat, trying to meld with the wooden shelf behind her. It dug into her spine.

Soft shuffles on the carpet. The slow but deliberate moving of furniture as if searching. For what? For her?

She felt rather than heard them approach where she sat crouched. Even though it was dark, she screwed her eyes shut

The Storm

as if the act of not seeing would make her invisible to her attacker. They were right behind her. She felt it. Almost felt their breath tickle across her skin. Down her neck. She shivered. She imagined it to be a man, but her mind wouldn't picture who.

Trying to shrink into herself, she curled her body inwards and crouching into a tighter ball, making herself as small as possible, and prayed that they couldn't see her. What was taking so long? Why weren't they moving? Why weren't they doing anything? Could they see her? She tensed her body ready to spring up in either a counterattack or to make a run for it. Poised, the wait was intolerable.

CHAPTER 90

Ellie felt as though she had been under the bed for an eternity, but in reality, it couldn't have been more than half an hour. Her body ached and cramped with the effort of staying in the confined space. She went through a cycle of stretching her limbs in turn – something she'd been doing on and off since being down here. Once again, she considered getting out, started inching herself backwards, then stopped. Panic kept her there. Trapped under her own bed.

She wondered where Lizzy had got to. Hoped she was ok. Prayed for her to come back soon. She stared at the door, willing it to open and be her.

CHAPTER 91

The bar had fallen silent albeit for the thumping of her heart. Lizzy stayed crouched, hidden, not daring to move, not trusting that whoever it was wasn't lying in wait. The silence stretched on around her. She hadn't heard them for a while now. She gave it a few minutes more, then put her hands to the sticky rubber floor and slowly crawled towards the hatch. Her movements, though quiet, seemed to resonate around the space and made her wince. Still nothing. She continued moving until her fingers brushed the joining strip and met with carpet. Out in the bar area, it was getting lighter. Not by much, but shapes were definitely clearer, more discernible. Morning was coming.

She took her time to fully take in the room. To make sure nothing was out of place and no one else was in there with her. Everything looked fine. Just tables and chairs.

She stood and listened. There was a faint sound that could have been coming from behind her – the direction of the dining room maybe. She had to move. As quickly and quietly as she could, Lizzy hurried through into the lounge, eager to get back upstairs to the safety of her room. As she weaved in and out of the tables, she caught one with her knee. She bit down a shout and winced at the sudden pain, but that was nothing compared to the loud knock it made. That sound alone would have been bad enough, but the empty wine glass that had been left on top toppled and smashed. It rang out in the silence of the room.

Lizzy froze. Her insides clenched in a tight knot and her eyes darted around maniacally, looking for an escape or somewhere to hide. The tables were too low in here to get underneath and she'd never make it to the door in time. Then she found it. An old-fashioned coat rack stood in the corner. She dashed over to it, squeezing herself behind and steadying the coats that hung from it. They felt heavy and damp to her touch. Musty in the residual heat of the room after being out in the storm.

Her heart thudded and her breathing came ragged. She concentrated on trying to calm herself. Tried to think. Maybe she had been mistaken. Maybe there was no one there. She had all but convinced herself that her mind had been playing tricks when she saw a shadow flit by the weak light of the window. Someone was in the room with her. Her breath caught, and she held it.

She followed them round the room with her eyes as best she could. They were in no hurry. Maybe they were wary of the glass, she reasoned, unless they were searching for her.

A crunch came as their foot found the broken shards, and they bent to examine the floor. They looked up suddenly into the darkness, startling her. Had she made a noise? She hadn't moved, hadn't disturbed anything, she was sure of it. Then they rose and started walking, coming nearer to where she hid. A sickening wave of terror welled inside her. She tensed her whole body, holding her breath, barely daring to look but forcing herself to. They passed by. As they did so, they left behind a familiar scent. Try as she might though, Lizzy just couldn't place it.

CHAPTER 92

The roamer left through the door to reception, exactly where Lizzy wanted to go. She considered her options. She could follow, keeping a safe distance away. They would be unlikely to backtrack and see her and there would be a possibility of seeing which room they entered, which could identify them. Or she could go back through the dining room and take the back staircase. This would take her in the opposite direction from them, reducing the risk of being seen. But not knowing exactly where they were or where they were going, she would risk running into them on the landing.

Feeling a higher risk for one option than the other, she set off after them, making sure to keep a good few feet back and stick to the shadows. She felt oddly exhilarated to be the one in pursuit. As though she had taken their power away from them.

She waited in the doorway to reception and watched them climb the stairs, waiting for the creaky step to sound and trying to note which one it was to avoid it. The roamer seemed to know which creaked, as they stepped over one step. She'd do the same. The stairs offered no cover, so she couldn't risk being on them at the same time as the roamer. As soon as they were out of sight, she hurried after.

She reached the top just as they were rounding the corner towards the front of the hotel. There were only two rooms down there – hers and Alex and Jenny's. She peered round to see them hesitating in the corridor. They held something in their hand, but she didn't think it looked like a knife. At least, not the knife she had seen earlier. The glint was all wrong. The shape off. They held it out – a key. Carefully and quietly, they turned it in the lock and silently let themself into the room. Her room. Lizzy turned on her heel and went in the opposite direction. She needed to get to Ellie's.

CHAPTER 93

Ellie's breath caught as she heard approaching feet. She curled into a tight ball and slapped a hand across her mouth to stop her from making any sound. They'd come back for her. She should have moved, should have found a different hiding place, a better weapon. Too late now.

The door opened and closed, but the feet that appeared were wearing trainers.

'Ellie?' Lizzy whispered.

She sagged under the relief and let out a shaky breath. 'Down here, just a sec.'

Ellie back-crawled out from under the bed, her hair wild and speckled with dust, pushing the hair straighteners along the floor and out her way as she did. Once she was out, she ran to embrace Lizzy, holding her tight, as though she were a long-lost lover.

'Hey, it's ok, you ok?'

'They were here... the killer... they came into my room.' Her words came out in hiccuppy gulps.

'What? When?' Lizzy held her at arm's length scanning her face, checking her over. 'Are you ok? What happened?'

Ellie slipped out of Lizzy's arms and dropped down onto the edge of the bed. It was so wonderfully soft after the confines of her hiding spot. Lizzy sat beside her.

'I don't know. Five minutes after you left. Ten maybe?'

'Did they do anything? Say anything?'

'No, nothing. They came in, looked around, and left. I was under the bed. Shit, Lizzy, I was so scared.'

Lizzy took hold of Ellie's face. Held eye contact. 'Hey, it's ok. You're safe, alright?'

Ellie nodded and wiped at a tear that had escaped in her relief. 'Did you find Poppy?'

'No. I've been in every room downstairs that I can access. I even looked in the pantry. I think she must have left the hotel.'

'Shit.'

'It's starting to get light out though. We can look for her again as soon as we can see out. I'd feel a whole lot safer in the daylight.'

Me too, thought Ellie.

This had been the longest night of her life. She wished they'd all listened to Lizzy now and stayed together, but she'd been too tired at the time to understand or argue. She could see now the comfort and protection it would have given. She longed to go back in time and make everyone see sense. No, she longed to go back to before they'd come on this damned trip so she could have stopped it from happening.

'So, what do we do now?' Ellie asked.

'We wait, I guess.' Lizzy looked to the door and swallowed hard. 'We'll be safer in here than out there.'

Ellie followed Lizzy's gaze and frowned. 'What is it? You're not telling me something.'

She bit her lip, seemingly debating some inner struggle, then relented. 'I saw them.'

Ellie paled and grasped Lizzy's hand. 'Who is it?'

'I don't know, it was too dark. I could only see shapes and movement. They walked around. The first time, they were purposeful – like they knew where they were going. They came from the kitchen, I think, and went upstairs.'

'To me?'

'I suppose they must have. It fits.'

'And then?'

'The second time, they were in the bar. I didn't see them that time – I was hiding. But I heard them. They got close at one point. I think they were looking for something.'

'Or someone…'

'Before I came up, I saw them again. In the lounge. I'm not sure what they were doing that time, but I followed them. They came upstairs and…' Her voice cracked, and she swallowed again.

'And what?'

'They went into my room. Ellie, whoever it is, I think they're looking for me.'

CHAPTER 94

'I think I should go.' Looking into Ellie's vulnerable face, the last thing Lizzy wanted to do was leave her, but they were in her room. They were coming for her. She couldn't put Ellie in any more danger by staying in here, in Ellie's room.

'What?' Ellie's face crumpled and her eyes instantly filled with tears. 'No. Why?'

Lizzy glanced over at the bedside clock. 5:06 a.m. She thought sunrise was about 6 a.m. at the moment. Nearly there. Come on, Luke, send the cavalry. We're counting on you.

'I have to see if they're still out there. It will be light soon. This might be my last chance to unmask them. They seem to strike at night when no one's watching. Once daylight hits, we've lost them. I don't want to go home from here knowing they're still out there. That they could come for me at any time.'

Lizzy stood, making her way determinedly to the door. She remained facing away from Ellie, not wanting to show her fear.

'I'll come with you. Two against one.'

Lizzy's hand hesitated on the door handle as she looked back. Ellie seemed so small sitting on the edge of her bed, and Lizzy couldn't help but see how young she looked. 'No, I can't let you do that.'

'Please. I don't want to be alone.'

Tears glistened as they began falling down Ellie's cheeks, and Lizzy had to look away.

The Storm

'I can't put you in danger like that. Let's go to your dad's room. You can stay with him.'

With a sigh, Ellie rose from the bed, wiped a sleeve across her eyes, and slowly limped over to join Lizzy at the door with a sniff. Extinguishing the light, they quietly opened the door and scanned the hallway. It may have been lightening outside, but the nearest window was in the reception downstairs and the lights were still out in the corridor.

Lizzy slipped into the hallway and knocked gently on Paul's door, hoping this time to rouse him. Nothing. She waited and tried again, a little louder. Tried the handle. It was locked and no answer came. She looked down the hallway, seeing nothing but darkness at the end. She couldn't be sure no one was there, already watching, but she sure as hell didn't want to bring any more attention to them.

She shook her head at Ellie and ushered her back into her room, closing the door behind them.

'Lock it behind me. I'll not come back until it's light and you can see through the peephole, ok? I'll knock and call out so you know it's me. If anyone else comes, hide, like before.'

Ellie dissolved into tears and grabbed Lizzy by the arms. Lizzy could feel the shake in her grip. It instinctively made her want to pull her close and make everything alright, and it tore at her heart that she couldn't.

'I need to do this.'

Lizzy willed Ellie not to make it harder than it already was. Ellie dropped her arms as she accepted what was to happen.

'Be careful,' she offered.

Lizzy left quickly before either of them changed their minds.

CHAPTER 95

Standing on the other side of the door, Lizzy took a deep breath. She needed a plan or a weapon. Definitely a weapon. She already knew they were armed and didn't fancy facing a knife barehanded. Hadn't she read somewhere that a weapon was more likely to be used against you though? Maybe she needed a shield of some sort, then. Something to deflect the blade and stop it penetrating.

Feeling her way as before, Lizzy started back to her room. She remembered there being a door by the top of the stairs marked 'staff only' that she hoped would turn out to be a store cupboard. Preferably an unlocked one. It was the only door on this side of the corridor before the turn, so she found it easily enough. Her fingers butted against the door frame, and she felt along the smooth wooden panel, searching for the handle. The metal was cool to the touch as she found and turned it. As luck would have it, it was unlocked and turned easily when she tried it, with only the barest creak.

She let herself in and felt for a light switch. A fluorescent tube flickered and buzzed into life overhead. After having moved around the dark corridor, it stung her eyes, and she gave herself a moment to adjust.

It was a storeroom. Quite a big one at that. Wooden shelves of bedlinen and towels lined the walls and cleaning products sat on the floor below. In the corner was a mop and bucket, a vacuum cleaner, and dustpan and brush. Perfect. She grabbed the brush – an old-fashioned wooden yard brush with

The Storm

soft bristles. She reckoned she could use the length to push someone away and keep them at distance. And if they did manage to get close, a kitchen knife wouldn't get through the wooden handle. It didn't exactly feel a fair fight, but she felt much better having something in her hands. At a push, she could always hit him, or her, with it.

She turned the light off before exiting and continued down the corridor. The closer to her room she got, the more jellified her legs became and the harder her heart pounded. What was she doing? This was madness. Still, she had to know. Had to face her fears head-on.

As Lizzy turned the final corner, she stopped and her heart leapt into her throat. There was someone outside her room. A cold shiver tingled down the length of her body as she decided what she should do. She couldn't tell if they were coming or going and she wasn't about to hang around to find out. Channelling a deep-seated rage, she held the broom in both hands across her body and ran at the figure, charging it into them like a battering ram and knocking them to the floor.

'Argh. Shit.' The figure lay winded, huffing and puffing. Lizzy recognised the voice, suddenly realised what she had been smelling earlier. Aftershave.

'Luke?' Lizzy's voice rose a whole octave.

The door on the other side opened, light spilling out from behind Alex, illuminating them in a soft glow.

It is Luke. Oh, thank the Lord.

Lizzy set the brush against the wall as she stared down at him, then back over to a startled and annoyed-looking Alex. The light coming from behind him cast his face into shadows that deepened his scowl.

'What the heck is going on?'

'Sorry.' Lizzy held her hands up. 'I'm sorry. Everything's fine.'

Alex looked daggers at them but was weirdly unperturbed by the strange man lying on the floor at Lizzy's feet. He said something under his breath and closed the door, taking the light with him and bathing them in darkness once again.

Lizzy bent to help Luke up. 'Oh my God, I can't believe you came. I'm so relieved to see you.'

'Funny way of showing it.' He laughed, brushing himself off.

'I'm so sorry, did I hurt you?'

'Nah. It's more the shock than pain. I'll live.'

Lizzy gave him a tight squeeze. She was so happy to see him. They were going to be ok; they were going to make it – help was finally here.

The relief she felt was so immense she momentarily forgot the reason she had been returning to her room. She popped her key in the lock and let them both in, then flicked on the light, motioning for him to go first with a wave of her hand. He went ahead, shimmying round the desk without questioning it with as much as a raised eyebrow.

'Oh, Luke, I can't believe it. So much has happened, I don't know where to begin.' She shut and locked the door behind them, squeezed herself round the desk, and joined him in the room. Her eyes brimmed with tears as she held his hands tightly in hers.

'Hey, it's alright.'

Luke pulled her into a hug and stroked her hair. A week ago, she'd have been dying to wriggle out of this kind of full-on embrace. Right now though, after everything she'd been through, she drank it in greedily.

'You got here faster than I expected.' She smiled into his chest, relaxed into his body as relief washed over her. He felt warm and safe. 'Where are the police? Are they outside? Are they on their way?'

'Police?'

'Yeah.' She pulled away slightly, looking up at him. 'You did call them, didn't you? When I didn't come home. That's why you're here, right?' Lizzy's eyebrows knitted as she searched his face. A blush crept up from his neck. He looked

The Storm

caught out or confused, stumbling over his thoughts, trying to form the words she'd want to hear.

'Please don't tell me you came alone.' She backed away, nervous energy back in control and coursing through her body.

'Look, I—'

'Shit, Luke, something horrible is going on here; people are dying.'

Lizzy ran her hands through her hair. Pinching the bridge of her nose, she sat on the bed. Luke quietly joined her.

'I'm sorry, that wasn't fair. You didn't know. I'm just so tired and so scared.'

Luke worked his jaw, looking down at the floor. He placed a hand on her thigh and slowly rubbed up and down. It was surely meant as a comforting gesture, but it just grated. Lizzy grabbed it and held it still, then felt bad and turned it into a hand hold.

'You came, and that's what matters.' She gave a watery smile. She didn't have the energy left to fully cover her disappointment. Maybe she had expected too much of him, pinning all their hopes on him like that. Now was definitely not the time to start falling out and laying blame. Then a thought perked her.

'Oh, the road. It's open?' Lizzy's face lit up as she sprang to her feet. 'You came through, which means the road is open. We can leave.'

Luke stood slowly but wouldn't meet her eyes. Something was wrong, she realised. Everything about him suddenly seemed off. She stopped, dread washing over her. Finally, he met her eyes.

'I can explain.'

Her whole body tensed.

CHAPTER 96

Lizzy felt fuzzy, as though she were two inches outside of her body. As though she were behind a glass screen, banging on the glass and shouting at the scene unfolding in front of her but no one on the other side could hear her.

'I've missed you,' Luke gushed. 'I love you so much, you know that.'

He stood and approached her. Held her again. The embrace was gentle and light. It would have looked loving should anyone have been watching, but to Lizzy, it was suffocating and restrictive. Her body went rigid at his touch, and she worked hard to relax it and not let it show.

'When did you get here?' Her voice came out weak, and she fought hard to force confidence back into it.

'I just couldn't stand to be away from you. A week is so long.'

'You've... you've been here a while?'

'I wanted to surprise you, be romantic and spontaneous. Surprise.'

He smiled down at her, and against all that she was feeling, she managed to smile back. She'd just told him people were dying and he hadn't questioned it. And if he hadn't just arrived today, he'd been here since... before the landslide. And if he had... oh God.

Realisation hit her like a sledgehammer. She felt winded. But she had to remain calm. Act natural. Not show that she was aware or scared of him. Of Luke. Her Luke. Luke

The Storm

who loved her to pieces. Luke who would do anything for her. But just how far did anything go?

'I've missed you too,' she managed to whisper.

He pulled away and held her at arm's length. 'You ok?' He suddenly looked concerned, worried.

'Yeah, fine. I… I just… I'm so happy to see you.' She couldn't stop the tears welling in her eyes, but she spoke with a smile. It was enough. He beamed back at her, clearly pleased with the emotional response and taking it the way he wanted to see it.

Her thoughts were going a mile a minute, but none of them supplied her with a reasonable excuse for leaving the room.

'So, tell me all about your retreat. How did you get on?'

'Er… good. I finished the edits.'

He took her hand again and gave it a squeeze. 'Oh, I'm so proud of you. I knew you'd do it.'

'Thanks. Er, Luke, listen, I've been helping a young girl here, Ellie, her mum drowned in the lake a few days ago.'

'Oh shit.' He looked solemn, but his words came out flat.

'Yeah, it's so awful. So anyway, I've been keeping an eye on her and I said I'd see her this morning. She's not doing well. Do you mind if I go and check on her, just quickly? I'll come right back.'

'But I've not seen you in so long. She can wait, surely.'

Luke nuzzled into her neck and started kissing her collarbone. Lizzy fought against the tremble in her lips. He brought his head to hers and kissed her full on the lips. She responded as best she could, reciprocating but not encouraging. The kiss became more heated, and he started to run his hands over her body and tug at her clothes. She prickled under his touch, the contact making her feel sick.

Lizzy held her arms up in front of her body and brought them down and out, pushing his arms off her as she stepped away from him, unable to bear it any longer. 'No.'

'What?' Luke's brow furrowed.

'I mean, not now. Sorry, I have my period. Rubbish timing, hey?' She tried to laugh it off.

'No, you don't.'

She felt as though the world froze in that moment. Her heart stopped beating and her mouth went dry. 'What? What do you mean?'

'You didn't bring any pads or towels. You're lying.'

'How do you...' Her face flushed angrily. 'Have you been through my bag?'

Luke had the grace to look sheepish, but only briefly. Then his face clouded over. 'What choice did I have? My girlfriend books a week's holiday without me. You've got to admit it sounds pretty suspicious. I needed to know you weren't meeting anyone here. I love you so much, Lizzy, I just couldn't bear the thought... and I would have missed you too much.'

'Would have?' The bottom of her stomach dropped suddenly, and she felt hot all over. 'Exactly how long have you been here, Luke?'

'You don't realise how much you mean to me, Lizzy.'

'How long?'

'I couldn't have lived a week without you.'

'How long?'

He walked over to her, tried to take her hand, stroke her arm. She moved out of reach.

'When did you come here, Luke?'

He spoke softly, embarrassed and bashful almost. 'I followed you up. At first, I just wanted to make sure you got here ok and that you were alone. I parked the car partway up the driveway and walked down. But then... I just couldn't leave you.'

Her barely contained fury bubbled beneath the surface. She'd known he was controlling, but this? This was a whole other level. Angry tears pricked at her eyes, but she refused to let them fall.

The Storm

'Have you been watching me this whole time?'

It was all slotting into place – the wet footprints in her room, her things not being where she'd left them, the presence in the woods.

'You don't understand. You mean everything to me, Lizzy.'

CHAPTER 97

Ellie was pacing her room. It seemed like ages since Lizzy had left, and she couldn't settle. Every so often, she would pause. Wait and listen to the silence. Listen for movements, for any sound of approaching danger or of Lizzy returning. A couple of times, she thought she heard shuffling feet. Once, she thought she could hear distant voices. No one came though, friend or foe.

It was nearly morning. More and more light was spilling into her room. Not daylight yet, but it was definitely dawning. She felt as though she'd been waiting her whole life for this sunrise. As though her whole life depended on today breaking. Maybe it did. She viewed the sun as her saviour – she couldn't be killed while it was up. She knew deep down that was silly, but she held on to it nevertheless.

CHAPTER 98

He was like Jekyll and Hyde, his responses swinging wildly from soft and comforting to angry retorts. Lizzy didn't know how to play him. In his softer moments, he was too loving and pawing, but in his angry moments? She knew she needed to get him back on side and play the dutiful girlfriend.

She let out a sigh, tried to make a show of softening and understanding. 'You mean the world to me too, Luke, it's just a bit of a shock to know someone's been following and watching you.'

'I know, but you see why I had to do it? You do understand, yeah?'

'Of course. It's just... well, you should have just said. We could have shared a room.'

He grinned at her then. It softened his face, and with it, his body relaxed. He sat on the bed, patted the space next to him. 'Come and show me how much you love me and how much you missed me.'

The thought made Lizzy sick to her stomach. She forced a smile, then stood in front of him and took his hand. 'Ok, but first, I really do need to check on Ellie, ok?' She bent and gave him a kiss that she hoped would pacify him. 'If I don't, she'll only come looking for me, and we don't want to be disturbed, do we?'

'Well, no, I guess not. Be quick, then.'

'I will. Warm the bed for me.' She winked, then quickly turned. She had to stop herself from bolting from the room.

Her movements felt awkward and forced, as if she couldn't remember how to walk normally.

Once Lizzy was sure she was out of sight and sound of her room, she broke into a run until she reached Ellie's room.

'Ellie,' she called in a loud whisper, knocking on her door.

It was answered almost immediately.

'Thank God, I've been so worried.' Ellie stepped aside to let Lizzy in.

'Oh, Ellie, oh, I'm so sorry.' Lizzy pushed the door quickly closed and scrambled to secure the lock.

'What? What for? What happened? Did you find them?'

'He was in the corridor outside my room.'

Ellie's skin lost all colour falling chalk white. 'Shit, are you ok?'

'I'm fine. Well, I'm not, but physically, yeah.' She ran shaky hands over her face. 'Shit, this is so messed up. It's all my fault, Ellie, I'm so sorry.'

'What do you mean? How is it your fault?'

'It's Luke, my boyfriend, he followed me up here. He's the one that's been stalking the corridors at night. He's been watching me, convinced I'm cheating on him or some other shit. It's him, he's the killer, and I brought him up here.'

Ellie's eyes flickered over the room for a few seconds as she thought it over, yet panic still predominantly shrouded her features.

'Where is he now?'

'In my room. My excuse for leaving will only buy me a few minutes. I need to get back, or he'll come looking. I'm going to get Gideon and Carl, see if they can restrain him or secure him in the room. I just needed to let you know I'm ok first.'

'Shit.'

'Lock your door again. I'll come back when it's safe.'

The Storm

Lizzy turned and fled through the door, not giving Ellie time to react or object. This time, she took the rear stairs. The front ones would involve getting too close to her room and risk her being seen.

CHAPTER 99

Dawn was breaking enough now that Lizzy could see her way rather than have to feel it. Now she knew who and where the threat was, she moved with confident ease and speed through the hotel. She burst out of the doors into the dining room and weaved her way round tables and chairs that seemed intent on being in her way. She knew she had to be quick, had to get Gideon and Carl up there before Luke grew tired and restless and left the confines of her room.

She had hoped that the hour was late enough that Gideon would have taken his post at the reception desk, but as she emerged into the room, her footsteps echoed around the empty space. The large oak desk stood dormant and unused. Where would Gideon sleep? Where would he be staying? All the bedrooms were taken now, unless he was using one of the crime scenes. As far as she knew, Evan was still in his, but Deidre had been taken away. He wouldn't though, would he? He surely wouldn't sleep where a dead body had lain.

Lizzy decided to try the doors behind the desk. The first was the office she had been in before. She gave a courtesy knock but opened it immediately. Or at least tried to. It didn't budge. Locked. The next opened into a small storeroom. One wall was stacked with office supplies and the other with cleaning paraphernalia and handyman tools. The whole room was only as wide as a corridor and she could clearly see no one was in there. She closed the door. The third and final room she hadn't been in before. Again, she knocked and immediately

The Storm

tried the handle. Locked, but this time, her efforts had summoned signs of life from within. A groan and a shuffle. A muffled, 'Hold on.'

The door opened a crack to reveal the head and shoulders of a dishevelled-looking Gideon. His dozy, sleep-heavy look changed to barely concealed anger on seeing it was Lizzy.

'Gideon, I'm sorry to wake you, but I need your help. The killer is in my room, but he won't be for long. We need to trap him in there or secure him somehow.'

Suddenly, he was fully alert, all signs of sleep lost as he took on a sharp focus. 'What? Who?' He threw the door wide.

'Never mind that now. Where's Carl? We may need his help too.'

'Shit.'

Gideon's expression fell to panic as he spun back inside the room, banging the door back on its hinges. Despite the situation, the sight of him scrabbling for his clothes in his vest and boxers amused Lizzy. He looked like a child who'd forgotten his school gym kit.

'The other office,' he called over his shoulder as he hopped and flailed into a trouser leg. 'Knock loud – he's a heavy sleeper. In fact, here.' He rummaged in his pocket and tossed her a set of keys. She caught them and hurried back to the first door.

There were five keys on the set. Naturally, it was the fifth key that opened the door, by which point, Gideon had dressed sufficiently enough to join her.

'Carl. Get dressed, now,' he spoke before Lizzy had a chance to get a word out. 'We've got him and need to contain him.'

Carl took a few seconds to register the words, then sprang from a makeshift bed of linen on the floor. He didn't ask for any further explanation or need one. Lizzy wondered if he was ex-military.

Lizzy turned away to give the man a little privacy to dress as Gideon brushed past her. He disappeared into the storeroom and started ferreting about. As Carl emerged ready for action, so too did Gideon, armed with cable ties and a hammer. Lizzy understood the cable ties, but the hammer? Her heart lurched at the sight of it.

'Just in case,' Gideon said on seeing the horror flash across her face. While she knew of all the terrible things he had done, he was still Luke, the man she had once loved, and the thought of Gideon using that hammer on him made her breath catch and her heart ache.

The three of them bounded up the main staircase. There was no longer any need for stealth or pretence – this was ending now. Lizzy reached her room first but stopped short at the door and let the two men step forwards. It suddenly seemed to occur to them all that they hadn't made a plan.

'Is he armed?' Gideon whispered to Lizzy.

'No. Well, he wasn't. And there's nothing in my room to use as a weapon.'

Gideon looked over to Carl. 'We rush him?'

'We rush him,' Carl agreed, grabbing hold of the door handle and wrenching it open at speed.

Carl barrelled into the room with all his weight behind him, closely followed by Gideon, who was probably aiming to match the gusto and intimidation of Carl but who waved the hammer around in such camp fashion that Lizzy thought even she could easily take it from him.

Nothing they did or had done mattered though. The room was empty.

CHAPTER 100

Ellie watched Lizzy go for the third time and felt utterly helpless. She hated constantly being left on her own. She wasn't a child anymore – she could help, she could surely do something. She stared at the door in frustration as angry tears prickled her eyes. She furiously wiped at them with the back of her hand, refusing to let them drop.

This is the last time, she thought. Next time, she'd go with Lizzy whether she liked it or not.

There was a knock on the door, and relief flooded her. Lizzy. She hurried over to it, forgetting that Lizzy had said she would call out to her. She turned the key and flung open the door. Her eyes widened in horror. A man she didn't recognise but took to be Luke stood before her, making her breath catch in her throat. He was a good few inches taller than her, and though his jumper wasn't snug, she could still see his strength beneath it. He seemed to fill the doorway. She stumbled backwards and let go of the door. Her blood ran cold as he took a step into the room, making her back away further.

'I'm looking for Lizzy,' he said.

No words would come. There was suddenly no air in the room. She shook her head, and he followed her further inside, pushing the door closed behind him.

'She said she was coming to see you. You're Ellie, right?'

She nodded as her legs met with the bed, and she fell back. Where were her weapons? Why hadn't she checked the peephole? Slammed the door when she'd seen it wasn't Lizzy?

Luke continued into the room and stood before her. Ellie couldn't read his expression. Annoyance? Anger? The walls seemed to be closing in, the room getting smaller, squeezing them together. Nowhere to go. Nowhere to hide.

'So, did she come here? I need to find her.'

Not angry, she realised at last. Annoyed. She could work with that. Be helpful – or at least seem helpful. Anything to keep him happy and send him away.

Ellie went to answer. Squeaked, coughed to clear her throat, then tried again. 'She just left.' It came out as a husky whisper, but at least she'd answered. 'She went back to her room.'

Luke looked towards the door, the way he'd come, then back at Ellie. His brow furrowed. 'You're lying. I would have passed her. I've just come from her room.'

He considered Ellie, but she offered nothing. Just shrank into herself as she tried to mentally locate the hair straighteners. Under the bed or on the floor somewhere. They must be. She remembered pushing them out but not picking them up when she'd crawled out. She wouldn't be able to find and grab them quickly enough to be of any use.

'So?' he probed, trying to elicit an answer.

Ellie tried to think back so she could give the right answer. What had Lizzy said? Think, Ellie, think. It needed to match.

'She came by to check on me and left. I don't know where she went. She said she was going to her room. Maybe she went to get a drink?'

Luke's split-second consideration of her answer seemed to take an age, but he finally turned and made for the door. She'd said the right thing. Or had she? She suddenly remembered where Lizzy was actually going and that she had

The Storm

just sent Luke down after her. She had no way to warn her, but it was too late now.

As Luke left the room, Ellie ran to shut her door and turn the lock. Then she scrambled on the floor for the straighteners. Sitting shaking on the bed, she hugged them close to her and wept. What had she done?

CHAPTER 101

'Where is he?' Carl was panting from the adrenaline and effort.

'He was right here. I left him in here. Shit. I took too long.' Lizzy sat down hard on the bed and put her head in her hands.

'I think you need to explain.' Gideon folded his arms and let out a huff. 'Who is this, and what the hell is going on?'

Lizzy looked up at the two men staring down at her. The anger in their faces. She couldn't believe this was happening. She'd let everyone down, put everyone in danger. This was all her fault.

'My boyfriend, Luke,' she said, her voice catching. 'I found him wandering the corridor tonight. He followed me here. Lord knows where he's been sleeping, but he's been watching me apparently. Stalking the corridors at night. It... it has to be him, doesn't it? He's the one who's...' She couldn't bring herself to say the words out loud. Couldn't bring herself to meet their eyes anymore. Her gaze fell to the floor as shame and guilt flooded her body.

'But why? What did he have against any of them? I mean, why would he want to...' Gideon paused, put a hand on his hip and rubbed his temple with the other. It was a fair question. One that was playing on her mind also.

'Maybe they saw him, caught him roaming around or watching and he had to silence them? I don't know. None of this makes any sense.'

The Storm

'The why isn't important right now,' Carl interjected. 'What matters is that we find and stop him. Before anyone else gets hurt.'

Lizzy sighed. 'I don't think he'll hurt me. I'll go and look for him, lead him back up here.'

'Take this.' Gideon offered the hammer.

'Thanks, but I think that might look a bit suspicious, don't you think? I'd better go as I am. No threat.'

'If you're sure. We'll wait here and grab him when you come in,' Carl said. 'If you're not back in twenty minutes, we're coming looking.'

Lizzy nodded, then left the room.

CHAPTER 102

Lizzy had told Luke she was going to Ellie's room, so surely that was where he would've headed. She started out that way. She would need to be quick. More daylight was spilling in, meaning time was moving on. People would be up soon. Whatever game he was playing, she needed this over with before they rose. Before there were any more deaths.

As she passed the rear staircase, she heard the tread of someone descending it. He'd moved on, she surmised, gone looking elsewhere. She turned on her heel and followed the retreating sound.

He was already at the other side of the dining room as she emerged from the bottom door. She debated whether it was best to call out to him or see where he was going and what he was doing. The decision was made for her as the door banged closed behind her. He whipped round at the sound. She faked a smile just as his eyes reached her.

'Lizzy, where were you? Where did you go?'

'To Ellie's, like I said. I came back to the room and you weren't there.'

'Oh really?' He raised an eyebrow and crossed his arms across his chest. 'And how exactly did you pass me in the corridor?'

She had no answer to that. Nothing plausible anyway.

'Come back upstairs,' she coaxed.

He moved closer to her, and her skin prickled. 'What's going on, Lizzy? What is this really about?'

The Storm

'What do you mean?'

He flung his arms out and started gesturing towards her. 'You running away, needing a week to yourself, not committing, never committing. Do you know how hurtful you can be sometimes?' He hugged his arms around himself and looked away as his eyes grew glassy. 'It's subtle, but I see it. The brush-offs, the avoidance, the excuses. I'm not an idiot. It's like you don't even want to be with me anymore.'

'Luke, it's not like that, I just…' Just what? What he was saying was true, wasn't it?

'Why did you need to come here, Lizzy?'

'I just needed some space.'

'From me.'

It wasn't a question. Despite everything that had happened this week, her heart broke for him. Her Luke. Her adoring, devoted Luke. She felt as if she were kicking a puppy. Then images of Deidre, Fiona, and Evan flashed before her eyes, the knowledge of him following and watching her… stalking her. It sickened her.

'Yes, from you.' Her voice grew loud, powered by the rage she felt at what he'd done.

He visibly recoiled, shocked by her admission. As if he hadn't really believed it until she'd voiced it out loud.

'Do you realise how controlling you are? Always right there touching and pawing over me, on the phone calling and texting whenever I go anywhere without you. It's suffocating.'

'Suffocating?' He leaned his head forward as if he hadn't heard her. He genuinely didn't understand. 'It's called love, Lizzy. It's how people show they care about one another.'

'No, it's not. It's too much. You followed me up here, Luke, and watched me. Stalked me. That's not normal.'

'I just needed to know you weren't seeing someone else. I needed to be close to you. I love you so much, Lizzy, and a week is sooo long. Too long for us to be apart.'

'Can't you hear how crazy that sounds?'

'It's not crazy to love another person.'

'What about the other guests?'

'What about them?'

'Deidre, Fiona, and Evan.'

Luke tilted his head. He couldn't grasp the point she was making, the question she was asking.

'Why did they have to die?' she whispered.

'How should I know?' He screwed his face up for a second, then his eyes widened in alarm. 'Wait... you think that I... Jesus, Lizzy, I didn't realise your opinion of me was that low.'

'Did they catch you? Is that it? See you skulking around in the night?'

'I haven't hurt anyone. I wouldn't. Couldn't. Come on, you know me, Lizzy, you know I could never do anything like that.'

'Do I? I never thought you would do any of this, but here we are.'

'Lizzy...' he began, taking a step towards her with outstretched arms. The epitome of no threat. Seeking forgiveness or an embrace. Lizzy instinctively backed away, but he was undeterred. As though if he could just take her in his arms, he could make it all ok.

She turned back to the door, flung it open, and ran through. She had to get as far away from him as possible.

'Lizzy, stop.'

As she started up the stairs, she heard the slap of his feet behind her. From the rhythm of his step, he was coming up fast, and her heart thudded at a pace that seemed to match it. Panting, she risked a backwards glance in time to see him reach out a hand towards her. She couldn't move away fast enough, and he grabbed hold of her leg, holding her tightly, instantly halting her motion and causing her to fall. She flung her hands out in front of her in an attempt to lessen the impact but only partially succeeded. Her left elbow slammed painfully against the steps, which managed to slow her descent but not enough to stop her chin from catching the edge of the steps above. The impact jarred her whole head and smashed her teeth together painfully. Her elbow radiated a deep throb and her chin felt sore and wet. Blood dribbled down her neck. She blinked the world back into focus, momentarily dazed, the fear coursing through her veins snapping her back to the present.

'I said stop.'

With a look of pure hatred, he pulled her roughly so that she bumped down towards him, and a scream lodged in her throat.

CHAPTER 103

Lizzy stared into the face of the man she had once loved, and her blood ran cold. He held her with an iron grip, his face set in a grimace. She kicked back desperately with her free leg, and her foot caught his face. He cried out and brought his hands up to his nose, which was instantly pouring blood. Lizzy took her chance and scrambled up the stairs away from him, arriving at the top on all fours.

Once she reached the landing, she righted herself and surged forwards, knocking straight into a shocked-looking Carl. She had clearly used up her twenty minute allowance.

'Shit. You ok? Where is he? What happened?'

Lizzy could barely catch her breath. 'In the stairwell. I bust his nose.'

Carl shot off down the stairs, followed closely by Gideon, as Lizzy collected herself and waited to see what emerged. She knew what he'd done, and she also knew he probably deserved whatever was coming to him, but she had no desire to watch and see him harmed. She hoped to God neither of them had brought the hammer.

Shouts from all three of them resonated up the stairwell and mingled together in a mash of voices. The sound mixed with the scuffling of shoes and dull thumps of what Lizzy could only guess was a fistfight. She turned away, as if the act of doing so would help to blot out some of the noise. Then the shouting subsided and three figures came slowly into view. A furious Luke flanked by Carl and Gideon.

The Storm

Luke had been 'cuffed' with cable ties that secured his hands behind his back. He also had a cut to the side of his head that hadn't been there when she'd left him atop a battered and puffy face. She guessed he'd needed a little 'persuading' into those cuffs.

'You bastards. Get off me. Lizzy, will you do something?' he shouted.

Lizzy looked on in conflicted horror as they manhandled him down the corridor and pushed him into the storeroom. She ran to catch up and looked on through the open doorway. Carl shoved him roughly to the floor and, producing more ties, secured his bound wrists to one of the shelves.

He looked up at her, his face a bloody and bruised mess, his eyes pitiful.

'All I've ever done is love you.'

Lizzy brought a trembling hand to her mouth. Unable to bear it anymore, she turned away, broke down, and wept.

CHAPTER 104

Ellie listened hard to the shouting down the corridor. Male voices, more than one, and she strained to pick out who they were. She thought one could possibly be Gideon, but she didn't recognise the other – or others – though she supposed one must be Carl. She couldn't quite tell how many she was hearing. Had they caught him? Was this finally over? She longed to go and see. Maybe she could open her door a crack and just have a peek? Several times, she made a move for the door, then stopped herself. What if he hadn't been caught? What if the sounds were another attack?

She moved to the door again. Tried the peephole. As much as she strained, the angle was all wrong. All she could see was the wall opposite. Then there was blackness as someone moved across in front of it. She jumped back as if scolded, heart pounding, debating whether to hide, what to do. Someone knocked. She stood perfectly still and held her breath.

'Ellie? It's dad.'

She breathed out and sent a silent prayer. Oh, thank the Lord. She rushed forwards and opened the door, falling into his arms.

'Hey.' He shushed. 'It's ok, you ok?'

'Poppy's gone missing, and Lizzy's found the killer, and, Dad, I'm so scared.' She hugged tighter, pulling him as close as possible and burying herself in his safety. 'He was in my room.'

The Storm

'What?' He suddenly moved them back into her room, where he could see properly, and held her away at arm's length. He cast his eyes all over her, looking for damage.

'I'm fine, Dad. He didn't hurt me. He just wanted to know where Lizzy was.'

'Lizzy? Why? Who is he?'

'Her boyfriend. Lizzy's gone to get Gideon and Carl, and they're going to trap him in her room. I think that's what all the noise is about.'

He let go of her, dropping his arms suddenly, his face flushing. 'I knew that bitch was trouble.'

'Dad.'

'Wait here.'

Paul stormed off down the corridor towards the ruckus. As he rounded the corner, he caught sight of Lizzy leaning against the wall by the storeroom, sobbing into her hands. 'You. You brought this here? You put us all in danger. My wife is dead because of you.'

Ellie appeared just after him, rushing towards them both. She grabbed at his arm, tried to pull him away. 'It's not her fault, Dad; she didn't do anything.'

Jenny and Alex had come out to see what all the fuss was about and stood watching the show. Mr Franks, in the corridor that ran in the opposite direction, lurked in the background, taking it all in from a distance.

Lizzy removed her hands from her tear-streaked face and looked frantically around at all the eyes staring her way. She pushed through the crowd and ran back towards her room, tears streaming down her face.

'Happy now?' Ellie shouted at her dad before turning and flouncing back to her room. She slammed the door as hard as she could.

She'd waited all damn night to be free and get out of this room and now she found herself stuck back inside it. She let out a frustrated growl and threw herself on the bed. She punched the pillow a few times for good measure, then stared up at the ceiling. How was this her life? How had everything gone to shit so quickly?

CHAPTER 105

He was right. Luke was her boyfriend, she had led him up here, and so those poor people were dead because of her. She leaned back against her closed door and shut her eyes, but all she could see was Luke's pitiful face staring back at her, begging, pleading. She opened them again quickly.

How could he have done this? How horrible had she been to him to make him snap so badly?

She went to her bed and lay down. For the first time since primary school assemblies, she prayed. She apologised for her sins and asked God for forgiveness. She didn't have anything left.

Lizzy sat hugging her knees to her chest on the chair in the bay window. Her whole body ached with tiredness and her head pounded with exhaustion. She stared out into the distance. Morning had fully broken, but no relief had come with it. It was far from the refuge she had dreamed it to be last night. She knew she would have to face everyone again at some point, but she delayed going downstairs. Would there even be a breakfast today? Carl had been pretty busy and she wasn't sure if he'd actually left Luke yet.

Would they leave Luke alone? He was secured, but it was possible they would want someone to stand guard until the police could come. She wondered when that would be. Now that word hadn't got out, they were back to waiting on the road being cleared. The phone lines wouldn't be coming back, not without an engineer.

The only thing she knew was she needed to see Luke. She needed to understand why and how this had happened. Once he had been arrested, she wouldn't be allowed to see him. And once convicted, she wouldn't be visiting him in prison. She was very sure of that.

Gathering all her courage, she forced herself to stand. Her body was heavy with tiredness and reluctance. Her elbow had settled into a dull ache, but her chin was shooting pain up through her skull. She welcomed it. It felt like penance. It was the least that she deserved.

Lizzy stepped out of her room and rounded the corner. The storeroom was dead ahead, the door half-closed. Voices were coming from within, but she wasn't sure who was in there with him. Should she knock or come back later? She really didn't want to face anyone again just yet.

She hesitated by the door for a while, hoping they would finish and go away, if they were going to go away, but the mumbling continued. Lizzy turned back to her room, decision made – she'd wait a while. It wasn't as though he was going anywhere. Not as though any of them were. No time soon at least. She cursed him again and the situation they were in. The road was still blocked, no one knew they were in trouble, no cavalry was coming. Today was supposed to be their salvation; instead, it felt as if her life had ended.

As she slipped the key back into her lock, there came an almighty crash followed by stampeding feet. Lizzy turned and darted back towards the storeroom. The door was flung open and the remnants of one of the shelving units lay scattered on the floor amid the towels and bedding it had been holding. She didn't need to enter the room to know he had escaped, but she did so anyway, just to make sure. No sign of him or the person he had been talking to.

The main staircase lay barely feet away and so made the obvious choice of exit. Lizzy darted down them as fast as

The Storm

she could, nearly tripping several times in her haste. At the bottom, reception was empty, the front door open. She looked around as Gideon appeared from the dining room, peering round the door frame towards the direction of the noise.

'Did you see him? Where did he go?' she panted.

'See who?'

'He's gone. Luke's gone. Who was with him?'

'Shit.'

Gideon's head disappeared back into the dining room momentarily, and he called out to Carl. The response was almost instant, as seconds later, the two men dashed into reception, where she waited. It hadn't been Carl with Luke, then. She was sure she'd heard another male voice.

'What happened?' Carl barked.

'I don't know. I heard a crash, and when I got to the storeroom, he'd gone. I assume he came this way – it's the closest exit.'

'Right, we need to find him quickly. Gideon, warn the others.'

Gideon went back into the dining room to tell the guests seated there to return to their rooms and lock their doors. By the time he returned, Carl had collected a number of various tools and blunt objects to use as possible weapons. He lay the heavier ones on the desk and held some hand tools out to Lizzy. She shook her head. She didn't want one. Didn't think she could use it on him.

Carl just shrugged. 'Your funeral.'

Gideon looked them over and took a fire axe. 'Right, there's three of us. I suggest we split up to cover more area and stop him roaming freely.'

A creak came from behind, and all three of them whipped round to face the stairs. Paul and Mr Franks, partway down, slowed their descent as they saw the armed mob. Lizzy closed her eyes and breathed out a sigh. They turned back as the newcomers joined them, both keen to help in any way that they could. Paul eagerly took a weapon from Carl, selecting a sledgehammer. Mr Franks was less forthcoming. He looked over the weapons, then up at Carl, who handed him a large knife. The sight of them all chilled Lizzy to the bone. This was not going to end well.

CHAPTER 106

The five of them set off in different directions, Carl and Gideon checking and securing the outbuildings and hotel, Paul the land to the front and the driveway, and Mr Franks the rear garden and footpaths. Lizzy had been given the wooded area in the back, then she was to help Mr Franks with the footpaths. She hoped she would find Luke first. She didn't imagine any of the others would hesitate or ask questions before swinging their weapons. Whatever he had done, she still couldn't quite let go of who she'd known before. He deserved to be punished severely for what he had done, but she didn't want to see him hurt. She also didn't want any of the others on the receiving end of a prison sentence. She felt responsible enough without adding to it.

Fern leaves slapped her legs and twigs cracked underfoot as she waded through the undergrowth. Everything creaked and groaned in the woods. Her vision darted in every direction as she tried to place each sound, which instantly disorientated her. Birds flittered across her view and squirrels scurried in the undergrowth, making her jump at every step. She was practically scared of her own shadow. She forced herself to stop and take a deep breath, to calm herself before moving on any further. She continued then, trying to be methodical in her search, mentally sectioning and searching the space before her. It wasn't a huge area, but it was densely populated with growth and there were many places to hide. The trees were well-established with thick trunks and the ground was littered with shrubs and dead wood. She supposed that would work in her favour too should she need it. She hoped she didn't.

She was nearing the patch where she and Ellie had stopped the day before when she felt eyes upon her, and she slowed to a stop. The hairs on the back of her neck tingled and stood to attention as a shiver passed down her spine. She started to move again more cautiously now, careful of where she placed her feet, being aware of the noise she was making and alert for any other sounds. The woods continued to creak around her, and her eyes darted left and right as she tried to get a glimpse or a sense of where he was. She felt rather than saw him. A telepathic link; a sixth sense. He was coming up behind her, slow but steady. She stopped walking.

'I know you're there. I'm alone and I'm not armed. I don't want to hurt you, Luke. Can we just talk?'

She was met with silence. Then the snapping of twigs underfoot as he came forwards and stepped out of hiding. Lizzy turned to face him. He looked sorrowful and scared. He remained where he was, close but not in her personal space. She felt wary in his presence but not afraid. He couldn't reach her from where he stood, not without moving.

'How did it come to this?' she asked. 'What happened?'

Luke looked in her direction but not at her. He looked so much smaller than he had last night; his shoulders rounded and his face drooped below hollow eyes. She wished so much that she could go back in time, to have voiced her concerns, told him how she felt. She tried to make eye contact, but he looked down.

'Luke, I'm so sorry. I should have said something sooner. It wasn't fair of me to carry on regardless and not let you know I was unhappy. I did try a few times but... I never... well, it always...'

'I know. I knew,' he said, his voice catching. 'I've known for a while you aren't happy, but my way of fixing that was to show you how much I love you. I guess my

The Storm

overcompensating was exactly what was pushing you away. I should have let you finish what you had to say.'

He looked up at her then, and she saw a flicker of the man she'd once known.

'Me coming up here, it was all about making sure you aren't having an affair. I'd convinced myself that someone else was involved – they had to be. And that well, if they weren't, then I could fix it. If it really was just you and me, then I still had a chance.'

'It was always only ever you and me. I would never do that to you, Luke, to anyone. But I need to know, and please be honest with me. Those other people, what happened?'

'Those... the dead people, you mean? I told you before, that was nothing to do with me, Lizzy, I swear.'

His eyes looked deep into hers as if he were pleading with her soul, begging to be believed. 'I never hurt anyone, Lizzy. I drove up here, left the car up the drive where it wouldn't be seen, and stayed in one of the outbuildings over there. I'd watch through the windows where I could and sneak inside at night or when you were out. Sometimes go through your room. Sometimes just lie on the bed to feel close to you. And I know, I'm not proud, alright? I can see how it looks, but I swear, Lizzy, I did not hurt anyone.'

She wanted to believe him, she really did, but all that skulking around... And she had seen him last night with a knife, hadn't she? She thought back over all the weird things that had happened. It was creepy and perverse. He was creepy and perverse.

Luke took a step towards her, and she instinctively stepped back. Her foot landed in a rabbit hole and went from beneath her. She fell backwards, landing on her backside, her hands shooting out behind her and keeping her upright. Pain shot from her injured elbow up her arm, reminding her of the altercation on the stairs. Her gut screamed at her not to trust him. He'd hurt her once, which meant he could do it again.

Luke offered a hand to help her up as a figure emerged from the trees to the left. Mr Franks strode through the short space towards them, his appearance halting Luke in his efforts. He'd appeared out of nowhere and was upon them in moments.

Luke stopped and stood straight, panic flashing in his eyes. 'Lizzy, run.'

Lizzy started to get to her feet, her eyes flicking between the two men in front of her. The other voice in the storeroom – had it been Mr Franks? What had gone on in there? What had he said?

He stood behind Luke with a sneer on his face. 'Don't worry, you're safe now, girl.'

Lizzy looked on bewildered as Mr Franks grabbed hold of Luke's hair and wrenched his head back.

She took a step towards him with an outstretched hand. 'No.'

Panic flared in Luke's eyes, and his arms reached up and backwards, trying impotently to reach Mr Franks. Without hesitation, Mr Franks shot his arm out, still gripping the knife, and drew it back across Luke's throat.

Lizzy stumbled to a halt as an arch of blood spurted from the slash and hit her in the face. Her heart was pumping, but she couldn't breathe. Couldn't move. She watched in horror as Mr Franks let go, discarding Luke. He fell to the ground, grabbing at the gash and gasping.

'No,' Lizzy screamed, dropping to a kneel in front of him. She pressed his hands harder against the wound with her own shaking ones, trying to stop the flow as the blood poured between their fingers.

'You're ok, you're going to be ok,' she comforted Luke as her tears fell, knowing deep down that he wasn't. 'I'm sorry, I'm so sorry,' she whispered.

He held her gaze, his face already deathly white yet somehow growing paler. There were gurgling sounds and

The Storm

then his eyes fell away, no longer seeing, and there was nothing. No noise. No movement. Nothing.

Lizzy gently closed his eyes. Getting unsteadily to her feet, she looked to Mr Franks. He stood there, panting slightly, looking down at his handiwork. Then he looked at Lizzy and smiled, and her world stopped spinning.

'It's better this way,' he said calmly. 'Everyone already thinks it was him. Case closed really. I did them a favour.' He let out a short laugh. 'Ha, I might even become a hero. How about that?'

'You?' Her voice shook. 'But... why?'

'I've seen you looking at me. The way you all look at me. With pity and disgust. But I'm a very important businessman. Well, I was until that bitch took it away from me.' He spat the word 'bitch' out as if it were a bad taste. 'I recognised her as soon as she arrived. She didn't know me, of course, the suits don't mix with us in sales. But it was her, Fiona, head of HR, the one who cost me my job.' His words dripped with hatred and anger.

Every hair on her body stood on edge and icy tendrils trickled down her spine. She was frozen to the spot. She daren't speak or interrupt him, daren't make a move though she knew she needed to. She had to get away, get help, get word to the others. All this time and it was him.

'Twenty-five years I've given that company. Twenty-five sodding years of my life, and for what? To be kicked to the side over one minor incident. Not only my job she took either, was it? Took my wife as well, my Kathy. She didn't want to know as soon as the money dried up, did she? When she heard their lies.' His jowls wobbled under the ferocity in which he spoke. 'Sexual harassment, my arse. It was just a bit of fun. Office hijinks. Everyone does it, but it doesn't mean anything, does it?

'And then Fiona stepped in, put her beak in where it wasn't wanted, and bam. Fucking bitch. It doesn't matter that it's lies when it's written in a report. Kathy believed every word. That bitch Fiona got what was coming to her.' He smiled then. 'I enjoyed that one. Took great pleasure in squeezing the life out of her, of holding her under until she slipped away. Can't ruin anyone else's life now, can she?'

She couldn't believe what she was hearing. A life lost over some stupid report. 'And what about Deidre and Evan? They can't have been part of that.'

His head shot up at her words, as though he'd forgotten she was there. 'Deidre was just a pain in the arse. I came here to get my life together, to write up my report and resignation for the investigation and source a new job. If I could do that, Kathy would come back to me, wouldn't she? Once I had my life together again, a life worth something. You saw what Deidre did to my papers. She did that on purpose. Ruined everything all over again.'

'And Evan?'

'Yeah, I felt a bit bad about him.' Mr Franks looked to the ground as he thought about it. 'The lad was alright really. Wet behind the ears and in need of a bit of a slap, but he'd have turned out ok in the end.'

'So, why did you kill him?'

'I heard you and him talking. He'd seen me, hadn't he? At night in the corridor.'

Lizzy thought back over their conversations, puzzled. Evan hadn't seen him. No one had seen him. And then it dawned on her. What Mr Franks had actually seen and what it must have looked and sounded like.

'No, no, he didn't; you have it all wrong. I was telling him that Ellie had seen someone.' A lump formed in her throat. She felt sick. If she hadn't told him or had just told him somewhere else, somewhere more private, another time even. That conversation had cost Evan his life. He had died for nothing. Her heart ached with such pain. 'She didn't even know it was you. It was too dark. She only saw a shape.'

For a moment, he looked genuinely remorseful. And then it was gone.

The Storm

'Well, now, that is a shame.' He gestured to Luke. 'And, well, this one, you know. Luke, was it? He just fell into my lap, really. I mean, what are the fucking chances? Perfect scapegoat if ever I needed one. Tied up nicely, really. All except for one last loose end.'

He looked at Lizzy, and her insides liquified. 'Sorry. You're actually pretty decent, but, well, you understand, right?'

The sheer terror she was feeling cut to her soul. She started trying to back away but found that her muscles wouldn't obey. Her movements came out jerky and stilted. She needed to look where she was going, but she also couldn't take her eyes off him. This hulk of a man held a knife and intended to use it on her.

Her eyes flicked left and right as she looked for an escape, for the best route that would take her away the quickest. She'd left it too late though. Her backing away suddenly had her up against a tree. And Mr Franks was in front of her.

'I'll take no pleasure from this,' he said as he pinned her back to the tree and readied the knife.

CHAPTER 107

Ellie strained to see out of the window. Most of her view was taken up with the storeroom wall opposite, with a few trees and grass off to the side of the hotel. Typical that she'd get the shitty room.

She'd been standing here for the past half an hour now, ever since her dad had ensured she was securely locked in her room. She knew what they were doing – they were out there searching for him. She tried again to see further past the wall by hitching herself up and onto the windowsill; however, from whatever position she craned her neck, she could never get the angle quite right. No one passed her little slice of the outside world and she heard nothing.

She hopped back down and sat on the edge of the bed, hugging her knees to her body. She hoped they got him. He needed to pay for what he'd done to her mum, and to Evan.

Knock, knock, knock.

She dropped her knees, spinning round on the covers to stare at the door.

Knock, knock, knock.

She slowly made her way over and looked through the peephole. Gideon was standing on the other side.

'Yes?'

'It's me, Gideon. I just wanted to let you know that the hotel is safe if you wanted to come out. The rooms have been checked and the hotel is locked. If you want some company, we'll all be in the lounge.'

The Storm

'Oh... erm... thank you.'

She put her head to the door and heard his footsteps retreating down the corridor. She desperately wanted to be out of this room, but part of her wondered if it was a trick. What if it wasn't Luke? What if it had been Gideon all along? She'd spent the whole night hiding and worrying, and she was exhausted. She could no longer tell if it was her overactive imagination stopping her or a gut feeling she should listen to.

Ellie slowly unlocked and opened the door. Standing on the threshold, keeping one hand firmly on the door, she looked down the empty corridor. With a thudding heart, she moved further out, letting the door close behind her yet still holding the handle.

Everything's fine. This is fine.

Finally, she let go and made her way slowly down the main stairs, to the lounge.

Everyone was huddled in a circle by the fire with a tea tray between them. Gideon and Carl were in armchairs and Jenny and Alex on a sofa.

'Every room has been checked and the doors are locked,' Gideon reassured her.

She smiled and sat on a chair by Jenny. Jenny poured her some tea.

Gideon lifted his own and sipped. 'I doubt that they'll find him, to be honest. We really are quite remote and the countryside that surrounds us is vast. At least we're safe though.'

No one really knew what to add to that, and an awkward silence ensued. Ellie sipped at her tea for something to do. To keep busy. Maybe it had been a mistake coming down after all.

Bang, bang, bang.

Tea slopped over her cup and Jenny knocked hers to the floor as they all jumped at the sudden knocking at the front door. Everyone looked at one another. Then Gideon and Carl rose and left the room. Jenny scooted closer to Alex and gripped his arm. Ellie felt as though she couldn't breathe. She shouldn't have come down. She should have stayed in her room, locked away, safe. She turned so that she faced the doorway and braced herself, ready to run. Footsteps approaching on the wooden flooring. No shouts. No scuffle. Calm and steady. And then they were back.

'Dad.'

Ellie leapt up to greet him, and he enveloped her in a hug.

'I went as far as I could. No sign, but then I didn't cross the river. He could have done if he was determined enough, but I wasn't going to risk it. There's a tree down across the road and it's pretty flooded, so if he did cross, he's still on foot. He'll not have gotten far if he did go that way, but it is possible for him to have gone up towards the road.'

'Thanks, Paul,' Gideon said.

'No worries.' Paul released Ellie, and they sat back with the others. 'Nothing from the others yet? They aren't back, then? Maybe they're having more luck.'

'Maybe. It's a bigger area to cover though. They could be a while.'

'Should we help?'

'We don't know where they've covered. I say we give them an hour and then head out. We've checked and locked the hotel. We're safe here.'

'Safe' didn't seem the right word to Ellie right now. She would never feel safe here. She wasn't sure that she could feel safe anywhere other than home again.

CHAPTER 108

The sun glinted off the blade as Mr Franks raised it across Lizzy's body, ready to bring it across her neck like he had with Luke. He'd taken a harmless old woman's life, he'd taken a wife and mother's life, and now he'd taken Luke's life. Her rage bubbled into the hatred she felt for this man and what he had done. No, she wouldn't let him hurt her too. She brought a knee up into his groin as hard as she could.

Mr Franks dropped the knife as he doubled over in pain, sucking in great lungfuls of air, his eyes streaming. Lizzy darted to the left towards the hotel, but despite his pain, he managed to throw an arm out and catch her foot. Her body slammed onto the ground, knocking all the breath from her. She rolled onto her side, desperate to pull some air into her lungs and to keep Mr Franks in her sights. He was crouched, breathing deep but shakily, hands clasped desperately between his legs. Despite his obvious discomfort, he looked over at her and smiled, confident she wouldn't be going anywhere for a while.

Her chest burned with the effort of breathing, but there was no time to let it pass – she'd got him good, but she had no idea how long a kick to the balls could keep a man down. Especially a man as desperate as he was.

She started inching her way forwards, grabbing handfuls of roots to heave herself across the ground. The pain was slowly easing, her breathing getting deeper, but it was still taking too long. She glanced back and saw Mr Franks straighten to his full height, and panic shot through her like a lightning bolt. She whipped her head back and began crawling faster, grabbing for anything to help pull her along the ground and away from him. She reached out a hand again as a shadow fell across her face. He stood in front of her, grinning. His hands were thankfully empty.

Using what little burst of energy she had, she turned to the side and scrabbled away from him and towards the knife. The woodland floor was littered with newly fallen leaves and debris. She dug away at them with her hands, frantically raking through until she hit earth. He'd only dropped it, so it couldn't have fallen far from the tree.

Though her limbs were quick, Mr Franks was quicker, and he was soon on top of her. She yelped as he grabbed her by the shoulders and heaved her out of the way. She quelled the panic that threatened to rise within her and kept hold of her rage. He was strong but clearly not as strong as he used to be or imagined he still was, and for all his efforts, he only succeeded in shoving her off course. She was quickly up on all fours again.

Undeterred, Lizzy scrabbled back towards the tree, sifting once again through the woodland debris. Mr Franks grunted in angry frustration, and as she heard him lumber closer, she spun onto her back and kicked out. There was no aim apart from his general direction. Any hit would be a win. Her foot caught his shin.

'Argh.'

He caught himself quickly, leaving the shout brief and quite stunted. Lizzy didn't think it would be enough to summon anyone, not from this distance. Her lungs still ached too much for her to spend any energy shouting or screaming just yet; she still needed to conserve what little energy she had if she wanted to get through this.

'You little bitch,' he spat.

He tried to grab her again, but Lizzy stayed on her back, kicking wildly. It worked in that he couldn't get near to

The Storm

grab her, but her legs soon grew slow and heavy, losing any impact they would once have had.

Mr Franks moved out of striking distance from her feet towards her head, but then past her altogether. He left her where she lay, and with a speed at odds with his size, he was down on his knees and digging around in the leaves.

The knife.

No. She had to find it before he did.

Lizzy flipped herself over. She surged forwards and started digging around too.

Mr Franks looked up at her approach, flared his nostrils, and dived over, knocking her onto her back. He straddled her and brought his hands round her throat. He was a big man, and heavy. His weight pinned her fast and crushed down on the small frame of her body. It felt as though just the weight of him was crushing her ribs and pushing all the breath out of her.

'Don't you worry about the knife – I don't need it,' he sneered, pressing harder.

Despite her desperate attempts to breathe, there was no air coming in or out of her lungs. Lizzy grabbed hold of his hands and tried to pry him off. They were too fat, too strong. She dug her nails in and tried to work her fingers under his to ease the pressure on her throat and allow some air to pass. But his grip was vice-like. She kicked, but her legs met with nothing but air. Her eyes bulged, her vision fast turning red and spotty, the edges blackening and closing in. She dropped her hands to the ground at her sides and searched desperately for anything she could use as a weapon, clawing at the earth. A rock, a stick. Anything. Her hands found nothing but dirt and leaves. And then everything went black.

CHAPTER 109

'It's been too long; we need to go out and look for them.' Ellie stood in front of the circle, hands on her hips. She'd spent what felt like ages moving around the windows in the room in turn, searching for any signs of those yet to return.

The others looked at her from their places around the fire, where they'd stayed seated the entire time with dull expressions, seemingly numb to the situation happening around them. Had they all forgotten there was a murderer out there?

'Just a little longer,' her dad urged. He reached out a hand to Ellie, but she moved away. 'We don't want to put anyone else in danger by charging out there into the unknown.'

'They're already in danger, Dad. Lizzy is out there.' Unease gnawed at her insides that they hadn't heard from her. She'd been out there too long.

Paul gave a small 'humph' and looked away. As if she was of no concern, as if she deserved whatever happened out there. Anger grew hot under Ellie's skin.

She charged towards the door. 'Fine. I'll go myself, then.'

'Ellie, no.' Paul was on his feet, following.

'We'll all go,' Carl said as he and Gideon rose too.

Jenny turned to Alex and grabbed him tightly, her face pinched and on the verge of tears. 'Alex?' she wailed.

The Storm

Her dad turned back to look, so Ellie took the opportunity. She slipped into the dining room, letting herself out the back door, into the grounds. She knew they'd catch her up, but she didn't want them slowing her down or trying to stop her. She thought she'd heard someone mention that Lizzy had gone into the woods, and so she scooted to the outbuildings and ran off to start there.

Once she became enclosed in the trees, her gusto deserted her. Her legs felt like jelly as she clumsily stomped through the undergrowth and her breathing became short and shallow. She forced herself to close her eyes for a moment and inhale deeply. Then she continued.

She'd only gone a few more feet when she heard rustling ahead of her, and she stopped to listen. Animal or person?

'Li—' What if it wasn't her? What if it was him – Luke?

She continued walking, slower now so as not to make any noise, towards the sound. As she grew nearer, she glimpsed someone between the trees. A figure in dark clothing knelt on the ground. She took a sharp intake of breath and stepped back behind a tree. Her heart stumbled over its own rhythm as it thumped in her chest. She closed her eyes and prayed that he hadn't seen her. It didn't appear to be Lizzy, but they also looked too big to be Luke from what she remembered of him.

Ellie gripped the damp bark with her fingers, opened her eyes, and risked a peek. She squinted with a furrowed brow, not understanding. It looked like Mr Franks, but what… and then her stomach dropped as she realised what she was seeing. Lizzy on the ground beneath him, fighting for her life, growing limp.

There was no time to run for help; it was all up to her.

Ellie looked around for anything she could use as a weapon. She moved from tree to tree, keeping hidden, until she found a fallen branch. She wasn't sure how much damage it would do, but it was big enough to have weight while small enough to swing. Steeling herself for what was to come, she felt adrenaline flush out all her fear, and hefting it above her head, she came at him from behind.

CHAPTER 110

There was an almighty crack-like gunshot, and the pressure on Lizzy's throat immediately released. Mr Franks slumped on top of her. She felt weak and dizzy as she pushed at his incredibly heavy weight in an attempt to get him off. His sour breath continued to flow just inches from her face. Whatever had happened just now hadn't killed him. The foul stench gave her the extra determination and power for one last huge push, and she managed to roll him off with a thump.

Lizzy scooted her legs out from underneath him and scrabbled into a sitting position, coughing and gasping and rubbing her sore throat. Ellie stood at her feet, holding a large piece of wood.

'El...' she tried, but all that emitted was a weak croak.

'Shit.' The wood dropped from Ellie's shaking hands. She stared at Mr Franks, her eyes unblinking, trying to process what she had just done. Finally, she tore her gaze away and locked eyes with Lizzy.

Lizzy tried to speak again, but her throat was too painful and wouldn't obey her.

Ellie wavered, hopping from one foot to the other in apparent deliberation of whether to approach or not. Then she turned her head back towards the hotel and screamed. 'Help. Over here. We need help.'

She turned back to Lizzy and Mr Franks as approaching footsteps grew louder. Suddenly, everyone was in the woods, surrounding them.

Lizzy's ears buzzed with sounds that blurred together as words and explanations were exchanged. She watched as Gideon and Carl's expressions changed from confusion to anger, and they were on Mr Franks like a shot, binding him with cable ties and a coil of rope they'd got from who knows where while he remained unconscious. Alex stood guard with a wrench, and Paul and Ellie embraced in the tightest hug Lizzy thought was possible.

Once they were satisfied Mr Franks wasn't going anywhere, Gideon turned to Lizzy. He was speaking to her, but his words were getting lost in an underwater world. He kept repeating himself, his words getting clearer each time until they finally broke the surface.

'Lizzy, can you hear me? Are you ok?'

She croaked, then nodded instead. He helped her up and guided her back to the hotel. The others followed, while Carl and Paul stayed behind with Mr Franks.

Back in the hotel, Gideon settled Lizzy by the fire in the lounge, covered her with a blanket, and poured her a sweet tea. She sat shaking, the shock rippling through her body. Ellie sat pale-faced on the sofa opposite, still in her father's embrace. He didn't seem to be able to let go of her.

'Did I kill him? He's dead, isn't he? What have I done?' Ellie's eyes brimmed with tears that fell silently onto a near expressionless face.

'I bloody well hope so,' Paul said, his words laced with his fury. 'He deserves to die for what he's done, so don't you ever feel bad, Ellie, ever. You did your mother proud. Though, Christ, why you had to go out there alone. If anything had happened to you too...' The last words choked in his throat, and he looked away.

'He was alive when we left,' Gideon reassured her.

'So what do we do now?' Alex asked.

'Well, for a start, I'd better go and give them a hand. Make sure they're ok out there,' Gideon said, rising to return to the woods. As he did so, the room lit in a blue pulsing hue.

The Storm

Everyone looked to the window in shock to see a police defender bouncing down the drive towards them. It pulled up hastily on the drive, and two officers got out. They were in the hotel before Gideon had even reached the lounge door.

There were a lot of hushed tones talking out in reception and looking over in Lizzy and Ellie's direction, then one of the officers got on the radio and walked from the room. He looked the younger of the two. All fresh-faced and eager to please. The other more senior-looking officer stayed. He didn't approach the group. Just stood watching, guarding. Gideon came back into the room and sat down.

Before long, the driveway was a hive of activity. Another two police defenders arrived with more heavy-duty-looking officers pouring out of them. They ran off in the direction of the woods to later return dragging a now conscious and furious Mr Franks with them. His face was beetroot and his mouth was working, though it was hard to tell if any words were actually coming out or if it was all just noise. He was helped into one of the vehicles and driven off.

There was suddenly a female officer at Lizzy's side. Lizzy could see her mouth moving, but there was just a hum of noise waving in and out, buzzing around her. The officer helped her to her feet and walked her out on wobbly legs. The pulsing blue was disorientating, and Lizzy wasn't sure where she was or where she was going. Still, the officer spoke; still, she heard nothing. Then she was in one of the defenders, heading up the driveway. Had she been arrested? She looked to her wrists, but there were no cuffs. She turned to her right and noticed that she was in the front seat, next to the officer. Not arrested, then.

She stared out of the window ahead of her as they bounced up the track and came to the point where she'd had to stop not all that long ago. The tree that had lain across the bridge was no longer there, dragged clear of the road. It now lay to the side, still trussed up to the vehicle that had removed it. A man in a high-vis jacket stood untying it.

Ahead of her, without the damming effect of the tree, the flood waters had receded. It revealed even more of the bridge and just how damaged it was, the sides completely taken out in a pile of rubble, half of it caved in completely.

The defender slowed and edged to the side, passing through the water. Despite the lower level of the river, water rose alarmingly high up the sides of the vehicle, and Lizzy felt herself instinctively raising her feet, expecting the footwell to begin filling. It didn't. They crossed safely and pulled alongside a waiting ambulance.

As Lizzy was transferred from one vehicle to the other, she saw Luke's car up ahead, parked in a passing bay. Tears prickled her eyes. He'd been obsessive, yes, but not a killer. He'd only really hurt her by accident, it turned out. She hoped he'd known she had loved him. She hoped he'd known at the end how sorry she was.

CHAPTER 111

'You were so brave, Poppy.' Lizzy held a limp hand that was still icy to the touch, attached to a pale, gaunt figure that barely raised the blankets covering her. 'Stupid but incredibly brave.'

Poppy gave a weak smile as she shuffled slightly in the hospital bed. At least her lips had lost their blue tinge now. 'I just wanted to go home.'

Her eyes were heavy and her words came out slow and deliberate, as if just the effort of talking exhausted her further.

'Thank you.' Lizzy gave her hand a small squeeze. 'If you hadn't left… if the workmen hadn't found you… ' Her voice caught, and she looked away, blinking several times to stop the tears from falling.

A trolley squeaked out in the corridor, and they both looked up to watch it pass. Lizzy tensed and felt the blood drain from her as she watched the figure upon it pass. Mr Franks, flanked by a uniformed officer and handcuffed to the bed, was wheeled by the open doorway. He didn't look in as he passed but stared resolutely at the ceiling. She swallowed dryly. It exacerbated the soreness in her damaged throat. It would be sore for a while, but she had been incredibly lucky to walk away with only bruises. She brushed away a tear and swallowed again, thinking of those who hadn't been so lucky.

She turned back to Poppy. 'I'm going to go now, let you get some sleep.'

Her eyelids were already closed. Lizzy stood and picked up her discharge papers, giving one last look down at the girl she owed so much to. The girl who, despite the sheer terror she had been feeling, had made it out to the road, alone and in darkness, and alerted the outside world to their plight.

CHAPTER 112

One week later

The flat felt incredibly empty without Luke in it. Reminders of him and them had been dotted all around – photos of holidays and nights out framed and displayed, notes written and left to each other stuck to the fridge, even the simple sight of their two toothbrushes side by side in the mug on the bathroom sink. She couldn't bear to look at them. To be reminded of what they'd been and what they had become. Or maybe it was what they hadn't become. She felt such guilt over his death. She was the reason he'd been up there. She was the reason he was dead. It ate her up inside.

The police were yet to release his body. His funeral lay heavy on her mind, and she dreaded it and the thought of seeing his family. It churned her stomach. So far, she had managed to put them off visiting, claiming she needed time to heal and recover. How would she ever be able to talk to his mother? To look either of his parents in the face? What would she say? She'd tried putting her own parents off, but they had rushed round regardless, bringing soup and casseroles and smothering her in hugs. They had asked but not pried when she'd said she wasn't ready to talk about it, then held her in comforting silence as she had wept.

Lizzy bent down under the sink and grabbed another bin bag from the roll. She moved through to the bedroom and opened the wardrobe they'd shared. The last of his things in the flat. A lump formed in her throat. She wasn't sure if what she was doing was healthy or not, stripping him from her life, but she knew it caused her further pain to keep seeing his things. She sighed heavily, looking at the hanging clothes he would never again wear. She started pulling them out and laying them on the bed.

Ping.

After fishing her phone out of her pocket, she smiled when she saw it was a message from Ellie. They had exchanged a few messages since leaving the hotel, and Ellie seemed to be doing surprisingly well. Lizzy clicked on it, and a photo of packing boxes filled her screen. An 'Almost time!' GIF flashed over the top of it. She beamed. So, she was going through with it, then; she was still going to uni.

```
Lizzy: Yay! I'm so excited for you - let
me know when you're settled, and I'll
come and visit.
Ellie: Defo! I can't wait!
Lizzy: Proud of you xx
```

Lizzy felt such happiness for her. Paul had tried to get her to defer for a year, but Ellie had held strong. She refused to let the events at Briar's Crag stand in her way, arguing that her mum would not have wanted her to miss her place. There was still a week left to go, and Lizzy hoped she really was as ready as she thought she was and claimed to be, although surrounding herself with new people and immersing herself in her studies could be just what she needed. It was probably harder being at home.

She sat down on the bed and looked around. The flat was hers again. Back to how it had been before Luke had

The Storm

moved in. Once she'd dealt with his clothes, all signs of him would be eradicated. She looked down, realising she'd picked up and was clutching an old jumper of his, and his last moments flashed through her mind. She screwed her eyes shut against the memory, trying to blot out the image as the nausea rose and her pulse quickened. The anguish in his eyes, the pain, and then nothing. Mr Franks' sneer, the malevolence. She breathed through it, slow and steady.

The police had kept her updated on the case against Mr Franks. He had been formally charged and was currently awaiting court. He had been caught trying to feel up one of the interns at work. He'd been immediately suspended, and Fiona, head of HR at his company, had launched an internal inquiry. In his desperation to avoid exposure and save his marriage, he had aimed to stop her and resign before they could start digging even further.

The events at Briar's Crag had made them look harder. So far, they had already found five more historic victims, all interns abused by his position of power. With three charges of murder, the attempted murder of Lizzy, and the six sexual assault charges, he was going to go to prison for a very long time. Presumably life.

Lizzy rocked gently back and forth, not even aware she was doing it, as she opened her eyes again. How quickly life had changed. How quickly it had been extinguished. A silent tear slipped down her face. Maybe she should take a leaf from Ellie's book and have a fresh start.

She stood and started bagging up Luke's clothes. Yes, she would, she decided. She'd get through this next week, deal with the funeral, and then she'd start hunting for a new flat. She'd been given another chance at life, and this time, she was going to live it without compromise.

ACKNOWLEDGEMENTS

First and foremost, to my wonderful publishers, a massive thank you to Cassandra and Cahill Davis for taking a chance on me. I will forever be grateful, and I hope you realise what a dream come true moment this is for me. Thank you also to Lauren for her superb editing. Her skills have made this into the book it was meant to be.

Huge thanks go to my good friend and neighbour, former PC Jeremy Carnell, and to former DC Darren Haynes, who happily answer all my legal and procedural questions, and to Jules Swain (aka @thereadingpara), for providing medical and paramedic insight. Please note that as a work of fiction some artistic licence has been used – all mistakes are my own.

A big thank you to first reader and now good friend Jo Simpson, whose opinions and comments I value greatly, and to beta readers Carol Page and Laura Pearson for helping me work out the finishing touches. I love you all.

Enormous gratitude to all my lovely reviewers on the blog tour. Thank you for taking the time to read and review this book. It is most appreciated.

And finally, thank you to you, the reader, for buying and reading my novel. I hope that you have enjoyed it – there is more to come!

ABOUT THE AUTHOR

Nottingham based Gemma began her career working in an artist studio illustrating children's books. The more books she worked on, the more she began to develop her own ideas, so she took the plunge and started writing her own books. The Storm is Gemma's debut novel.

You can follow Gemma on X (formerly Twitter) @gemmaEdenham

THE INHERITANCE

By Gemma Denham

Inheriting a house at a time of financial crisis seems to be the answer to their prayers, but before long strange things start happening, and the house of their dreams becomes the start of their nightmares.

Kate and Patrick are struggling through life. After living on one wage since the birth of their son, Riley, Patrick is suddenly unemployed. Bouncing from one bad interview to the next, the family are suddenly offered a lifeline when Kate receives a phone call. Her aunt has passed away and left her house to them. Patrick is reluctant but Kate is buoyant – this could be the fresh start she's been after. The new start she knows they all need.

Excited for the change, the family move hundreds of miles from their Beaconsfield home to the northeast coast. The Victorian townhouse needs a lot of work, but that doesn't deter Kate. She is excited to be there and determined to make it work for them.

However, it isn't long before Kate starts noticing things going missing and being moved. At first she blames forgetfulness, the disarray of the move, her young son; but once night falls and the house becomes dark and quiet she hears footsteps. Terrified, Kate becomes convinced there is someone in the house. Upon searching the house is empty. There are no signs of an intruder. All the doors and windows are secure. Night after night Kate hears these noises...and then she starts to receive messages. Is someone really in the house, could it be haunted, or is she losing her sanity?

Out 12th June 2026